THE SOUND OF HER VOICE

NATHAN BLACKWELL

ORION

First published in Great Britain in 2019 by Orion Fiction,
an imprint of The Orion Publishing Group Ltd
Carmelite House, 50 Victoria Embankment,
London EC4Y 0DZ

An Hachette UK company

1 3 5 7 9 10 8 6 4 2

A CIP catalogue record for this book is
available from the British Library.

ISBN (Trade Paperback) 978 1 4091 8634 2

Designed and typeset by Mary Egan Publishing

Printed and bound by CPI Group (UK) Ltd, Croydon, CR0 4YY

MIX
Paper from
responsible sources
FSC® C104740
FSC
www.fsc.org

www.orionbooks.co.uk

GLOSSARY

1D	*Domestic violence incident.*
3T	*Traffic stop.*
10-10	*Emergency radio call. Immediate assistance required.*
2I/C	*Second in charge / command.*
AOS	*Armed Offenders' Squad.*
ASAT	*Adult Sexual Assault Team.*
Caustic soda	*Used in the manufacture of methamphetamine.*
Charlie	*CIB call sign.*
Chem Desk	*Gathers intelligence on precursors, materials, and chemicals used in the manufacture of illicit drugs.*
CIB	*Criminal Investigation Branch.*
CID	*Criminal Investigation Database.*
Clan Lab	*Clandestine laboratory, i.e. a meth lab.*
Clan Lab Team	*Specialist unit that responds to and safely dismantles clandestine drug laboratories. Staffed by Police and ESR.*
Comms	*Police communications centre.*
CPT	*Child Protection Team.*
D	*Detective.*
D Senior	*Detective Senior Sergeant.*
DC	*Detective Constable.*
Deodar	*Police launch.*
DI	*Detective Inspector.*
DS	*Detective Sergeant.*
Eagle	*Police air support unit.*
ECL	*Electronic Crime Lab.*

Ephedrine	*Precursor used in the manufacture of methamphetamine.*
ESR	*Institute of Environmental Science and Research.*
EVI	*Evidential interview for special victims, recorded on video.*
FLIR	*Forward-looking infrared.*
GA	*General Aviation.*
Gear	*Drugs. Often methamphetamine.*
Homebake	*Heroin produced from morphine.*
Hype	*Hypophosphorous acid. Used in the manufacture of methamphetamine.*
I	*Iodine. Used in the manufacture of methamphetamine.*
JB	*Junior boy / bitch. Term of endearment.*
I-Car	*Frontline patrol car / incident response. HSI – Henderson I-Car. GFI – Glenfield I-Car, etc.*
NIA	*National Intelligence Application.*
NVGs	*Night-vision goggles.*
O/C	*Officer in charge / command.*
OCEANZ	*Online Child Exploitation Across New Zealand. A Police unit that investigates offences against children with an internet component, such as the making / supplying / possessing of objectionable material, or online grooming.*
PM	*Post-mortem.*
Pseudoephedrine	*Precursor used in the manufacture of methamphetamine.*
RHIB	*Rigid-hull inflatable boat.*
Section	*Frontline Police staff.*
Senior	*Uniform Senior Sergeant.*
SOCO	*Scene of Crime Officers.*
Speed	*Early term for methamphetamine. Same drug, more impurities.*
SSG	*Specialist Search Group.*
STG	*Special Tactics Group.*
Telcos	*Telecommunication providers.*
TF	*Territorial Force. Now called the Army Reserve.*
Toluene / Tolly	*Solvent used in the manufacture of methamphetamine.*
TSU	*Technical Support Unit.*
Witpro	*Witness Protection.*

PROLOGUE

August, 1995

The chill cut right through my duty jacket. A downdraught before the storm front. The rain started to fall, cold. I shivered and looked up, staring at the night as the water started to splash across my forehead. We were parked up near the pool hall on Target Road. It offered a decent view over the Wairau Valley and Link Drive industrial area. A regular favourite of commercial burglars. I glanced over the roof at Andy and raised my eyebrows. He nodded, stamped out his cigarette, swept the water from his ginger hair and got back in the driver's seat. I slid in on my side and pulled the door. I fired up the heat and the car warmed up while the rain hit the windscreen, harder now. Brief comfort was broken by the radio. The Comms operator was panicked, worked up. A 10-10 call. Something going down in Kumeu. Another patrol car, or I-car as they're known, in trouble. Someone was seriously hurt, or about to be. No cars free up there. West all tied up. Another car on the Shore called for details. I reached up to the console on the dash and twisted the black dial. Flashing reds and blues lit up the dark around us and the siren wailed as Andy put his foot down, taking us out of the valley, up onto Wairau Road and then north toward the Hobsonville turnoff that would take us west.

I'd been out of Police College a little over three months. A skinny eighteen year old, green as. I'd been dicking around in my final year of high school less than twelve months ago. I definitely hadn't come to grips with the job yet, was struggling to find my feet. *How did I end up here again?* Luck. No other way to explain it. I hadn't had a clue what to do with my life. Unsure what to study. I'd wanted to help people, but I wanted excitement. Challenge. Relative terms those. Subjective. Life behind a desk? No thanks. Seeing my mates filling out their uni timetables and getting ready for yet more bookwork, I'd looked for something else. I'd seen the recruitment ad for the cops and gave it a crack. Now here I was, having fudged my way through the recruitment process and the College, no more certain of my career choice than I had been six months ago. But it was exciting. And challenging. And I had a hell of a lot still to learn.

We hit the seventy-K area north of Sunset Road, heading for the turnoff onto Upper Harbour. *How can I make this easy for Andy?* I adjusted myself in the seat and leaned forward to the glove box, pulling the map book out and flicking through the pages. I got motion-sick doing it. I didn't travel well when I couldn't see out. *Suck it up, you little bitch.* Andy was now throwing us in and out of the turns on Upper Harbour with his foot on the floor. Streetlights, trees, houses and big yards flashed by either side. There wasn't much traffic this time of night, and besides a couple of oncoming headlights we shared the road with hardly anyone.

I'd been listening to the radio, and was fucking about with the map, trying to find Deacon Road. I knew Andy would be taking us up State Highway 16 into Kumeu, but from there he'd be relying on me. Kumeu was a rural area on the urban fringe, north-west of the city. My knowledge of it extended to the bakery, the pub, and the girl I'd had a thing for back in fifth form. So, not much. I found the page I needed and picked out the intersection of Riverhead and Deacon. Andy was focused on the road so I gave him simple directions.

"State highway sixteen, then right into Coatesville-Riverhead Highway. It's off that."

We accelerated over the Greenhithe Bridge. Normally at night you can see across the water to the Whenuapai Air Force base, but tonight the winter weather had destroyed all visibility. As the rain hammered the windscreen we passed some fields on our left, and some shops on both sides, before heading right into Brigham Creek Road. Up a gentle incline, then skirting the edge of the airbase. Through the rain and low cloud I saw halos round the big floodlights, and I could make out the hangars and a few large dark shapes on the tarmac.

Comms was trying desperately to get more out of the unit in the shit but nothing was coming back. That wasn't good. Andy was tearing the road up, pushing it as far as he could without losing it completely, as we hit State 16 and turned right, heading north. I gave our position to Comms over the radio in the hope the crew in trouble could hear us and would know we were close. But as we took the right into Coatesville-Riverhead Highway, the words cut across the channel, strained and forced through gritted teeth:

"Comms, HSI . . . we've been shot at . . . status one . . . I've got gunshot wounds, we need ambos . . ."

Fuck me. Confusion. Both shot or just one? Someone was status one. Fuck it, we'd soon find out. There was some back and forth between Comms and the unit, clarifying that it was safe for others and attempting to get some more info about the shooter. I could feel the frustration from the guy who'd been shot, was getting frustrated myself. Because fuck it, I didn't care what was where.

Despite the fact we didn't have firearms, Andy and I were going straight in regardless of what anyone else thought.

"It's clear, my partner's dying, I'm hurt bad . . . ambulance here . . ."

Holy fuck. Both shot. Odd as it sounds, coming all the way from the Shore we were still gonna be the first car there. There's a disturbing lack of Police available to patrol the streets at night. Often only one or two cars out and about in west Auckland. They were always busy. All it took was an arrest, or a victim, and they couldn't cut and run. And Rodney District, where we were now, this area was covered by the Orewa station. They were a long way away, and always tied up. I felt like I was shaking, but I wasn't really. That adrenaline hit, knowing you're heading into something bad, but you wouldn't back out even if you had the choice. You're only focused forward, on what you're running into. Cops got assaulted all the time, people got hurt. But getting shot was something out of the movies. Yeah it had happened before, but this wasn't the USA. It wasn't a common thing out here.

I directed Andy left into Riverhead Road, and straight on toward the Deacon intersection. I saw the red and blues from HSI flashing through the rain further up, where Riverhead Road bent left and Deacon carried on straight. Andy came in right behind them. As I got out I could smell the tyres, feel the heat off them. All I could hear was the rain splashing off the bitumen. I ran toward the flashing lights through the downpour. I forgot about safety, didn't wait for Andy. I ran past the rear of their car. Noticed the holes in their back windscreen. *Fuck. Fuck, fuck, fuck.* A cop was leaning over someone in the road in front of their car, lit up by the headlights. "Help me with her!" he was yelling as I moved in. He was fucked. He'd taken a round in the shoulder and was bleeding heavily. His blue shirt, already dark from the rain, was covered in a darker stain, running down his arm. He was on his arse in the mud beside the road. Another dark, shiny patch spread over his lower trouser leg. I was frozen to the spot, hadn't seen a colleague hurt this bad.

What the fuck? What the fuck? I was going around in circles in my head, trying to assess the situation, plan a way forward. *Right . . . he's conscious . . . let's try and stem the bleeding. Shoulder first? Leg maybe. Could be an artery.* Then I remembered why he'd yelled at me. My vision expanded, widened from the dark tunnel it had been. I looked down at the person lying on the ground beside him, and my world went shiny grey at the edges, then black. I leant forward to try and get some blood back into my head. *Fuckin' hell. Gabby.* She'd been on my recruit wing. We were at the College at the same time. She'd joined straight after high school too. Yeah, we were close. Her eyes were open but they were vacant. Blood flowed out of her mouth and bubbled as it pooled at the edges. *Round through the chest? Through her lung?* The blood soaked her uniform and I glanced back at her car. More holes in the front windscreen. My vision narrowed again. Windscreen. Bullet holes. Lashed by the rain and wind. *Is this happening?*

I looked back down and realised I'd gone to my knees beside her. Rain was splashing around us. Her long dark hair was plastered across her face and I pulled the wet strands aside. My fingers on her carotid, but I felt nothing. Andy had brought up the first aid kit we had and, taking it all in, flung the kit at the guy and got in with me beside Gabby. They teach you to assess the surroundings, plastic shields, gloves, all that safety shit . . . but this was real, not a training day. It all went out the window. I didn't have Ebola. And neither did Gabby.

I scooped what blood I could out of her mouth with my fingers, and wiped it on her uniform. After that did fuck all, I tried to turn her head, letting the red mess run out of her mouth onto the road. I rolled her head back and delivered breaths while Andy pumped her chest. I was trying to force air past the blood in her mouth, could taste metal and salt, could feel the warm stickiness staining my face as I tried to get her breathing, stopping all the time to scoop more blood away or tilt her head sideways again. *We're getting nowhere pretty fuckin' quickly*. This routine went on for a bit before Andy began tiring. We swapped around and I did compressions. He also struggled to push his breath past the red froth coming out of Gabby's mouth and had as much luck as I'd had. The rain splashed down and there was a shallow pool of water around us now. The smell was so out of place – one of the few details I really remember. A weird, sickly sweet coppery combination of fresh rain and blood.

We were just speeding things up, pumping the life blood out of Gabby quicker. No way of effectively stopping the bleeding, and unable to get any air into her. We needed shit we just didn't have. A lot of the bleeding was internal. We were fighting a losing battle, but we weren't doctors – we couldn't make the call, and we sure as hell weren't going to stand around and not try anything. Not when our mate was dying beside us. Her partner was in a bad way too, he was losing blood fast but had somehow managed to bandage up his leg. He was now struggling with his shoulder. I continued compressions and Andy stopped with the breathing, giving the guy a hand to tie off the bandage and check the pressure on the one on his leg. My vision was filled only with Gabby's face. The only calm, serene thing in this total gang-fuck. That image burned itself into my head as I kept on doing compressions. Looking for some change in her that I knew wasn't coming. I didn't know it then, but it was an image I was never going to shake.

I don't remember much more of the night. Things blurred into one and I couldn't be sure of the order of events. The rain didn't let up. More cop cars came from somewhere. Paramedics arrived and took over. Gabby had been dead a while by then. Detectives from the CIB turned up and took charge of the scene.

Tents went up to protect what little of it hadn't already been washed away. Some big bosses walked around. Cordons went up and I ended up back at one of them, out on the Highway. I was soaked through. Rain. Mud. Gabby's blood. Her partner's blood. The water stopped the blood from drying. It covered me – face, neck, uniform – had flowed down across my arms. I didn't know what I was supposed to be doing. Didn't know what was going on. People raced around but nobody gave me too much attention, I don't really remember. My head spun, and my vision began to close off again. Nausea. I leant against the car at the cordon, but the feeling kept rising from inside me. I pushed myself up off the bonnet and saw the red impression I'd made with my upper body. The rain diluted the stain, and my vision closed off completely for a brief moment. I dropped my head and it returned. Then the ball of sick rose too far.

PART ONE

"Sometimes we stay in hell a long time because we've learned the names of the streets."

– MICHAEL LEVINE

ONE

July, 2011

Missing person, homicide investigation, re-investigation – it doesn't matter. They don't fade. Faces burn into your memory. You don't shake them. But you don't want to anyway. Churchill said something about being in the arena. That's where I needed to be. I couldn't watch from the sidelines – go to work, read the paper, watch the news – like every sane person. A life of that shit would've bored me to death.

I'd been pulling a file apart at my desk, and started searching my drawer for one of those crocodile-looking things that rip the staples out. I saw the photo I kept. The guilt hit me, as it always does. I stared at her face, locked forever, fourteen years old. Samantha Coates had gone missing in March 1999. She'd have been twenty-six now, if she was still here. But I knew she wasn't. She'd been walking home from school towards Hillcrest when she'd disappeared. I'd been a Constable attached to the CIB at Henderson then, a baby investigator, far from a qualified Detective. It had been all hands in the District to the pump. After initially chasing a few leads I was made the file manager when the previous guy went on leave. That job was usually a shafting, because you were the bitch. But you got your head round the file well as you sorted all the incoming information. Suspicious very early on, obviously. But an eighteen-month investigation with thirty CIB officers on-and-off had turned up nothing. We'd had fuck all leads, and they all ran out. No forensics. Nothing firm. We never found her body. Like she'd disappeared into thin air. You'd think that probably wouldn't happen in little old New Zealand, but there have been plenty. So I held on to her photo. It reminded me of my incompetence. I couldn't let this slip into some dusty old archive. Homicides never get filed or inactivated. Unsolved, they remain assigned to a Detective until they are solved, even after the investigation proper winds down. Missing person files were different. They did get closed. But I'd held on to this, because I knew there was only one way to explain the fact she had vanished. The case was mine until it was solved or I left the job and handed it on. I never felt I'd done enough.

The dead and missing leave a pretty big impact. Faces, names. I always remembered the victims, but struggled with offenders. They did fade. No cop takes the killing of a human being lightly. So, the photo reminded me. Of my obligation to Sam and her family. No one else in the Police was going to be her voice twelve years on. The twenty-six ring binders that made up the hard copy file were still sitting on the bottom few rows of the shelf next to me. I found the staple-ripper thing and closed the drawer.

I was working with Dan tonight. A good mate. Bright guy, solid investigator. Five years younger than me, he had a short sharp haircut and always had the latest shirt or shoes. But a better Detective than I'd ever be. It was late, and I was on my sixth Nescafé instant. I could feel the kidney stones forming. Or was that just the big shit I needed to take? My phone rang and the on-road Senior Sergeant was on the other end. It was

Stef, an ex-Detective who'd been promoted and gone back into uniform. That meant the call was good and bad. It meant he'd be all over it. It also meant that if he couldn't sort it himself, it was pretty serious.

The Orewa station was all one level, so I left my desk and wandered up to the front reception area where he'd said she'd be arriving. She'd beaten me to it. Jeans and T-shirt, feet up on the chair in the front counter area, hugging her knees. Light brown hair loose around her shoulders. Her parents were sitting beside her. Their faces pale. Unsure. Looking for direction. *Join the club.* Dealing with a rape was never easy, not for me anyway. I was always so shit scared of fucking up in front of them, and losing their trust. This girl had just survived something horrific, and I was supposed to have the answers. Tough gig. But I guess I could have been on a building site if I'd wanted. My mind wandered. *That'd be the life.* But you expect certain things when you speak to a Detective. Like answers, and professionalism. So I held my shit together on the outside, while on the inside I was a nervous wreck, hoping like hell I was going to be the person this girl needed me to be. I introduced myself.

"Kelly, I'm Matthew, a Detective here. Thanks for coming straight in. Let's get out of this reception area and go somewhere more comfortable." Kelly followed me and I opened the door, guiding her through, followed by her parents. We chatted a bit and I shook hands with her dad. Late forties, balding, glasses. His eyes were uncertain, searching mine for answers. I explained to the three of them about speaking to Kelly in private, the importance of getting a brief recollection of events from her. We call it a preliminary interview. There isn't much detail, you just get the basics. I wouldn't ask many questions or clarify too much, that'd come later when a cognitive interviewer sat her down for a few hours. Tonight I just needed what, where, when, and, if possible, who. The last thing Kelly needed now was to relive it all over again. I needed to get her to a doctor, so I didn't want to linger here at the station any longer than was necessary.

"Kelly, it's your call but I'd like it to just be you and me at this stage. If it's just us, I'm a blank canvas, you can say what you like to me, it won't get repeated without your say-so. But if your mum and dad are there, you might not say something that's really important, you know, to protect their feelings about what's happened."

That was part of it anyway. The rest was that I knew she wouldn't tell me everything in front of her parents, because they wouldn't know the half of what really went on in their daughter's life. But I sure as fuck wasn't going to say that in front of them. All three of them nodded, and Kelly's parents went into the room next door where Dan was all ready to sort them out with the coffee machine.

As they left I looked back at Kelly. She was fifteen. Not much older than Hailey. I felt a brief flash of anger, but suppressed it before it rose and my face gave anything away. *Fuck! If anyone ever . . .* I cut away from it though. *Hailey's fine. Focus on Kelly.*

"There's some things that I'd suggest doing, because it allows us the best chance of securing the evidence we need to move forward. But Kelly, these are suggestions, okay? Nothing happens tonight without you. Nobody's going to force you to choose or do anything. If you want to talk to your parents, or go home, or stop, or you want or need anything, you tell me, right?" She nodded. "We won't be long here. I want to get you to the doctor. But when did you last eat or drink?"

Easy question. *Let's just get her talking. Build some trust.* She found her voice.

"The lady on the phone told me not to eat or drink anything. She was pretty firm about that."

"Yeah. That's because there's a chance some evidence may be washed away if you eat, drink or get changed. But that's all that is. I'd rather make sure you're okay right now. How long has it been?"

"I had a drink this morning . . ."

Fuckin' hell. "I'll be right back. One minute."

Evidence could get fucked for all I cared. At this stage, building a trusting relationship with Kelly was more important than anything else. Fuck that up, and this would go nowhere fast. I went to the kitchen and sent Hailey a text as I went, letting her know I'd be late:

> **Don't wait up for me, just got a job. It'll probably be a late one, so I'll see you in the morning. I'll drop you to school. Love you.**

Hailey hated it when I spelled whole words out in my texts. So I did it all the time. I didn't get *War and Peace* back though:

> **Swt**

I returned with a glass and a roll someone had left in the fridge. *Tough shit for them.* Kelly ate and drank. Then I took the prelim. I let her get out what she wanted to get out. I got the what, where, and when, but not the who. I struggled like hell to keep my face neutral, not giving away how I felt.

Kelly had been at a party in Stanmore Bay. Lots of kids, range of ages, fourteen through eighteen. Advertising a party on Facebook could be a whole lot of fun or a recipe for disaster, depending on a number of variables. A lot of older guys there, and everyone was getting pissed. Kelly remembered passing out, waking up to two guys on top of her in a bedroom. She had screamed, tried to push them off. A few people came into the room and got into a fight with the two. They left and Kelly didn't remember much else. She rang her dad. He came to the party and found her, heading home initially before changing course to the Police Station once Kelly started talking. They'd met Kelly's mum here.

Right now, the "who" was probably the least important. That'd be easy enough to work out once we started interviewing other people from the party. I called Helen, my Detective Sergeant, and briefed her. She said she'd come in and coordinate the rest that night. The scene needed securing, preserving for tomorrow. There were a lot of potential witnesses to track down too. Me and Dan, however, we were taking Kelly to the on-call forensic doctor at Greenlane. Her parents followed us in their car. It was a pretty long drive, onto the motorway south, cutting through the rural areas and then Silverdale and Dairy Flat.

I hated silence, hated someone sitting awkwardly in the back. It didn't need to be like that, this shouldn't be harder on Kelly than it already was. So we talked the whole way about other stuff. The best way to build rapport with someone is to talk about them, and be genuinely interested. Yeah, sounds obvious, but everyone's shit at it. Kelly was Year Eleven at Orewa College. Decent netballer, shit at science, liked English and history. I was telling her how Dan was a rocket scientist, but I'd been average at pretty much everything. "Yeah they had to tighten up on their recruiting standards after I joined the Police . . ." That got me a laugh.

We crossed over Oteha Valley Road, still heading south through Albany. Under the Sunset Road overbridge and passing through the North Shore suburbs of Sunnynook and Takapuna. We climbed the Harbour Bridge, the bright lights of the CBD clear across the water on our left. We dropped down into the city fringe and continued on. Arriving at Greenlane Hospital, we parked in the emergency space and waited for her parents. We then all got buzzed in by the security guard, took the lift to the right floor and found the team of specialist doctors and nurses in the waiting room. They're awesome, these people. Kelly looked confused as the motherly doctor opened another door for her, beckoning her in. The doctor explained.

"Your parents will be right here. The Detectives aren't going anywhere either." Kelly relaxed and went through the door.

Now I had to make small talk with her parents. This was hard, because normally now Dan and I would just joke about other things to take our minds off what we were actually doing for a few brief moments. *No chance of that.* We chatted about Kelly, about her school and sports, her hobbies, her friends. Then Kelly's mum asked what would happen if we caught the guys. I felt like a right arsehole because I was glad she had said "if" and not "when". "When" is a difficult thing to answer. I really wanted to tell her the truth. The two guys would be arrested. They'd be charged. They'd plead not guilty. There would be a trial. Kelly would have to give evidence. The defence lawyer would attack her character, call her a liar, make her out to be a slut, in front of a jury of twelve. The offenders would be wearing suits, looking sharp and innocent. Young men on the verge of becoming something great, they just needed a chance . . . *won't you twelve men and women give them a chance?* The jury would be unsure. So, to be safe they'd probably acquit them, and they'd walk. And Kelly would wear that scar for the rest of her life. Even with counselling, it would ruin her relationship with her parents, with her male friends, make future romantic relationships difficult. It would make school hard. It would make life hard. *But fuck, get it together, Matt. Enough about the truth.*

"I don't want to overload you with information. But I'll never lie to you, so on that, I don't want to promise anything, or get you or Kelly thinking about anything that may turn out differently. We'll do this one step at a time. The next step is to get what happened from Kelly on video, in more detail. We'll aim to do that over the next few days. In the meantime we'll be getting hold of everyone at that party, and talking to them to find out what happened and who those guys were. We'll be in touch every step of the way."

When the medical team had done their thing Kelly's parents

took her home. Before they left I gave Kelly my card. She took it and looked at it.

"Cell, landline, and email. Whatever's easiest for you, Kelly, I don't mind. Get hold of me anytime, and I mean that. I'll answer anything as honestly as I can." I gave a couple more to her parents. Outside the hospital they were grateful. But as her dad shook my hand, he held my arm at the same time. He looked at me hesitantly, expectantly, glancing at his daughter. His face said, "Tell me what the fuck I do now? What do I do?" and his eyes said "I'm lost here." I thought of Hailey, what I'd do in this situation if I was him. And I had nothing. Because I had no idea what I'd do. He knew how to be a dad. I couldn't think of anything to say that wouldn't make me sound like a fucking idiot. So I just nodded at him, gripped his hand and turned to leave.

Kelly called from behind me. "Thank you." I definitely had no idea what to say to that. At a complete loss again, I just turned, nodded at her and smiled, and then walked back to the car with Dan.

Sixteen years in, and it still shook me every time. I found my brain worked overtime trying to choose all the right words, trying not to fuck up in front of someone vulnerable. I always ended up with a headache from the pressure. *What the fuck was wrong with me? Surely not everyone felt like this every time.* Thing was, I probably wouldn't deal with Kelly again as this file would go to the Child Protection Team, based out of Albany on the Shore. They worked the whole district – Waitakere, North Shore, and Rodney. They'd investigate and run the prosecution.

I crept in through the front door, clicking it shut, careful not to wake Hailey. She wasn't getting a day off school just because Dad worked late. I checked the fridge, couldn't be arsed heating something up. *Fuck it.* I ripped open the pack of Toffee Pops and sank six of them. I set my alarm for early and was out like a light.

TWO

I parked up the end of Haigh Access Road, near the start of the Okura bush track. Rain lashed the ground and I pulled my jacket up around my neck, meeting up with the Sergeant standing on the gravel where the road met the track. I shook his hand and he pointed out toward the mudflats.

"About twenty metres into the mangroves apparently. We tried to recce it to save you guys a callout, but didn't get far before it became too hard on foot." It was then I noticed a young chap shivering under a towel over near a patrol car. *Spot the JB. Poor bastard.* But I couldn't hide my grin. The Sergeant carried on. "Deodar are heading this way to support with one of their RHIBs if you need it."

A kayaker trying his luck with spearing flounder had found the bones in an old tarp tied to a mangrove trunk. Half the material had rotted and he reckoned it looked human. He'd phoned 111 and was being interviewed by Dan back at Orewa station. Helen and I had come out to the scene. From what Dan was reporting back, the guy was pretty adamant it was human so we got to work locking the scene down. The Sergeant offered his section's services. "I can put two at the end of Haigh Access on East Coast Road, and send a few door knocking?"

"Cheers mate, that'd be perfect." We didn't know anything at this stage and needed to preserve as much of the area as we could. "We'll need to send a couple along the bush track too. I know the weather's shit but we'll make sure everyone's out, either back this way or up to Stillwater, once we have their details."

Helen was looking serious as she spoke on the phone several metres away. Her greying blonde hair and harsh features completed the "don't fuck with me" look. She was a tough bitch, but one of the best supervisors I'd had. She put the troops first, job second. I could hear she was getting the fire service here with their lighting and rigging equipment. That may come in handy a bit later. But for now, I could only see one way into the mangroves without getting too stuck, and that was the same way the kayaker had. Scene control was a bit fucked. The primary scene was in the middle of a mangrove swamp, difficult to access and difficult to cordon. The mangroves clogged the estuary, which flowed between private land on one side and the public track on the other. East of the mangroves the estuary led out to the ocean. Going south of the immediate scene, a tributary weaved back between several properties and then went under East Coast Road. *Should we cordon that off too? Nah.* Although some fuckwit would probably say I should have later on.

As we waited for the RHIB I helped one of the frontline guys put some tape up across the entrance into Haigh Access from the highway. I left him with a scene log and the usual instructions – no one in or out without a signature and a phone call to me or Helen. We could always bring the cordons in. But you can't make them bigger if you've already contaminated evidence and fucked it all up. But it didn't really matter what I did here, in the early stages. Later on, that same fuckwit with twenty-twenty hindsight would tell me I did it all wrong anyway.

I heard the low rumble of turbine-powered rotors and looked south. The weather had lifted slightly and the Air Support Unit must have taken their chances. I got on the radio and spoke with one of the observers on board *Eagle*, asking them to check out the primary scene from above before directing us in. They would try to grab some imagery if they could too. I watched the chopper come over the water and lift its nose slightly as it descended, losing forward speed and settling into a hover above the mangroves. It was still quite high, they weren't wanting to disturb anything with the downwash. Their powerful onboard camera meant distance wasn't an issue. My radio sparked up.

"Charlie, Eagle, will call you on cell."

I thumbed the switch on my radio. "Roger."

Then my phone buzzed. I could hear the engine noise in the background still, but whatever noise-cancelling gear they had was pretty good. The observer's voice came through reasonably clearly.

"It's right in the middle of the swamp, mate. We're pretty much directly above it if you're looking at us. Looks like a blue bag or tarp tied to a mangrove trunk. Can't make out much but there could be some bones hanging out. Can't get there easily on foot, it's mudflats and mangroves in every direction. Water's down a bit now too. I reckon if you want to do a recce, get the RHIB to take you far as they can, then kayak the rest. We'll stay over the top and direct you in."

Sounded good to me. We had to get up close to the body pretty smartly, confirm what it was. Even though the kayaker had been pretty adamant, there was no point locking the whole place down and kicking things off big time if it was a sheep. But I struggled to think why someone would wrap a sheep carcass up and tie it to a mangrove trunk. *Yeah. This wasn't gonna be a good day out.*

Helen and I kitted up in white forensic overalls and blue rubber gloves, but we went with wetsuit booties from the launch crew on our feet rather than the forensic ones. Those would come off in the mud in no time. We boarded their RHIB near the bridge at the start of the track. They'd picked up a kayak from their Mechanics Bay base on their way over and were towing that behind them. One of the guys helped Helen into the RHIB, and I made a nice controlled stumble in after her. We sat up the front and the guy driving opened the throttle a bit and we headed toward the mangroves. I still had the radio link to the chopper because I'd need it once Helen and I boarded our kayak. I was listening to the observer and held my arm pointed in the direction we needed to go for the driver's benefit. My earpiece was receiving *"left"*, *"right"*, *"straight"*: shit like that. We didn't get far into the mangroves before the trunks got too close together to keep going. I called up the observer. "Eagle, Charlie, any other way in that will get us closer?"

The radio crackled a bit, then: *"Not really. Looks similar all the way round. I reckon that line is as good as any."*

With the help of the RHIB crew Helen and I got seated in the kayak and started paddling gently. Fuck, we looked ridiculous. *Only in New Zealand.* Bet the FBI would have some contraption to lower their people in from above. Not us. If it was a sheep, I really would laugh. The radio crackled in my ear again. *"You're about twenty from it, keep that line."* I couldn't see fuck all beyond the yellows and greens of the mangrove leaves, and the new shoots poking up out of the water. These raked across the underside of the kayak, but bent easily. The water was only about a foot deep here but it was enough for the kayak. It was the low branches that were the issue. We really had to bend and twist around those, sometimes taking a detour around a trunk or two before getting back on track. But it got to the point where we were going to have to get out and try our luck walking, because the kayak wasn't going to squeeze much further through this shit.

"Eagle, Charlie, we're going on foot. How far now?"

"Close, no more than ten in front of you." The chopper thundered above us as we picked our way forward, feet sinking into the dark mud and coming out caked in the stuff. It stank. We bent branches and tried to step on the new shoots where we could to avoid getting our feet stuck. *"Right in front now Charlie. You should see it."*

Then I saw the blue tarp a few metres ahead. I stopped and pointed it out to Helen. She was right on my shoulder. She had her DS hat on. "Slow down, Matt. I'll walk in your steps."

We were always trying to minimise disturbance. The tarp was stained with mud and looked rotten, but the most recognisable bit was the rib cage sticking out the side, dark brown, not white as you'd expect. Not a piece of flesh on it. No knowing how long it had been there. I gently moved some of the tarp aside with a gloved hand, and saw the human pelvis. I looked back at Helen and my face must have said it all. I got on the radio to the observer and reported back. I extracted the camera from the small backpack slung on my front, and took a heap of general photos and close-ups of the tarp and bones. I didn't want to move around too much in case there was other evidence in the mud, so we backed out the way we'd come in. I asked the observer to try to plot my track on their GPS somehow so we could follow it back in later without disturbing anything else.

Back at the car park area we changed out of our mud-caked overalls. I phoned Dan to get someone to bring the scene tent and equipment down. Helen briefed Tim, the Detective Inspector, on the phone and explained what we had. Then she called the pathologist while I called the duty scientist at ESR. Within just over an hour the area near the cordon was humming with uniformed officers, plain-clothed detectives writing shit in their notebooks, and photography and forensic experts setting up their gear. The fire service had arrived and had begun setting up their lighting equipment to illuminate the scene come nightfall. There was a big discussion and it was decided that tomorrow was a new day, let's kick the scene examination off then. *Thank fuck for that.* I returned to Orewa and documented everything I'd done. The scene team tomorrow would use it to formulate a plan.

By the end of the next day, after several hours painstakingly moving through the mud, the D's doing the scene, along with the ESR staff and pathologist, had uncovered a total skeleton inside the tarp, minus three crucial parts – the skull and both hands. The pathologist reckoned the skeleton was female from the hip construction. He couldn't approximate an age or how long it had been there, that would only come with further testing. The area search started the same day, and officers were called in from far and wide to assist. Search and Rescue were the experts here, as well as the Specialist Search Group. The entire bush area and swamp at low tide was searched over the course of the following week, as well as all entry points and neighbouring properties. As per usual, when you wanted to find stuff, we found sweet fuck all.

THREE

The homicide investigation was named Operation Ariel. It had been running for four weeks now, and we hadn't got very far. There was a team of fifteen, local staff plus extras from the Shore and West. I'd landed on the general enquiries team, interviewing people and chasing leads. The skeleton was female, and the experts reckoned she'd been aged around sixteen years when she'd died. They'd been able to extract some DNA from the marrow, but there wasn't a match to anyone on the database. The missing persons unit in Wellington had several teenagers from the greater area on record – but we had DNA on file for all of them, and there was no match there either.

So we had no ID. We couldn't go down the dental path without the skull. Nothing in the area search; no teeth, no other bones, no nothing. Skeletons lose bones all the time – weather, animals, erosion. But you find other fragments nearby usually. This scene had nothing. Yeah it was tidal, but all indications suggested that the head and hands had been deliberately removed. There were also fractures to the pelvis and right leg.

I was sitting in with the bosses. Tim was the Officer in Charge. Helen, being the DS, had been made the 2I/C. We'd been discussing the media release. The story was out, with just enough detail to get people calling in without leaking anything too sensitive. But we weren't progressing far on the ID front. For all the searching and speaking to people in the area, and for all the people phoning in with suspicious vehicles and dodgy neighbours, we had nothing.

The smart people used radiocarbon to date the bones, and they reckoned the girl had been dead for fifteen to seventeen years. *That was a fuckin' long time.* Then I got the shit job I knew was coming. While everyone else was out chasing real leads, I, with the help of Rebecca, the young, bright intel analyst, searched the Police system for everything that had occurred in the area from September '93 until March '97. We'd been using a different computer system then and not everything was recorded properly. When I say that I searched with Rebecca's help, really what I mean is that she did it herself. When it came to anything beyond Microsoft Word, I was a fuckin' idiot.

She found over eight hundred events in our National Intelligence Application (NIA) and a few other databases I couldn't figure out. I made a coffee before sitting down to sift through them. I did the lazy version first, skimming over anything that didn't immediately stand out. Crashes on the main highway, all resolved. Disorder jobs from parties in the area, and they would have been decent parties too – the neighbours weren't exactly on your doorstep. A lot of burglaries reported over that time period, which could have some linkage, but I was looking for something glaringly obvious. There had been drug dealers recorded stopped in the area but nothing untoward. I wanted something quick and easy, and, as per usual, nothing. Nothing stood out from the pile. *Well that's me fucked for the next few days*. I refilled my mug and began again, firing up the computer to cross-check everything.

After a day and a half of reading and looking into all the Police systems I could, I got on the road with a much smaller pile of shit to do. But it was a pile that was still too big. I pulled up the drive toward a single-level bungalow, two streets back from the beach in Mission Bay. It was newly painted, well landscaped. Someone had definitely blown out their paving budget. My long grass and cracked concrete at home weren't quite the same. I knocked on the door, which was opened by a well-dressed five-year-old kid. He was wearing more coin than I had, total. "Evening, mate." I smiled. "Are Mum or Dad home? I'm with the Police." He nodded and rushed back into the house, calling for Mum. I heard snippets of the exchange.

"Who?"

"It's a Policeman."

"What?"

I heard footsteps. Then a woman in her early thirties appeared behind the door, looking worried.

"Mrs Campbell?" She didn't correct me. "Hello, my name is Matt, I'm a Detective with the Orewa Police. Sorry to bother you, nothing's the matter, I'm just following up on something from years ago."

She relaxed, but I'd hit her curiosity button. She brushed a strand of dark hair back behind her ear and nodded. "Okay, sure, please come in. Don't worry about your shoes." But as per usual when someone says that, I was already balancing on a socked foot fucking about with my second shoe. I stepped across the hard-wood floor foyer and followed her into the open-plan kitchen and lounge. A guy appeared from the other end of the house. "This is Brad, my husband."

I shook his hand. "Matt." They offered me a seat and I picked a single leather chair. They took the matching couch across from me. "I'm working on the girl found in the Okura estuary, you've probably seen that on the news?"

They both nodded. Brad shook his head as he spoke. "The skeleton? Bloody shocking, it's unreal. Do you know who she is yet?"

"Not yet. That's our main focus though. Look, this probably has nothing to do with it, but Nicole, you lived with your parents on Haigh Access Road when you were younger?"

She smiled. "Yeah, my whole childhood really." Then her smile dropped. "Is this from way back then?"

"Yeah, the pathologist reckons she could have died as far back as '93, '94."

"Oh my god . . ." Nicole put her hand up to her mouth. "I would have been . . . seventeen?" she looked at her husband.

I kept talking. "I've been looking through all the events in our system from back then, but the records aren't particularly detailed. Do you remember a party you would have had back in November '94? There was a call for an ambulance. Somebody needed an ambulance?"

The record had actually said: *Attempted suicide. Female caller requests ambulance. Police assist.* But I didn't want to make Nicole uncomfortable, so I figured I'd give her just enough, and invite her to talk about the rest. I had no idea who had needed the ambulance, and, for all I knew, it might have been her. She racked her brain, and then nodded. "Yeah, yeah, I probably had quite a few people from school over to celebrate the end of the year. Mum and Dad had gone away for the weekend. One of the girls, she . . ." Brad was looking at his wife. I doubt he'd heard this before. He was as interested as me. "She'd broken up with her boyfriend shortly before I think, and he was there with another girl, you know, teenage . . . stuff. I found her in the bath, she'd taken some pills, I called the ambulance. But when they came, she was awake, got a bit stressed out. They called the cops."

"Right. Did they take her to hospital? Can you remember?"

"Um, not really. I think they took her but all I remember is the ambulance guys saying she'd be okay, I'm sure she was okay. The cops sort of calmed her down, they didn't end up doing anything. I just remember her being all right after . . ."

"Did you see her after that?"

"I don't think so. She wasn't a close friend, more like a friend of a friend. I can't remember having much to do with her after that."

"Can you remember her name?"

Nicole looked at her husband then back at me. She was doing pretty well here. Ask me what I had for lunch yesterday and I'd be struggling. Seventeen years ago? No chance. But she had a better head than me. Clearly. "Laura. I'm going to say Laura Booth? I think that was her surname. Booth."

I made some notes, took their details and left them my card. "Thanks Nicole. Like I said, it's probably unrelated. We're just following up anything where the records aren't perfect. I'll be in touch. Cheers Brad." I shook his hand and stepped off the porch onto the driveway. I phoned Rebecca from my car and asked her to run Laura Booth, aged around thirty-four. *Was that right? Seventeenish in '94. Yeah.* The system could do a wide search a few years either side. I drove back along Tamaki Drive, past the marina on my left and Mechanics Bay on my right, home of the maritime unit and Eagle helicopter. The cranes and stacked shipping containers dominated the skyline behind. I kept the docks on my right as I continued along Quay Street into the lower CBD, before joining the northern motorway just past Vic Park at the Fanshawe Street on-ramp.

Rebecca called me back as I was crossing the Harbour Bridge. "Matt, I think I've found the most likely: Laura Douglas, maiden name Booth. Born in '78, apparently now living in Campbells Bay on the Shore. Definitely alive . . ."

"Thanks Bex."

She gave me the address and a landline, but I didn't call. I figured I should probably do Mrs Douglas the decency of a face-to-face for something so personal, if she was the right person. I pulled into the cul-de-sac off Beach Road, and drove to the end, turning around in the keyhole and parking in the direction of the way I'd come, with the houses to my left, the playground and park to my right, and beach behind me. I walked up the driveway, past the Holden and the Audi and knocked on the solid aluminium door. I took a guess it was her when she answered. "Mrs Douglas? I'm Matt Buchanan, Orewa Police."

"You're working on the Okura body?" she knew right away.

"Yeah, and it's nothing for you to worry about, but I'm just covering off some loose ends from old records as we try to identify the victim."

"Yeah, I used to live up in Dairy Flat."

"Look, I apologise for bringing this up after all these years . . . but I just need to make sure I've got the right person so that we don't go chasing something we don't need to. Back in 1994 . . ."

"Right. Party? Haigh Access? Yeah. That was me. I think the girl that lived there called the ambulance, they took me to hospital and I was okay. I did get referred for an assessment though, which was actually a good thing. Got me on the right meds at last."

She was pretty switched on. I looked around the property and smiled at her. "Things look like they're much better now."

"Yeah they are. Shit, that was a long time ago. You must just be following up everything."

"Yeah, just following procedure. I'm really sorry again, there are big holes in our records from back then. I just had to make sure it wasn't . . ."

She put a hand up and smiled. "No worries, I understand. Good luck, Detective."

"Thanks. Goodnight, Mrs Douglas."

Another dead end. I wanted something to start happening. But that was how homicide investigations generally rolled . . . one slow foot in front of the other. It sure wasn't as glamorous as TV pretended. *And the main characters were a shitload uglier too.*

FOUR

She was sitting at a table at the window, looking out over West-park marina. She hadn't ordered, and she stood with a smile when I walked through the ranch slider entrance. She looked the same as she had for the last twelve years. Shoulder-length blonde hair, well presented. But now with a tiredness behind her eyes that she wouldn't shake anytime soon. I greeted her with a kiss on the cheek. "Great to see you, Karen." I always made a point of visiting Sam's parents in person. I couldn't treat them as another thing on my to-do list and deal with them on the end of the phone. For them, I was the one remaining chance of ever finding out what had happened to their daughter. They knew it and I knew it – no one else would ever give them, or the case, the attention it deserved. Not that I'd done it any justice recently. *Or ever, in fact.* We ordered at the counter and took our seats back at the window. Even on a wet, grey day, the view was pleasant. I didn't know much about life on the ocean wave, but I had always liked boats, fishing and marinas. Something I wished maybe I'd learned more about. It was calm, peaceful.

The recent case in the media had unsettled Karen a bit. "Another one for you."

"We don't know who she is. We just know it isn't Sam."

We chatted about the Okura area. I'd run that track plenty of times. It was a popular place, and she knew exactly where the media reports were talking about. We didn't know of course whether the girl had been killed near the swamp, or killed somewhere else and then dumped there. I wouldn't have told Karen even if I had known. But regardless, she was thinking of the girl. "She would have been so scared. So, so scared. What a horrible, horrible place to end up."

I didn't want to think about it. My flat white arrived and I stirred in a sugar. I thought about my own cold, robotic appraisal of crime scenes. Police were clinical – who did this, how did it happen, how do I find the person responsible, how do I go about locking them up so they can't do it again? We had to be. Otherwise it'd be a shambles. Follow a logical process, cut away from the emotional side. Start getting emotional and you're fucked. The job suffers.

The public thought differently though. Karen, for example, was putting herself in the victim's shoes. And, if I was honest, I was starting to realise that after sixteen years of policing, and sixteen years of cutting away from the emotional side and bottling everything up, maybe it hadn't really worked for me the way I thought it should. Cracks were appearing at the sides. I gave my five cents. "I guess we can only pray it was quick."

She looked into her cup. "Mmm. God." She shook her head. "They really exist, don't they? Evil people."

I stared out toward the boats. Dark clouds hung about above. There wasn't any blue sky in sight. Beyond the masts there was no sign of the city skyline. I couldn't even see Hobsonville Point out to the left. It was all grey. I considered what Karen was asking. As much as I've come across some horrible events, some truly brutal things, I don't think I've ever encountered someone truly *evil*. To me, that was a strong word. I'd interviewed murderers, rapists, child abusers. I'd managed to have a conversation with all of them. They'd committed horrific acts, sure. But at different periods in their lives they'd had friends, families, people who loved them. They drank beer, socialised, did favours for mates, all the things that normal people do. Then, because of a combination of things: genetics as well as circumstances – maybe abuse, maybe tragedy, often a skewed moral compass, perhaps a dose of psychological unravelling – they'd snap, and become a killer. There were a lot of factors. Don't get me wrong – most had made definite, culpable choices. But I don't think I'd ever sat across from pure evil before. "I guess, even the worst, they're all just people. Flesh and blood. I think that's what keeps me focused, but at the same time . . . it's probably what scares me the most. We're actually capable of this shit."

"Not us, Matt."

I looked back from the window at Karen. "Not us, no." I changed the subject. Sam's dad was usually present at these catch-ups too, but he was away currently with work. "How's Rob doing?"

"It never gets easier. Well, the pain eases. Well no, no it doesn't ease, it shifts, morphs into something more bearable. It's hard to describe to people who don't understand, who haven't been here. That's why we keep bothering you, Matt. You know better than most. You understand."

"Different circumstances for me though, Karen."

"I know, but I often think, maybe that's far worse? No rhyme or reason, no intent, just . . . just something awful out of the blue. Kate—" she trailed off. "I'm so sorry, Matt."

Rob and Karen had met my wife years back, when this all kicked off. They liked to remind me. Not that I needed reminding. "I think Kate wouldn't have had too much time to think about it."

Karen held my hand. *Weird.* "You need to look after yourself, Matt. You aren't as bulletproof as you think. How's Hailey?"

I laughed. "She's a teenager. What can I say?"

"Difficult?"

"Not really. Sometimes. I can't complain. Her mates are everything at the moment. But that's good. That's important."

"She'll get back to you when she's twenty."

"Yeah, I know." I looked out at the boats again. *Who the fuck was counselling who here?* I changed the subject again. "And Holly?" Holly had only been ten when her older sister had disappeared. She must have been twenty-one, twenty-two now. I hadn't seen her for years but I knew it would have been tough for her.

"She's working in town. Small law firm, they treat them harsh early on."

"So I hear. Long hours, weekends?"

"Yeah, she's doing eighty-hour weeks, poor girl. But she likes it, it's mainly commercial work, employment and some property."

"Tell her to stay on that side of the fence. If you hear she wants to head down the criminal law path, get hold of me. I'll put her off."

Karen smiled. "I don't know if she wants to." She turned the conversation back to the morbid. "Her sister is a huge part of her life. She keeps her photo in her wallet. Always talks about her, it's a hole she'll never fill. But I think the memory of Sam helps Holly make the right decisions. She's doing okay."

I fidgeted. Turned my mug on its saucer. *I can't do this sort of conversation.* We finished our cups and parted ways at the café entrance. Karen spoke first. "Always nice to see you, Matt. I know I always apologise, but I am sorry. To keep bothering you."

"I wouldn't see you if I didn't want to, Karen. It's important to me, you know that. Call me anytime. And if Rob and Holly want to catch up, or have questions, just let me know."

"Thanks, they'd love to see you."

I turned my back on the marina and headed for my car. Just as I reached my door it started to spit. *Yeah, fuck you Winter.*

FIVE

I got a breather from the homicide a day later to help the Organised Crime Squad out. They tackled drugs and gangs, and I'd rotated in and out of the squad a few times in the past, always enjoying the proactive nature of the work. Steve Prentice, one of the D's there, was a really good mate of mine. He'd called up the night before.

"Hey mate. The squad's knocking a lab over tomorrow morning, in Glenfield."

"Someone I know?"

"Pete Childs. Thought you might be keen to have a chat with him afterwards . . ."

Steve and I had worked together on and off for years. We'd recruited Peter Childs as an informant back when he was a car thief and low-level meth dealer. We'd tried to get him to clean himself up, but that world sucks you in and he couldn't dig himself out of the meth rut. It was a dependency he couldn't afford. He'd learned to cook, became one of those guys hoping to cook just to feed his own habit, maybe flick some gear to his mates to earn money for bread and milk. But it doesn't work like that. Once word gets out, you're hot property, whether you like it or not. He'd run foul of that dark world, been forced by the clubs to cook at gunpoint, beaten and bashed for not doing their bidding, losing everything several times over. As a result, he had a few enemies, which is where we came in. We were a sounding board, the voices of reason, guys who could be trusted in an otherwise fucked-up world. We fixed problems where we could, and where the law allowed us. It wasn't business; it was mutual gratitude. He'd provided some pretty good information over the years, on some pretty big players. But he couldn't keep on breaking the law. That was always made clear. Meth is meth. Hence the warrant on his place.

Steve passed a few more details. "Doors in at 6 a.m. They don't have much on his phones so will just be going on what's found there. Shall we see him after he's interviewed? He'll be taken to Henderson."

I'd run it past Helen and she'd given me the morning off to do it. I'd taken my own car to Henderson.

We sat in a triangle – Pete, Steve and I. This wasn't an interview, it was a catch-up. We had a cover story. You had to keep this sort of shit tight. No one knows who your informants are, and that includes other cops. The rest of Steve's squad thought I wanted to talk to Pete about another meth lab up my way. I didn't. But I had a big ringbinder labelled "Manufactures Class A – Makarau – CHILDS/ Peter" to prove I did. It was actually just full of random shit to bulk the ring binder up. Gotta look right. Look after those that help us out. The only people who knew we talked to Pete off the record were Steve and me. That's just how it worked.

"Long time no see, gents." He laughed.

"You look well, mate?" I said. "Been off the gear?"

"Yeah. Trying to, you know how it is. Doing my best. But those cunts in the club needed a place, needed a job done and I was it."

Steve piped up. "We've told you how it goes though, mate. You should've called us weeks ago, we could've stopped this. Taken some pressure off you."

He shook his head. "I know, I fuckin' know. Sorry, guys. I just got caught up. What a fuck-up."

"You've been here before though, Pete. Take the consequences and we'll see you on the other side. Next time, keep us in the fuckin' loop, will you?"

He nodded. Then he frowned, looked at the desk, fucked about with his fingers. He looked up at us. More serious now. This wasn't about him. "There's some shit you guys will want to know about. Not normal stuff, but it's linked up with my scene. There's a group, on the face of it they're cooking gear, flicking it. But I heard they're into some heavy shit, dark web, kiddie porn, that sorta thing."

I hated the phrases "child porn" and "kiddie porn". It was child rape – just recorded. I didn't know too much about computers. "Dark web?" I looked at Steve.

He gave me a look that asked if I lived under a rock. "Don't you read the news? The shit you access on Explorer, Safari, Firefox – that's just the tip. Dark web's the rest. You need special programs to access things like Tor networks . . ."

"Eh?"

Pete nodded at Steve. "Yeah, yeah, you can't get it on the normal internet. But that's what they're doing. It's fucked up."

I was still a bit confused. "So, what, are they watching it?"

"No! Fuck." Pete shook his head. "No, mate. They're fuckin', you know, making it. Producing it."

I glanced at Steve. He wouldn't tan in a sunbed, but he'd gone paler than even his normal complexion. He ran a hand through his short ginger-blonde hair. I looked back at Pete. "Who is?"

He looked sheepish. "I don't know. 'They'. I've just heard rumours. I don't want to fuck you guys round. I wouldn't – you've known me a while. I don't have any more than that really, but it's something I thought you guys would want to hear about."

"Of course. Where did you hear the rumours?"

"A mate. I probably shouldn't tell you who he is, but look, he's not in their group. He spoke to some mate of his who told him about it. This mate of his saw some of the films apparently. Totally freaked out, wasn't happy about it. Told my mate. He told me."

"He going to the cops?"

"Fuck no. The people involved are . . . no. That's why I'm telling you guys."

We had a lengthy chat then, asking Pete to look further into this. Whether he got bail, or was remanded inside, we needed more. If there are two things that really light a fire under cops' arses, they're murder and sexual abuse. Filmed sexual abuse of children is about as big a fire as you can get. He agreed to do some snooping, either in prison or when he got out, whichever way it went.

Steve spoke on our way out. "Look after yourself, mate."

I shook Pete's hand. "You know the drill. Nothing you wouldn't normally do or say." He grinned and slapped me on the back.

Steve spoke once we were outside the room. "Two of the other lads will process him and I think they're charging him with equipment, materials."

"Not manufacturing?"

"They found a boxed-up lab, bit of 'I', some hype, but no ephedrine."

No trifecta, no full lab. "Depends if the ESR swabs come back positive too, I guess."

As I walked down the CIB corridor past a few more of Steve's crew, Jas, one of the more senior Org Crime guys smiled at me. "Any luck?"

"Nah." I did my best fucked-off-looking impression. "Denied it. I know he was the cook though."

Jas grinned. "He's old school, Childs. He'd never own up. Never talks to cops. After this morning, didn't think he'd be saying much about another one."

I grinned to myself on my way out. You had to protect your sources. Or the Police wouldn't get anything done. Some cops didn't know how to talk to people. Treat people like a piece of shit, and you'll go nowhere fast. Treat people right, and you'll be surprised. I pushed through the red metal door and exited out the back of Henderson station by the vehicle gate. It was pissing down and I jogged across Sel Peacock Drive. It was a long run through the rain along Buscomb Ave to my car. Parking round here was shit. I slid in, cranked the warm air con, and headed for the McDonald's on Lincoln Road. There was a McChicken and a caramel sundae with my name on them.

SIX

At my desk. Trying to look at the screen. Eyes glazed over. Mind wandering. *Killed somewhere else, then dumped in the estuary.* That was the most likely scenario. I mean, it was good to keep an open mind and all, but if she'd been killed near the mangroves then that would be a spur of the moment thing, which meant mistakes, which meant we shouldn't be as fucked as we were right now. *But if she was killed elsewhere, then the job I'm doing – sifting through hundreds of events in the immediate area – is pretty fucking pointless.* Still, no stone left unturned – someone had to do it. But something else about it was doing my head in. *How does a teenager go missing for more than a decade and a half and no one reports it?* Family involvement? That's usually how. Not always. But without knowing who she was, we wouldn't know who they were either.

I focused back on my screen, opened the next incident Bex had earmarked and started reading the few lines of information. A traffic entry from 1995. Crash on the old highway, now East Coast

Road. The file had come about back to front. A rental car had been returned with front impact damage. The driver had done a runner. The rental company had laid a complaint and Police had looked into it briefly before writing it off as an insurance matter. I phoned the insurance company. It took poor Caitlyn several minutes to dig it up because, like us, they'd migrated to a new system from the one they'd had back then.

"Yeah, that was eventually resolved. Our records say the driver hit a stock animal on the road, the impact matched his statement and he eventually paid the excess we needed. The Police weren't involved after the excess was paid."

I thanked her and went back to my screen. I stared at it for a while, but I couldn't put this to bed quite yet. I requested the crash file from Records, and then phoned Caitlyn back to request the file the insurance company had. They needed a production order, so I spent my afternoon typing that out and getting it signed at the Court. I read through both files two days later.

On the 5th of September 1995 a Toyota had been returned to Hertz with major damage to the front bumper, bonnet and windscreen. The driver, a Jared Clayton, had dropped the car and left, without filling out the paperwork, and Hertz had got the Police involved. Forensics officers had gone to Hertz and photographed the car, swabbed blood from the windscreen, all that shit. But Clayton came to the party after a polite visit from the cops, and gave a statement about hitting an animal. Paid up all the costs. Nothing else came of it and it was filed. I called the cop who'd had the file back in '95. He was an Inspector now, based at the Harbour Bridge traffic base. Showed what a little ambition could do for you. He had to think hard when I queried him, and I didn't blame him at all. He would have dealt with hundreds of crashes in his time. I kept adding bits of information to help him out, describing the location, the type of car, the insurance company.

He got there eventually. "Yeah sorry, I think I remember that. I remember going to have a look at where the guy said it had happened. That long straight heading south on the old State Highway One, near the road that goes to Okura. This something to do with the body?"

"I'm gonna say no. I've just got the unenviable task of looking back through all the files from around the time the girl died, so cheers for helping me out. Anything odd about the driver's explanation that you can remember?"

"Well, it was bloody ages ago, but funnily enough I do remember it being odd. He was cagey as. I'd been on Highway Patrol for several years before I went to Enquiries – I'd seen plenty of stock animal hits and this didn't look like that to me. I mentioned my concerns, but nothing happened – cos, you know, no one fronted in hospital saying they had been run over around that time or anything like that. So, nothing to refute his story, no reason to believe anything otherwise. The insurance company was happy so I shelved it."

I had a hard-on for this now. Jared Clayton had been twenty-one at the time. He'd be thirty-seven now. I checked NIA and saw he'd made a recent complaint about tools stolen from his garage. Which meant I had an address and a cell. I gave it a ring. "Jared, Detective Matthew Buchanan from the Orewa Police. How are you this morning?"

The standard hesitant, what-the-fuck reply: "Um, hello, yes, good thank you."

"I wanted to have a chat about something from years back, your crash on what used to be State Highway One, near Okura back in '95? The rental car. I'm working on the body found in the estuary near there and am going through events around the time they reckon the body ended up there, just as a matter of course. There might be some things you can help me with."

"Don't think so. My memory isn't so good now. That was, what, fifteen, no sixteen years ago? I gave a statement back then – that will probably help."

"Yeah, I've got it in front of me. But I'd like to catch up in person if you could?"

"Ah . . . I'm pretty busy. Not trying to be difficult, you know, but I just don't think there's anything I can add. I mean, I don't see how it'll help with that girl – I saw that on the news. Fuckin' horrible. I'll have a think though and if there's anything that might be useful I'll let you know."

"I'd rather just have a chat—" and he hung up on me. *You giant horse's cock.* I wanted to pay him a visit but first I rang the SOCO office.

"Rick here."

Rick was a good bastard. He'd been doing forensic and scene-of-crime work for years. He was in his late forties now, and, like me, he had no wish to do anything else. "Hi mate, Matt Buchanan. Just querying an old file. I'm not holding out any hope, but I figure it's worth checking out . . . it's about some blood swabs taken back in '95."

"Geez, okay, shoot."

He wasn't making any promises from that long ago, but I quoted the file number and said the notes indicated blood swabs were taken, but didn't indicate where they ended up. He had a think. "They would have been destroyed, I'd say. I'll call you back."

Four hours later, my phone rang. "Do you want the bad news or the good news?" I chuckled but said nothing. He carried on. "The bad news is that the officer filed his file and confirmed on our sheet that he destroyed the swabs." *Fuck. Ah well, on to the next one . . .*

"But the good news is that he took the lazy option and never actually retrieved them from the exhibit store to do it. They're still here."

SEVEN

I sent the blood off with an urgent request. No full analysis required, just whether it was human or animal. I went back to sifting through more files, ticking off NIA occurrences and following other leads that went nowhere.

ESR came through two weeks later with a result. I opened the envelope and skimread the statement from the scientist – name, qualifications, yup, scientific analysis yup . . . I skipped to the conclusion…and stared at the words. I breathed out hard. *Finally, the break.* Human DNA. *Fuck! That lying little cunt.*

The heavy-hitters were in the middle of a meeting when I barged in. Helen and Tim looked round at me. They were mid-conversation but I cut them off.

"I've been looking at a car crash from '95. Early September. Car hit an animal, insurance write off. On the old highway, near Haigh Access." Helen raised her eyebrows, but my face was saying "it gets better". "I phoned the driver. Didn't want to see me." Tim folded his arms, waiting. "The O/C of the case never destroyed the blood samples forensics took from the area of damage. I sent them to ESR two weeks ago."

Tim stood up from his chair. "You're fuckin' kidding me."

"Nope. Human blood."

I gave them the start to finish on the crash. I detailed my conversation with the old file holder and how he reckoned something was up with the driver. I then went through my phone conversation with Jared Clayton. The bosses decided to form a proper suspects team under Dean, the DS running Organised Crime at the moment. They put me and Dan under him. The three of us got together and had a brainstorm about where to from here. Jared had to be pulled in for an interview. We didn't have a match to our body yet but it was looking likely enough to warrant stepping things up. We had what looked like a person run over in the right time period, never reported. A lying driver. And a body in the mangroves less than a K away.

I suggested we go live on his phone first, and they agreed. We had enough. We had grounds probably for careless driving causing death, at the very least. But with the hands and skull missing, the offence we put on the application for the interception warrant ended up being murder. Tim called the evening briefing and the investigation team was brought up to speed. Once we had the wire up and running we'd pull Jared in for an interview and see what fell out.

EIGHT

The rest of Dean's Organised Crime crew, Steve included, ran the wire for us. We couldn't spare the staff necessary to monitor that 24/7, and they were the experts in that area anyway. Listening live is more resource-heavy than people think. We needed five officers – Dean's whole team – just to monitor one guy. And that was just a landline and a cell. We didn't have the capability to monitor his computer shit too, but even if we could, we didn't have the people to do it. We also can't just flip a switch and listen to whoever we like for shits and giggles, though that'd be nice sometimes. A warrant application goes to a High Court judge. We outline to the judge who we want to listen to, and why. We have to show that criminal activity has either happened or is happening, and prove that listening to their conversations is going to get us some evidence. These applications often run into the hundreds of pages. If we're granted our warrant, we work alongside the telcos, who give us the access to listen. It's like a safe needing two keys – we can't listen without their say-so, and they can't say so without our warrant. Some very average technology our side then feeds the audio to our office computers so we can listen at our desks. Since the Police are generally stretched at the best of times, we only did this for serious shit.

With the wire up and running, Dan and I went to Jared Clayton's place in Red Beach early in the morning. We drove up the driveway to the two-level, plaster-cladded house – the back one of two similar-looking ones on the section. There were kids' scooters lying in front of the front door, and a tramp set up on the lawn to the right. *Great. More lives affected.* But I was switched on and on a mission, and this guy had already lied to me. There wasn't going to be any arguments or fucking about here. I was straight into it when he answered the door.

He had messy brown hair, the wrinkles on his forehead and the stubble not hiding any clues to his age. Big nose, face that had seen a lot of sun.

"Jared, Detective Buchanan. We spoke on the phone. Time for a talk. You're under arrest for careless driving causing death." I gave him his rights while he feigned complete disbelief. His wife came to the door and started protesting. Then she started yelling. Not at Dan and me, strangely, which was the usual story, but at Jared. *Parents must have raised her right.*

"Jared, what the hell is going on? Tell me what's going on!"

He called from the driveway as Dan led him to our car. "It was a crash, honey, years ago. It's nothing, honestly. I'll see you later today."

Dan had got Jared into the back seat, and I took the opportunity to try and calm Jared's wife down a bit. It always fucked me off, what the partner and kids went through. But we had a job to do. I walked over to her and she pushed her hair back from her face, breathed in, trying to calm herself. But she was welling up. "Emily, is it? My name is Matt Buchanan, and that's my partner Dan. Here's my card. Your husband hit someone with a car years back, in 1995. Hit and run. At this stage we're trying to establish the sequence of events, work out what exactly happened, and get Jared to explain what he did. He won't be staying with us tonight. We'll bring him back. Then you can ask him all about it. If you have any issues before then, give me a call. But he'll be back later."

She thanked me, which was nice to hear. That might sound odd, but it's the little things. Her fear was the unknown, including not knowing how long Jared was going to be away for. Now she knew she'd get her answers from her husband later that night.

The car trip started with questions, obviously.

"What the hell are you guys doing?" Jared was asking as we drove the few K's to the station. Up to Hibiscus Coast Highway and down the hill over the Orewa river. "Honestly, this has got to be some sort of mistake. I never hit anyone, anywhere." He didn't seem agitated or angry, just confused. We pulled into the station, parking at the rear after negotiating the security gate. Dan marched Jared into one of the interview rooms and I made us coffee. While opening the tin of normal shit, I noticed someone had left their prized jar of Moccona out on the bench. *What a dumbarse.*

When I came through the door Jared was seated, looking up at me expectantly, eyes flicking across to Dan as he set up the DVD recorder. I gave him one of the cups and spoke gently. "We need your version of events, Jared. That's all. You don't have to worry about this process . . ." I waved at the DVD unit, ". . . it's nothing special, we record all our interviews like this." I went back out and grabbed Dan's cup. Coming back in, I passed it to Dan and switched the DVD unit on. Jared nodded at his rights as I gave them again, and agreed to talk to us.

"September, 1995. You dropped a rental car back at Hertz, front impact damage. When the Police caught up with you later, you told them you'd hit a stock animal." He was looking at me, frowning. He'd been here before, but far more casually I'd say, back in '95. This looked a whole lot more serious, and he couldn't figure out why. He thought he'd covered his tracks. He was trying to figure out where he'd gone wrong – where he'd fucked up. He probably wouldn't say much, but we just needed something. "Tell me about the crash. The impact. Everything you remember."

Normally people begin fucking about by telling me their whole life story, steering well clear of the important shit. But he surprised me and went straight into it. "I was coming down the highway. From Silverdale. Past Stillwater. I was going quick, right, but I can't remember the speed obviously. But quick. Straight roads, right, not many blind corners on that highway. Just dark, real dark in some places. Coming down the hill toward Okura, I couldn't see anything. I don't remember seeing anything, until it hit the car. I remember feeling the impact, I don't remember hearing anything. I must have hit the brakes, eventually came to a stop. Car was fucked. I had a good jolt, but was okay. So probably a sheep, I'm thinking. I checked around, found the sheep in the drainage ditch running by the highway. Now, look, I don't want to incriminate myself here—"

I interrupted him. "I'm not interested in whether you were pissed or not, Jared, that's not why we're here. Can't really prove that this far along, can we? It's the crash itself I'm concerned with. What you hit. What did you do next?"

"Well, I panicked. The car was fucked. I thought someone might call the cops. Then I'd get breath-tested. I was young, I was freaking out. I got back in the car and took off, slowly mind you, because the windscreen was fucked. Window down, head out a bit all the way home."

I had been leaning in, listening intently. I sat back at that point and studied him. Determining guilt or innocence isn't an exact science, of course, but experience is experience and there were two things I'd found to be generally true. An innocent person with nothing to hide will be adamant about their innocence from the moment they're arrested. They won't get aggressive, but they'll do everything they can to get themselves out of the mess, so they'll offer anything to convince the cops they didn't do it. They'll be vocal, use their hands, lots of body language. And when interviewed, they'll spend a lot of time talking about the main event, explaining their alibi, getting right into the detail. If left alone, they'll be fully alert, agitated, stand up, walk around. I haven't dealt with many of these people. But a guilty person, well, they're different. They might become aggressive and abusive, but not always. But they'll always be pretty unhelpful. They talk about everything except the key moment. They stay away from that, because that's where they're fucked. And if left alone, they'll put their head down on the desk and rest, or actually go to sleep. Because they know what they did. And they can't change that. So Jared was surprising me. After going over it again in detail, I called a break and had a chat with Dan outside the interview room.

Dan was thinking ahead. "He might not do anything if he thinks we have nothing."

"Yeah. We need to show our hand. Show him how serious this is. Get him worked up, and set him loose among the pigeons." We wanted him to get on the phone after this and chat to someone about it. If he thought he'd sold the sheep story well, he might not bother. Dan and I went back in and I leaned into him, talking slowly. "Thanks for your recollection Jared, it's pretty consistent with your statement from '95."

He leaned in to me, mirroring my body language. This was good. He was concentrating. "Well, of course it is. But sorry my memory is probably a bit worse now than it was."

I extended the pause, got him focused on me, waiting for me to say he could leave. "But we've got a bit of a problem here, Jared. The thing is, the blood on the car you returned was swabbed by forensics staff back in '95. And they held on to those samples, even after the matter was dealt with." *Confusion on his face.* "See, they weren't destroyed, Jared, those samples of . . . what you're saying was sheep blood." I saw his brow flicker slightly as he pieced this together. This was new information for him. But it shouldn't have been. I took him off balance, in another direction. "You've seen the news? Seen the body, in the estuary at Okura? That's at the end of Haigh Access. Less than a K from your crash. They reckon the body was dumped there between '94 and '96." I let that hang. He started to screw his face up as he realised where this was going. "We got your 'sheep blood'" – I made quote marks in the air around that – ". . . tested. Results came back a few days ago. And guess what, Jared? The blood on your rental car? Human."

I shut up and just watched him. Confusion spread over his face again. Followed by panic. He started to look distressed, and could see he'd been boxed in. The fear looked genuine.

And he kicked into super-helpful mode. "No, no, that can't be right. I never hit a girl! Look, it's like I said . . . fuck!" He looked around the room, hands open, palms up. "Fuck!" he said again.

I locked eyes with him and didn't move. "Human blood on the car, blood you lied about sixteen years ago, Jared. You lied and said you hit a sheep. You didn't. You hit a girl. Now we've got a body in the swamp that's been there sixteen years. Let's put the bullshit behind us. We're over that, forget it, I won't take that personally, mate. But you've got some explaining to do now."

He started crying. He started mumbling and I couldn't make out what he was saying. He seemed genuinely upset that he'd been confronted with the human blood on the car, it all seemed new to him. "There must be a mistake with the testing, must be a mistake . . ." he was shaking his head, looking at the desk, looking up at Dan, then at me.

My cue. "Look, the investigation is ongoing, we're looking further into this. We're not charging you with anything, not today. We've got a lot of enquiries to follow up on. But we're going to talk to you again, and we'll need you to work with us. This isn't going away and you've seen the news. I wouldn't bother booking any overseas holidays. They won't let you past passport control. Take my card. We'll be in touch."

Before dropping him home I spoke to Helen and we phoned the Organised Crime guys to let them know the cage had been rattled, and that hopefully the phone would start running hot.

It did. Within minutes of dropping Jared home, he was on the phone to another guy. Steve called us once Dan and I were back at Orewa and gave us the rundown. With Steve on speaker, Dan, Dean, Helen and myself gathered round.

"Jared phoned a guy he called Dylan. We can't identify him from the cell-phone number, but he's polling in Takapuna. Jared was pretty wound up. Accused Dylan of hitting a girl on the highway back in '95. Told Dylan he'd just been interrogated. That we'd tested the blood. Told Dylan it was on him, that Jared had never agreed to cover for this. He was yelling at this guy Dylan to go talk to the cops about what had really happened."

"Was there confirmation from this other guy, this Dylan?"

"Sort of. He didn't argue when Jared accused him of being the driver, but that's about it. He kept telling Jared to calm down, that the cops must have it wrong."

This was gold. We needed to go live on Dylan's phone too. While that was being arranged, Dan, Dean and I jumped into a car and raced down the motorway to the Organised Crime office on the Shore to listen to the conversation properly. We pulled our chairs close to Steve's computer and played the recording. Jared had really let Dylan have it. He definitely wasn't happy. It was pretty clear this Dylan had been driving and that Jared had taken the fall for some reason.

While we listened to the call, Steve was monitoring the live feed beside us and suddenly called out: "Dylan's calling Jared back!" He turned the speaker up so we could all hear. The live feed crackled and we could hear the ringing of the phone. Then it got picked up.

"What the fuck are you doing?" Jared's voice crackled out of the speaker. "Go talk to the cops, you fuckin' idiot. Get this shit off of me. Emily's gone ballistic. I'm trying to tell her it's nothing to do with me. Whatever I say means nothing unless you go up there and tell them—"

Dylan cut in. "Mate, what was the end of your convo with that cop?"

"What?"

"What did he say, what are they going to do?"

"He said they were still investigating."

"Okay. Fuck. What though, what are they looking at? Would they get onto me?"

"Well, fuck, man . . ." I imagined Jared throwing his hands up in the air, ". . . yes, yes they fuckin' will, because if you don't go talk to them, I . . . this is nothing to do with me. I did you a favour cos you were pissed. That's all. I'm not taking the rap for whatever the hell this is if they're looking at charges. They said careless causing death. They know you hit a girl. This isn't going away. And I'm not involved. Fuck you, you lied to me. I can't believe someone's dead, you never told me, you . . . fuck, man. This isn't you. This isn't you. How could you do this? If you don't talk to them, I'll have to tell them the truth. I've got kids."

"But it was dealt with, it's done. How have they linked it!?" Dylan was sounding pretty panicked himself now.

"Do you watch the news, dickhead? They found a girl in the swamp. In a tarp. It's all over the TV, the internet. It's murder, Dylan! A murder case! That's what they're looking at! He didn't say the blood from the car matched her, but it's pretty obvious they're going that way . . . he was a detective, right? Not a traffic cop. Don't you get it? It's a murder case, and you're fucked. And I'm fucked if you don't tell them what happened. This has nothing to do with me. What the fuck did you do anyway?!"

"Man, I fuckin' hit her but, honest to God, I didn't do anything else! It was so dark, pissing down, huge storm . . . I couldn't see shit, it wasn't my fault! I just hit her, bam, I stopped, panicked, looked back and I could see she was moving in the middle of the road. She wasn't dead. I shat myself, I was pissed, I fucked off. There was nothing on the news that night, so I assumed she was all good, nothing had been reported. I didn't think anything bad had come of it, so I just covered my arse with the car, that's all—"

"What the fuck?! Are you fuckin' serious? Oh my god . . ." Jared's heavy breathing came through the speaker. It sounded like he was having a panic attack. "You fuckin' stupid prick. That's not you man, that's not you. You don't fuckin' do that. Drive off? How the fuck am I supposed to believe you didn't drag her out to the mangroves? I wouldn't have believed you could hit a chick and leave her on the road, so what the fuck am I supposed to believe now?"

"I was pissed mate, I was a young pissed cunt. I didn't have my shit together . . ."

"Ditch your cell-phone. Get rid of it. I'll come and have a chat. You gotta sort this out. You. You have to talk to the cops. You aren't a crook. Tell them the full story. Not me." Jared hung up.

We looked at each other in disbelief. Dean broke the silence. "Twenty-one years I've been doing this, never heard of a case solved with one of the first conversations."

I got on the phone to give Helen the news. She said she'd come down with Tim to have a listen. As I hung up, Dean got a call from the surveillance team. They were following Jared. If there was any luck left to go round, we'd have Dylan identified shortly.

NINE

Jared was sitting in the chair across from me again. He'd been crying, and it looked weird on his weather-beaten face. His hands were running through his thick curly hair. *C'mon mate. You're almost forty, for fuck's sake. Stop acting like a little bitch.* To be fair, I had arrested him at dawn for being an accessory to murder, so maybe it was fair enough. He'd looked like he'd been shot when I said that.

We had a bunch of recorded phone calls confirming the facts, but we didn't have the full picture, and we needed some answers. I knew Jared was motivated to tell the full story. ESR had come back two days earlier with a positive on the blood swabs, matching marrow from the skeleton in the mangroves. There's no such thing as a coincidence, but getting that confirmation was the nail in the coffin for Dylan Manning. Jared's statement was just going to be the earth piled on top.

I'd just played the recordings to him. From that initial call after we picked Jared up the first time, through to him telling Dylan to ditch his phone, and several further calls we also had. Despite telling Dylan to toss his phone, Jared had kept his own. This had helped us carry on with our listening. We probably wouldn't get enough to satisfy the Crown Solicitor with an accessory charge for Jared. We might, if we looked hard enough, but if he turned witness against his old mate, we wouldn't go searching. Dan was in another room interviewing Dylan for murder. We were pausing both interviews every so often, and having discussions with Dean in the breaks so that we all stayed on the same page.

As hoped, Jared distanced himself fully and went over his actions around Dylan's crash in as much detail as he could remember. Not everything was spot on, of course, but the general sequence of events made sense. He'd got a panicked call from his mate late one night, September '95. Jared's car had been getting serviced and the garage had paid for a rental because there'd been a delay or some shit. Dylan had borrowed it one night, and managed to pretty much write it off while driving pissed. Paranoid the cops would track him down and breath-test him, he'd asked Jared if he could drop the car back at his place. The next day, they figured the damage was the least of their worries. But driving pissed was a big issue. So was an uninsured driver. So Jared held on to the car for the agreed time with the garage then just dropped it off at the rental place, leaving in a hell of a hurry. He sorted the story with Dylan, and Dylan flicked him all the coin necessary to cover the excess once the cops got involved.

I'd asked Jared exactly what he remembered Dylan saying about the crash location. He thought hard. "I'm trying to remember exactly what he said. He was driving south, from Silverdale down to the Shore on State One. It was dark, the weather was shitty. It wasn't long between the crash and him calling me from his house. I'm pretty sure he said it happened in Redvale, which is just there near Okura, so just south of Stillwater, I guess. I don't remember too much more about where he said it happened, but I remember telling the cop – when I was interviewed and took the blame back then – I said the straights just after Okura heading south. I'd made that up though, all I actually remember Dylan saying was Redvale."

"What about the supposed animal? What did Dylan tell you about that?"

"I don't think he said what it was . . . just that he hit an animal. I told the cop it was a sheep, I think. I can't really remember. But I don't remember Dylan telling me what animal it was, I just made that up."

"Did you ask him later on?"

"Probably, but yeah I can't recall. It became one of those things, you know, you joke about it later on, have a laugh, because it could have gone so, so wrong. Driving drunk, you know . . ." he shook his head. "So fuckin' stupid." He looked at the table. "I never questioned his version of the story. Why would I? He was a mate. I'd never have expected he'd lie to me. Never thought he'd be capable of something like this. Nothing came of it for so long."

"Yeah, well, something did go wrong, horribly wrong, Jared." It was time to mention the specifics. "This wasn't just a crash, just a hit and run. Nah." I breathed in, did my leaning in trick, got eye contact. "I'm afraid it's much worse than that." Jared frowned and looked toward the ceiling. He breathed in and rubbed his forehead. What more could there be? I let him breathe for a few more seconds. "Her skull and hands were missing, Jared. The pathologist's opinion is that they were cut off. Those are the parts we use to identify someone. So, if we know Dylan hit her, and was the last person to see her, then he cut those off her for a reason. To cover something up." Jared snapped his head down, looking right at me. Questioning. Looking for meaning. Thinking it through. Fear broke out on his face. I carried on. "That's right, mate. He didn't just hit her and leave her behind. He did something horrendous. He cut her up. He's staring murder, and life imprisonment, down the barrel."

Jared held my gaze, and I saw the tears start to well at the bottom of his eyelids. He put his hands together in front of his face, and looked at the desk. "Oh god." He leaned back, looked at the ceiling again. He put his face back in his hands. "Oh my fucking god." He grabbed the tissues and had a good blow. He wiped his mouth and looked at me through bloodshot eyes. "Look, I know Dylan, he was a fuckin' idiot back then, bad at making decisions, but . . . he isn't a murderer. No fuckin' way. You're saying he hit her, then dragged her into the swamp? He isn't capable of that, or at least I didn't think he was. Guess there's always things you don't know about a person. But cut her up? You've gotta be shitting me . . ." He ran his fingers through his hair.

"We don't know the full story yet. He's still being interviewed. It's possible he killed her on the road. Panicked. Drunk. Wanted to slow the identification down. Who knows? People are capable of all sorts of things when they panic, Jared. It could have been sexually motivated. But because it's been so long, because of the state the body is in, there's no evidence to prove anything like that. But regardless, it's not looking good for him."

"You can't argue with the facts I guess." He didn't phrase it as a question, but he was searching me for an alternative.

"No. You can't."

I broke the interview and went out to talk with Dean. He was watching the live feed from Dan's interview on a monitor in the room next door. He got me up to speed. Up until that point Dylan had admitted to hitting a girl, but insisted she had been okay, that she hadn't died. Dylan had explained in detail how she'd come out of nowhere, on the straights heading south past Okura. He'd hit her, and because his windscreen had shattered he'd stopped and got out. He'd seen her moving, saw her getting up and falling over, and he'd panicked. He'd cut and run before she could get his rego. Dan had listened and nodded, pretending to accept Dylan's bullshit story, probing, asking for detail. He wanted this version for when he hit Dylan with the full facts. I watched the monitor screen. Dan was talking.

"We still haven't identified her. What did she look like? Tell me everything about her."

Dylan was a smaller guy than Jared. Late thirties also, but dark hair, cut short and receding. He had these bulging eyes and he kept covering his face with his hands as he spoke. "I, I can't remember much. I saw nothing when I hit her. Just felt it, heard it. When I stopped and got out, I looked back on the road. It was dark. It was pissing down, like, really pouring. Not many lights on that stretch, you know? Dark hair maybe? Not short, I remember seeing it around her shoulders. Fuck, it was a long time ago now."

Dan was getting wound up. I was too, and I was just watching. "Bullshit, Dylan. You've had this hanging over your head for sixteen years. This is probably the image you've had in your head every single night since. A girl you should have helped. Think. What did you see?" Dylan kept on insisting he hadn't seen her close enough to be able to describe her. And now Dan was starting to get pretty fucked off. "I know you got a good look at her, so let's stop dancing around the issue here. You've admitted hitting this girl. The DNA matches. It's the girl we pulled from the estuary, from the mangroves, only several hundred metres from where you hit her. Wrapped in a tarp, Dylan. Dumped there, abandoned there, by the last person who saw her. And guess what?" Dan leaned right in, engaging Dylan fully. He flicked some photographs onto the desk between them. Two, three photos. I knew what they were. Dylan went whiter and put his hands up to his face. Dan kept going. "The body had no head and no hands. Not lost, Dylan. They were cut off. You cut her up, Dylan. You cut her up, and dumped her in the swamp. Was it because you raped her? Or you panicked again? Cut the shit. You obviously saw her up close because you put her in the car. Took her to the estuary. Wrapped her up. Cut her up. Carried her into those mangroves. So I want you to tell me, Dylan, what she looked like."

"Fuck off! I fucking did not cut her up! No fuckin' way!" Dylan was out of his chair, standing up. "I hit her man, I hit her, and then I gapped it, I gapped it cos I was shitting myself. No fuckin' way did I hang around, fuck no!" Dan had moved backwards out of his chair as soon as Dylan stood up, and was on his feet with his hands up. But Dylan just sat back down and put his own hands up, palms out, in apology. "Sorry man, I'm not having a go, I'm just, fuck, no way. No fuckin' way." Dan pulled some papers out of his folder and dropped them one by one on the desk between him and Dylan. I couldn't see detail on the monitor screen, but I knew what was in the package Dan had. A map of the Okura estuary, and the old State Highway One, with the location of the crash and the location of the body marked. Dylan was shaking his head, tears streaming down his face as he looked at the maps, and the photos already sitting on the desk. "I didn't fuckin' do this, I didn't fuckin' do this."

Dan exploded. "You dragged her into your car! Killed her, cut her up, and dumped her in the swamp! You got a good fuckin' look, all right. So what did she look like?!"

Dylan was crying. This was getting close to the line and I looked at Dean, but he was just glued to the monitor. He knew what I was thinking though and spoke without looking at me. "Won't get anything more if we don't try." *Fair call.*

Dan went in for his final attempt. "Dylan, you're in trouble. You've admitted hitting her. Problem is, we've got her DNA on the car you drove, and now her headless, handless body in the mangroves. You've put yourself at the crime scene. There was no one else involved. You can deny it all you like, but it isn't going to change what has happened. We're going to charge you with murder. But you can still do some good here. It's not all fucked up, Dylan. I get that you panicked. We all make shit decisions sometimes. Believe me, I know. I've made plenty. We just have to take the consequences that come. But you can still do right by this girl. You can still do right by her family, mate. What did she look like? Where did you dump her head and hands?"

Dylan was a mess. I could see the snot, even on the monitor. "I can't tell you, because, I didn't do that, I didn't . . ."

Dan concluded the interview and we all had a chat. Dylan was charged with murder. If by his own admission she was alive after he ran her over, then unwittingly he had put his hand up to ending her life. Jared was released without charge, but signed up as a witness.

Emily's relief was tangible as I reversed out of their driveway after dropping Jared home. I doubted there would be hard feelings between him and Dylan. Jared had never known the actual truth, so Dylan couldn't really expect him to cover his arse now. Still, people are capable of some crazy things when they panic, and this was an example. *What a fucking waste.*

Dan and I drove Dylan down to the cells at North Shore station, in Albany. We processed him there. He'd appear in the North Shore District Court the next day. Though it had been more than a decade and a half, we'd still be opposing his bail, in case there was some evidence he could fuck about with that we hadn't uncovered yet. We were still searching, still chasing his movements and interviewing his old mates.

We got back to Orewa station after dark. The bosses had prepared a media release. We had a few beers in the office. Not to congratulate ourselves, but to let off a bit of steam. We'd been at it solid for months, and had all been dealing with some emotionally heavy shit. Normal offices had pictures of sunsets, cats, and harassment awareness posters on their walls. Not us. We'd had to look at pictures of a headless skeleton, pulled from the mud and silt, as a reminder why we were there. It was a relief to have some sort of result. The beers were just how we dealt with the subject matter. I cracked a Speights and checked the sports question under the cap. *League? I wouldn't know anything about that blue-collar rubbish.*

TEN

The window above my kitchen sink was taking a battering this morning. The rain smashed in sideways and slid down the glass, drops joining together and disappearing out the bottom of the pane. I focused beyond the glass and the grey haze sharpened. A bit. Wind and rain whipping the trees and bushes along the fence-line. I couldn't see fuck all across the valley where normally I'd see down towards Browns Bay. Vis was just shit. I looked down and realised I'd been stirring my coffee for a good few minutes. I shook my head clear, and took it into the lounge.

The TV was talking about Dylan Manning making his second appearance in the District Court. Name suppression of course though. Not Guilty plea. They'd put it off again for some pre-trial arguments – there wouldn't be a High Court trial until at least mid-next year. I wandered through the house, pausing at Hailey's open door. It was the holidays and she was still at Sarah's, after a sleepover last night. Apparently. God, I worried about her, all the time. Not that she gave me much to worry about. All things considered, I couldn't believe she'd come through Kate's death the way she had. She was a hell of a lot stronger than I ever would be.

School would be finishing up in a couple of months' time. She'd be fifth form next year, time to get serious. *Yeah. Like I had when I was her age. Not.* If she'd kept a diary, I'd have monitored her life through that, nosey detective parent that I was. But she was smarter than me. Also, there was Facebook these days, and that shit was beyond me entirely. I felt the best I could do was make sure she could always come to me. The way to achieve that was to remove the threat. Remove the threat of angry dad, turn him into problem-solving dad. It was how I approached work and home, and it seemed to have worked so far. But I knew that some things Hailey would just have to work out for herself.

I carried on and went into our bedroom. *Our bedroom?* My bedroom. There were still a few pictures of Kate and me, of course. Engagement, wedding. Family photos. Almost five years, it had been. Seemed like yesterday that she'd been calling Hailey and me in from shooting hoops for dinner, before she got on the road. Hailey had only been ten. Back when I could still kick her arse at netball. Not anymore though. I returned to the lounge and there was a message on my phone:

> **Friends r talkn bout th**
>
> **arrest. Proud daughter xx**

Ah well, at least she wasn't off her face. I checked the time. 10 a.m. *Yet.* It was brief moments like that that anchored me into the real world, showed me what was actually worth my time. If only I could keep her from this sort of shit, but that time had passed. Kids, you could shield from the world pretty effectively. Teenagers? No chance. I sent her a short one back.

> **Who do you mean?**
>
> **You don't have any friends**

I got an emoji doing the fingers back. I thought I'd better come clean.

Love you too xx

My head drifted. Kate. I'd taken a few months off following that, but work grounded me, provided structure, so I had dived back in. The trauma psych reckoned normally that'd be okay, except that the subject matter at my workplace probably wasn't ideal. I'd never taken the hint though. My mind wandered from Kate's car crash, to the one at hand. An unidentified sixteen year old. No missing reports. *How the fuck does that happen?* Hailey meant so much to me. It didn't make any sense. Someone had to know who the girl was. I thought about other work. Other pain. Of young Kelly. Her rape trial would be starting in several months. *Did she know what she was in for?* I thought about Gabby too. Too much loss. Fuck it, life was what it was. Right?

I answered my buzzing cell. Helen. "Are you sitting down?"

I was sprawled across the couch. "Yup. Tell me you've identified her?"

"No."

I didn't say anything, but sat up straight. There was something in Helen's voice that made me do it. I waited and she filled the silence. "Dylan Manning hanged himself in his prison remand cell this morning."

ELEVEN

It was like I'd been electrocuted. I stood up. "What?"

"Yeah. Gone. Left a note. Addressed to the girl's unknown parents, of all things. Apologising. He just couldn't bring himself to talk about what he'd done. He just couldn't accept it."

I held my cell after Helen ended the call, turned it over and over in my hand. *Fuck.* Guess he couldn't handle it after all. And here I was thinking he was handling the whole thing fine, had even kept it secret for sixteen years, no bother.

That evening, the media had already swarmed all over it. The public comments I read on the news sites crucified him, calling him a coward. Apologising to the girl's parents? *We don't even know who they are. You should have done the right thing back in '95, you arsehole.*

Hailey had arrived home in the afternoon and was glued to the TV. She had even taken a break from her iPhone for a bit. Though she was your average teenager, she did have moments of insight. Very infrequently, let's be clear, but moments nonetheless.

She didn't glance up initially, but spoke toward the telly. "So, you still don't know who she is?"

"Not yet. Awful, eh?"

She looked around at me. She had Kate's brain, thank God. My light brown hair though. It fell over her face and she flicked it back. "You've got Sam's DNA, right? So it wasn't her." It wasn't a question. Hailey knew all about Sam and the Coates family. Probably a bit too much. She knew I had it in the back of my mind.

I changed the channel. "That's right. Not her." Flicker of a frown on Hailey's face. She studied me as I stared at the TV to take my mind elsewhere. "What?"

"Nothing." She pulled out her phone and got busy.

The next day we had a discussion in the office. Helen didn't have a trial to prepare for now, but what would the public make of that? We discussed Jared. Whether any charges could or should be brought against him now. *No.* We'd made a call on that months ago. We weren't going to change that decision just because the killer had hanged himself. Besides, Jared had now lost a mate too. Still no ID on the girl. That, more than anything I think, upset the team. I know Helen was heavily affected by that. She had four kids, two girls and two boys. The oldest were in their mid-teens. Like me, like the rest of the team, Helen couldn't understand how a sixteen year old gets murdered, and no one notices. We'd continue some work around her identity in the background, but the wider criminal case was put to bed.

I spent the rest of the day going through the motions, helping Helen get rid of some operational shit around the office, tidying up files. But my mind kept going back to the case. Maybe Dylan had run her over intentionally. Maybe he even knew who she was. I might never know. That was the shit that really got to me. Scared the shit out of me. The stuff we would never, ever know. Often only two people have ever known the full facts. The killer is usually your best shot. Because the other's always dead. *But he can't have run her over intentionally, could he? It was still an accident initially, wasn't it? Before he cut her up and dumped her in the mangroves?*

It continued to bother me.

What the fuck had she been doing on that road in the first place? In that storm? In the dark?

TWELVE

May, 2012

There wasn't much about the court process that I enjoyed. In fact, I'd rather cover myself in chocolate sauce and offer myself to the nearest bidder on K Road than sit in a courtroom. But I understood the end-game well enough. Too well. What I had never embraced was how a visceral, traumatic event that had permanently scarred multiple people was reduced to nothing more than a game between two opposing teams. With the judge as the referee and, oddly, the jury deciding the final score, whether they'd observed all of the goals or not. I didn't have a solution, I just knew I didn't like what we had. I was sat at the back of the public gallery, next to Kelly's parents. I wasn't a witness – I hadn't gathered any of the evidence that was being put forward, that was being given by others – but they'd asked me here at Kelly's request. I don't know why, maybe because mine had been the first face they had seen last year when this all happened.

Kelly was giving evidence via video link from a room next door. It was supposed to protect the young and vulnerable, to make it less imposing than taking the stand. But it was still awful. The other people in this room, professionals and jury alike, this was all they saw. The end-game, the showdown. Not me. My enthusiasm, my drive, everything that kept that fire burning when I was working a case, it was all extinguished by the time I got to trial. My job began with the event, and continued through all the pain. But it ended here, when the Crown Solicitor's office took the case. My focus was always on the victim, and on the investigation. Nothing else.

A lot of lawyers think that cops just don't get it, that we don't care about the finer points of law, or what "actually matters". They're right, we don't, because we know the facts. The courtroom is just where the facts get bent and twisted. You can never predict the outcome of a trial, no matter how solid the case. You just never know. Which to me is ridiculous. If someone can be excused because of a technicality, then they're sometimes deemed not guilty. Cops can't make that illogical leap in logic. If someone did it, they did it – regardless. Believe me, there are a frighteningly large number of murderers and rapists walking free, having never entered a programme or served any time.

I could see Kelly on the video screen at the front of the court. She was in tears, mouth creased in a grimace, raw pain. But he wasn't done. "This didn't happen the way you've told the court, did it Miss Thornton?" The defence lawyer looked at the men and women on the jury and gave his best eye-roll.

"Pardon?" Kelly frowned, the word forced through some snot and salty water.

"You'd had a couple of drinks . . . and you were fifteen at the time." He let that hang, just to show the jury that Kelly was the real criminal here. "You got a bit amorous, Miss Thornton. You were seen touching a few of the other guys, hugging them . . ." He raised his voice for effect. I often had a hard time keeping my thoughts to myself. *You're a showman, mate. You should be wearing tights and quoting Shakespeare. Wouldn't pay as much though, would it?*

"You saw my client, and you saw my learned colleague's client, and you decided to have sex with them that night, didn't you, Miss Thornton?" He finished with a grin, pleased with himself.

She started crying again. "What are you talking about?"

He charged ahead. "Let me put it another way, if you're having trouble answering." Again, eye-roll to the jury. Hopefully they thought he was a right cunt too. I mean, I did. And I'm not even that bright. "You told them you were sixteen, and you had consensual sex. But then, your boyfriend turned up . . . and you were nowhere to be found." He turned to the jury, arms out, palms up, turning side to side to mimic her boyfriend's supposed search. "You reckoned you were in a bit of trouble with him, so you made up this story, because you didn't want him to find out the truth. Isn't that right, Miss Thornton?"

Kelly shook her head, crying towards the floor. I was starting to get fucked off. Which, surprisingly, doesn't take much, but I thought it was warranted here. I looked at the prosecutor. *C'mon mate, ask the judge for a fuckin' break.* I looked up at the judge. *C'mon judge. She's a teenage rape victim, and you're going to let this carry on?*

The lawyer kept going. "You lied to your boyfriend, which seemed like a bright idea at the time. But it got serious when he decided that you should talk to the Police, didn't it? Your little plan was spiralling out of control, but you had to go with it now, making your statement, telling your story . . . it's not the fault of the Police. They did their job. They had to listen . . ."

It always fucked me off when lawyers did that. A throwaway comment, but it made it look like they were standing up for the Detectives involved, on the Police's side. No-one likes a cop basher in a courtroom. But I could see the veiled meaning behind it. It was everyone versus Kelly. And a suggestion the Police were incompetent. But he was here, thank Christ, to shine light on the truth. *Well done, you articulate fuck.*

"Yet here we are, with these young men facing serious criminal charges, and you're still making this all up, aren't you, Miss Thornton?"

Kelly was crying uncontrollably now and she was starting to shake. The prosecutor rose and she started to speak, but the judge was already on the same wavelength and called a pause. The jury were excused and Kelly was escorted off camera. I left the court with Kelly's parents, and James, the CPT detective that held the case. We gathered in the small Police room around the corner.

Kelly's dad turned to James. "What would happen if we just took her home now? Just removed her from this shit?"

James answered honestly. "We'd lose the case. The judge would order her back, she wouldn't be here, I'd have to explain why you guys left, which I'm happy to do, but then the judge would possibly dismiss the case. There's a chance it would be adjourned but I couldn't say that would definitely happen. And if it did, we'd have to go through this all again."

I couldn't watch the rest so I just sat outside the courtroom instead of in it. I wasn't helping Kelly by being there, she couldn't see anyone in the courtroom anyway, except the lawyers. The cross-examination of victims was unbelievable. I understood the need to clarify things, but how it was done in court was shocking. One rule for the cops, another for the lawyers. We received so much training on how to deal with sexual assault victims, how to do everything we possibly could not to re-traumatise them. Held up to very high standards and expectations, and rightly so. We'd made some horrendous fuck-ups investigation-wise in the past, and it didn't help when some pieces of shit who called themselves police officers committed horrific sexual crimes too. The public and media had a field day whenever we slipped up, or, even if we hadn't, but it was interpreted that way. Fine. But here, right at the end-game, this lawyer was free to do pretty much whatever he wished, against everything we know and are schooled up on. He could just chew Kelly up, and spit her out. And no one cared. No one spoke up to say it wasn't okay. *Unreal.*

Six days later I headed back in for the verdict. I looked straight at the jury members as they walked in. Most were looking at the floor. I caught the foreman's eye and he immediately averted his gaze. *Ah, for fuck's sake.*

"On the charge of sexual violation by rape, do you find the defendant guilty or not guilty?"

"Not guilty."

"On the charge of sexual violation by unlawful sexual connection, do you find the defendant guilty or not guilty?"

"Not guilty."

It was a repeat for the second accused.

I got up and left, waiting near the car for Kelly and her parents. I knew I should stop doing this to myself, beating myself up. I didn't have a hell of a lot of faith in the jury system. People will always prefer to let a guilty man walk than have an innocent man imprisoned. That's just human nature. But beyond reasonable doubt is the threshold. Not no doubt whatsoever. There would always be some doubt, unless we could play high-definition video and quality audio of the whole crime. I've had judges speak to me after acquittals, shaking their heads at how the jury managed to come to a certain conclusion. I've even had members of the jury send me emails, saying they thought the accused had done it, but couldn't convict him because of some random aspect of the case that actually meant nothing. The system won't change though.

The ride back north to the Thorntons' Gulf Harbour home wasn't comfortable. I felt like the biggest cock ever. We were the link between the so-called justice system and them. James was the one who had to explain to Kelly and her family why things had turned out the way they did. At the Silverdale lights I took a right, taking the road out along the Whangaparaoa Peninsula. Gulf Harbour was a pretty flash area with a lot of new development. Miles away from anything else though. I liked it. The marina dominated the harbour in front of the houses on the hills behind. We pulled up their drive and James and I got out with them. We stood on their tiled porch, in front of their large aluminium and glass door. We weren't gonna go in, but there was something I believed quite strongly and Kelly needed to hear it. "Kelly, just because the jury returned that verdict, it's not because they didn't believe you." She was looking at me, waiting for more of an explanation. "That judge, he believed everything you said. From the way he spoke to the defence lawyer, to the way he addressed you, and issued directions to the jury. He believed you. So did the registrar, the woman in front of the judge that controlled the court? You should have seen the looks she gave to that guy. Even that defence lawyer – he believes you too. He knows those two fuckwits did what they did . . ." I got a sideways glance from James. And Kelly's dad. *What, she hasn't heard someone swear before?* "That's why his only option was to try and attack your credibility. That was all he could do. He got to the jury that way. But it's important, I think, that you know that the people in that room believed you. Nobody in there, none of the professionals in there, thought that you were lying. You have to remember that."

Kelly stepped in and gave me a hug. Tears were still flowing. I was actually a bit shocked and stepped back, dragging her a couple of feet before she released me. Her dad gave my hand a solid shake before doing the same with James. James headed for our car and I turned back to the Thorntons. "You've got James' details if you have questions about the case, but remember you've got my number too. James is a pretty busy man, because he's so good at what he does. But it doesn't matter what it is, day or night, you are welcome to get in touch with me. Whether it's Police stuff or just advice you want. And that continues for as long as you can remember my name or number. Sometimes it's quite handy to have a Detective's number in your back pocket."

I joined James on the driveway and got in the passenger seat. He dropped me at Orewa station. I chuckled. I'd be cracking a Speights while he enjoyed the motorway traffic all the way back to his office in Albany.

I didn't dwell on it, but more of whatever keeps us ticking along left me that day, I think. To have Kelly's family put so much trust into the Police, and the system, just to have it come crashing down around them . . . I was becoming more and more cynical, but I was also starting to feel a bit too much. And I couldn't do a thing to stop it, because I couldn't really pinpoint the issues. Hailey had noticed me change over the last few years. I'd seen that look the other day. But there was no simple solution. *Was there?* Cops cut away, shut it out. That's just what you have to do – you have to be the professional. You maintain your composure. That's what everyone expects. So you cut away from the brutality, the blood, the bodies, the trauma, the pain – job in this box, emotions over here in this other one. Then you bury that box. You bury it deep. What you don't realise at the time is that the shit in there creeps back in, initially in ways that aren't obvious. But the faces reappear. The crime scenes playback. And so many cops box on. Why? Because a lot of them can't do anything else. And usually people don't recognise they're slowly losing it.

I fell asleep easily that night, for the first time in several months. But my head filled with awful images. Hailey stuck in the mud at Okura, struggling to dig herself out. I just couldn't get to her. The acrid smell of the mangrove swamp curling around my nostrils and burning my throat. Sam Coates, whispering something to me, but I couldn't hear her. I sat bolt upright and checked the time. 3 a.m. *Fuck's sake, man. Get a fuckin' grip.* I got up and had a shower. I couldn't shake the images from my head and didn't want to go back to sleep. *Can you be scared of your own head?* Cos tonight, I was.

THIRTEEN

I attended the morning briefing with about fifteen others. I hadn't been on-call, but Helen had given me the heads up overnight. She'd lined me up to do the scene this morning, so I already knew the basics. A group of forestry workers had found her small body in the dunes yesterday evening, several K's north of the Muriwai Surf Club. By the southern end of Woodhill Forest. She hadn't been dead long, maybe a few days at the most. Buried in a shallow grave. Well, more like someone scraped some sand away and threw her in, kicking some on top. The constantly shifting sands had uncovered enough of her to be seen.

After the group briefing I took a car, loaded up the scene kits, and headed west. I'd be meeting up with two D's from Henderson that I knew pretty well: Derek Rakete and Erin Thomas. They were both good at what they did. I don't know why I was O/C scene – Derek had more experience than I did, and Erin was junior to me but a better investigator. Rodney job, I guess. That stretch of black sand beach disappears all the way north to the

Kaipara Harbour. Woodhill Forest parallels the coast there, but between the forest and the beach, there's a wide strip of grass-topped dunes all the way up. That's where they'd found the girl.

After filling up at the BP I drove down the Silverdale hill, ignoring the motorway by crossing over it and then heading west on Kahikatea Flat Road, a rural open road with farms and life-style blocks running along both sides. I was thinking through the possibilities with this scene. It was going to be a bit of a cluster. A gravesite in a shifting dune area. The search around the body would be painstaking. But it would be methodical. I could do that well enough. I thought about the little girl. *Who the fuck could do* . . . then I told myself to cut away from that emotional bullshit. I could return to that later, with a few beers in me. At the moment I had a job to do, and I needed to do it right.

I hit the FM button for the radio, and Layne Staley let me know he was heading into the flood again. I turned the volume up. *Great song.* I turned left when I hit State Highway 16 at the other end of Kahikatea Flat, and headed south. Passing through Helensville and then cruising further south toward Waimauku, I found McPike Road on my right. Turning into it, I crossed a culvert and I saw marsh extending left and right from the road, dotted with clumps of toetoe. Their cotton-topped stems were bent over in the wind. As I continued, the marsh gave way to a few houses on both sides, and a couple of large weeping willows on my right. A few hundred further on and the sealed road became a mix of gravel and mud as I took a right into Lyon Road, following it west toward the forestry block. Some of these roads weren't for public access, and up ahead I saw a patrol car parked at a gravel crossroads, pointing me in the right direction while preventing others from being nosey. I dropped my window as I pulled up alongside. It was a young pair of Constables, a guy and a girl.

"Hi team. Matt Buchanan from Orewa." I showed my ID because I knew they were obliged to check, and I signed the scene log the guy passed to me. "I'm going the right way, obviously?" I handed them the two coffees I'd grabbed at the BP. *Scene guard was a shit job. It was the little things.*

The girl came alive with a smile. "Yeah, follow this road. It's called Pulpit Rock Road if you pull it up on your GPS. It follows the edge of the forest, south, but then it sorta bends west again. Eventually you hit a four-way – Pulpit Rock Road keeps going straight ahead. Follow it till you hit the T-intersection on the other side of the forest, right by the dunes. That's Coast Road. Go left, so south again, and you'll see the scene a few hundred metres down."

"That road, Coast Road, you end up by the golf course if you keep going south on it, right?"

"Yep. That's the one."

Good. Because I didn't trust myself to remember much of the directions she'd given. The mud and gravel track bordered the forest which rose on my right, the pines catching the morning sun and giving no hint of the horror they shielded on the other side. The road turned west under the trees and it was darker, wetter. The sun wasn't hitting the ground in here yet. As I went through the four-way intersection the girl had described I noticed the road turn from gravel and mud to gravel and sand. The dunes had retreated this far back, but the forest still thrived and grew here. About half a K further on I hit the T-intersection with Coast Road, and the forest fell away on both sides. In front of me I saw dunes and scrub, and though I couldn't see it, I knew the ocean was out there just ahead. Looking left I saw several more Police vehicles in the distance, so I turned that way and joined them. As I got out I saw Derek and Erin standing at the edge of the inner cordon.

Derek was on the phone to ESR, talking them in from the south. There was another car guarding the scene in that direction, further south on Coast Road by the horseriding place. I kept clear of the cordon tape but walked up the dunes a bit. I gazed across the wind-whipped mounds toward the surf. I could hear the breakers, but could only just see the water from here. In both directions, left and right, it was just rolling grey sand, covered in marram and other shit. Desolate.

"Seems familiar." Erin had followed me up. Cute was probably the best way to describe her. She was short, and always wore her brown hair in a ponytail. There was only a touch of ginge in there too, but she took even more Ron Weasley jokes than Steve did. She used to wear glasses but I know she'd got her eyes lasered recently, so they were no longer a feature. She stood next to me and gazed out in the same direction. "The A-team back together."

I grinned, but swallowed. "I'd say we're probably the B-team." Erin and I had been on the generals phase of Operation Mist, Sam Coates' disappearance. That was early on, before the file manager went on leave and I was given that job. We'd both attended the only real lead the case had. Two items of Sam's clothing were found on this stretch of beach, just a bit further south, the other side of the golf course. Her top and a shoe. We'd both searched those dunes for a week and a half, looking for any sign of Sam. We'd found nothing more. And we'd got no forensics from the clothing. A dead end. Erin touched my shoulder and looked sideways at me.

"I haven't forgotten her. You know I'd be keen to get on that again, give it another nudge."

I nodded. "Cheers. We'll see if we can do better with this one first."

We walked back to Derek just as the ESR crew turned up, and the forensic photographer. Derek wasn't huge, but he was ripped. He also had a knack for lightening up the mood regardless of the circumstances. Big toothy smile. "Hey bro. Dress yourself this morning? I see you're still wearing your sister's shirts, eh?"

I looked down at my tightish shirt. "You can talk." I gripped his bicep. "All that kaimoana you've hauled in over the years, I reckon." He laughed.

The on-call guys last night had done all they could. They had set their cordons pretty wide, and got the frontline crews to guard them overnight, so that was taken care of. Our focus was the primary scene. You establish a common path in, to minimise the fuck-ups. We chose the same path the on-call guys had walked. Whether it was the best or not, no point contaminating another way in. We set up the scene tent near the cars. The tent floor was marked with hot, warm and cold zones. These were just to remind you to change out and into forensic clothing, and not drag shit around contaminating everything. It was always about not fucking things up. *So yeah, dunno how I'd survived in this job for so long.*

I gowned up and, with an ESR scientist and a photographer behind me, I started placing the stepping plates. Aluminium rectangles about A3 size, and a few centimetres thick. I checked the ground, then the photographer behind me snapped some pics, and then I placed the plate down before stepping onto it and looking to place the next one. Derek and Erin followed us in a chain behind, bringing more stepping plates with them to pass to me. Yeah. Slow, methodical. Painful. Not like TV. You didn't have multiple people tramping through the scene, wearing their normal clothes, maybe just pulling on a pair of gloves. Picking shit up, moving it, fucking about. Nah. *But then again, they'd be fuckin' boring TV shows if they were realistic.* We were ready for the Ebola epidemic in our white overalls, booties, gloves, face-masks and hair nets.

Slowly and carefully as I could I placed stepping plates from the hot side of the tent, west through the dunes, then turning south slightly to approach the primary scene from the north. The body could have arrived from any direction – the road, the beach, any direction over the dunes. But fuck it. We had to make a call and do this. Some of the plates sunk into the loose sand as soon as I put them down, especially if it was near the base of a dune. I tried to trace a path between the dunes rather than go over them, otherwise by this afternoon half my fucking plates would be buried.

I placed them all the way up to the grave. If you could call it that. I stopped just a few metres from her small body, still half buried in the sand. I couldn't really tell, from her size she could have been any age between about seven and twelve. It definitely looked like she hadn't been dead too long. She was pale but there was no sign of decomposition. Half her face, some long brown hair, and a shoulder were visible, but caked in sand. The rest of her I couldn't see. She looked completely at peace. No indication of the horror she must have experienced in the final moments of her life. She had totally let go, and maybe I envied her a bit. It was over.

The photographer snapped a lot more photos up close, and then we backed out to the tent. We had a discussion. We needed the pathologist before we touched or moved anything. Our priority was to preserve and remove the body. After that, we'd go wider and search the rest of the area. I checked the weather and texted Hailey.

This job isn't good. Late.

Catching the bus home?

The no-texting-in-class rule didn't apply to her.

Nope. Stoppin off in th park

with older boys and a bong

Well she had her Dad's wit, I'd give her that. If she ever texted something normal, I'd know she was up to something.

The pathologist arrived. We gowned up again, and I took him in along the stepping plates. He checked the body and made some comments. "Her throat's been cut. Quite deep by the looks. I can't see any other major injuries but that's only what I can see without moving her. She would have bled out from that, but no blood deposits I can see here in the sand. She's probably been here a day, maybe three at the most? Enough for the sand to shift a bit, but obviously not enough for decomposition and animals to get to her."

We set up a metre-by-metre grid system in the dunes with string lines, so that every item we found could be tracked back to a specific place. We searched the sand around her first, and the ESR people took samples from different depths as we searched deeper. We brushed the sand carefully from around her body, measured her depth in the dune, looked for anything left behind. They swabbed parts of her body and collected whatever they found on it. Once she was fully exposed, we placed a forensic sheet alongside her and transferred her onto it, packaging her tightly. She then went into the body bag. We took her out of the dunes, through the tent and into a wagon. Derek and Erin would continue with ESR, searching under the area her body had been for foot impressions, or anything else that may still be visible from when the shallow grave was dug and loose sand thrown on top. I escorted the body to the Auckland Hospital mortuary, and once it was safely locked away I returned to the scene to carry on. The post-mortem, the PM, would take place tomorrow.

FOURTEEN

O/C body is a shit job. The victim is searched and dissected by the smart people – the pathologist, assistants and ESR. As the detective – AKA dumbarse – in attendance, you document and receive every piece of evidence, unless it's something the scientists want to look at harder. Mostly you just stand there like a dickhead, trying not to sway or vomit. Well, that's what I end up doing anyway. With Erin and Derek at the scene, and more than able to handle it, I'd volunteered for this PM to save some of the more junior DCs the job. Let them start with a drowning or a medical death. To give a junior member this – a young girl with her throat cut open – was pretty grim. Better to ease them into this shit.

The mortuary always reminds me of an abattoir. Cleaner, but the smell is still there, butcher's-shop-meets-bleached-bathroom. I did my dickhead impression for the early stages, as the girl was photographed and then searched again. They took swabs from all over her. The tiniest things were important, some dirt might later prove she had been in another place, and then moved. Nothing was overlooked. Normally I'd receive all the clothing and package it up. But there was none. She'd been dumped naked. No jewellery, nothing. So, my main task was to observe and report back to the investigation HQ. When ESR were done, the pathologist washed down the body before beginning the cutting.

Once again I got more than a little pang of jealousy. Wherever she was now, this girl was free. Of this. Whatever had driven her, whatever powered her thoughts, actions and memories, it was long gone from this cold, sterile place. *Get your shit together, Buchanan.* I looked around. This room had seen plenty of death. I tried to think of her body now as a scene, something to help us catch her killer. But when I looked at her face, pale and at rest, it was still her. And I couldn't cut away from it emotionally, not this time. For the first time ever, I found myself looking away for the most part, something I hadn't had to do in the past with PMs. I was an interloper. *I shouldn't be here.*

None of it was pleasant, but there were two parts of this process I specifically couldn't stand. I'm not sure if it was more an intangible thing – the invasiveness, the fact a human life had been reduced to this – or whether it was physical, maybe my stomach had just grown weaker as I got older. I dunno. The first was the garden shears that they use to snap the ribcage so they can get to the heart and lungs. That sound, the snapping – the harsh, fast crunch of bone – it went straight through me every time. The second was the high-pitched whining and grinding of the electric saw as it cut into the skull so they could get to the brain. When the bone saw started burying itself into the crown, my skin just prickled and I found myself screwing up my face involuntarily. But there was more. I got that jelly-like feeling in my legs and extremities when the organs were removed. You know, that feeling you get when you think about how easily you could drop dead? I watched the guy lifting the bits out. *Is this*

really all that keeps us going? Everything seemed fragile as fuck:
the heart, lungs, brain. Lungs reminded me of glad wrap, inflated
plastic film. As if a poke with a finger would collapse them like
a bubble. The brain, a grey rubbery mass, just sitting in the skull,
responsible for so much. How does a person – how did it all just
get snuffed out? A mass of flesh and organ tissue on a cold slab
in a hospital basement. *Shut the fuck up, and do your job.*

As each organ was removed, the pathologist took it to a table
and dissected it. He was trying to identify cause of death, and
eliminate other causes. I thought the deep, dark cut stretching
front to back on the right side of her throat was probably a safe
bet, like he'd said yesterday. I got his preliminary conclusion at
the end, but as they do, he qualified that by saying the full report
would have everything, including toxicology, which would be a
few weeks away.

I phoned Helen. "Twelve-centimetre-long cut to her throat,
through her carotid. She was also strangled, a bit of bruising
around her upper throat, petechial hemorrhaging in the eyes.
Lividity around the back, shoulders, backs of the thighs. She'd
been prone a while after she died. She could have been sexually
assaulted, but he can't be certain."

"Okay, I'll pass that on to Tim and update the board . . . fuck."
Helen didn't swear often. I could feel her pain here. She said what
had been on my mind since yesterday morning. "Who the fuck
does this to a kid?" She breathed on the other end of the line,
pulled herself together. "You're heading back out to the scene?"

"Yeah, a lot of work still to do at the gravesite. We'll be finished
the immediate scene today, Derek reckons, but the area search
will take the rest of the week at least."

"Okay. We've identified her by the way. Brianna Darwen. She
was nine."

As soon as Helen said it I tried to block it out. *Fuckin' nine.*

I didn't say anything. I just hung up.

FIFTEEN

The teenage girl we'd pulled out of the mangroves the previous year was an exception, but people generally notice missing kids immediately. Unlike missing adults. Brianna's mother and some extended family lived on a rural block north of Puhoi. The longer it had taken them to report her missing, the more suspicion fell on them. It had been four days after her approximated death when the team identified her, and none of the family had subsequently come in. The principal of her primary school had phoned the station to say Brianna hadn't been in on Monday or Tuesday, with no call from her mum saying she was sick, which was odd. Brianna fitted the age of the girl in the dunes and he was worried. They'd sourced and matched dental records to the body and confirmed it was her.

I drove with Dan beside me, and we had Derek and Erin with us as well. There was nothing to suggest there were any firearms at this place but it was rural, so Derek and I had shooters with us – Glocks on our belts – as a precaution. Six more investigation staff followed in convoy in a couple of vehicles behind us. North of Puhoi I turned right onto Mahurangi-West Road, and headed out towards the east coast. A couple of K's in I pulled over, waiting for the convoy to catch up behind me. When they were with us I pulled out again, looking to the right side of the road for the driveway to match the Google Street image I'd seen at the briefing that morning. I found the one with the distinctive white letterbox and turned right down the long, winding gravel drive. It weaved and twisted, following the contour of the land. A few other driveways branched off it to other properties, but we were heading to the end. As the ground flattened out, the driveway skirted a patch of bush, and then the target address appeared in front of us: a large main house, two-level weatherboard job, a collection of smaller dwellings and sheds nearby, and a couple of barns further off in the distance.

As we pulled up in front of the main house a guy came out to see what the fuck was going on. *They must all be aware something's wrong, surely?* We were going to play it casual, but I still placed my right hand on the Glock secured to my side.

Derek did the talking as we got out. "Morning. Derek Rakete, Henderson Police. Is Nicola Darwen home?"

"Sure. This about Brianna? What the hell has she done now?" The guy didn't bat an eyelid. He was big with broad shoulders. Close-cropped dark hair, cauliflower ears. Rugby player probably. He had stubbies and a singlet on. It was fucking freezing. *Rural hard-arse.*

Derek was confused. "Pardon?"

The guy looked confused too. "Sorry. I mean . . . I'm her uncle. David. David Kitson. Bree's at a friend's, I thought this might be about her."

Eh? Maybe we had this wrong. Maybe the family was unaware.

The uncle went inside, then reappeared a few minutes later looking apologetic. "Sorry, detectives. Nicola has . . . she's sick. If you wouldn't mind, will you come in? She's in the far bedroom."

There had been little doubt in my mind that someone here was responsible, or at least knew something. But this guy appeared open, honest, inviting. I was expecting aggression and refusal. Some of the people here might be in for a shock shortly. The guy showed us to Nicola's room and then Derek took him aside to grab some details.

I went ahead with Erin and pushed the door open. "Nicola? Police." The room wasn't big and I saw her straight away. She was on her bed, shaking. I tried to introduce myself but got no reaction. She kept her face hidden. I kept talking anyway. "We're here about Brianna."

At the sound of her daughter's name she twitched and looked at me, her dirty blonde hair a mess, covering her face. She shook her head, kept shaking it, repeating to herself: "No, no, no, you can't, don't . . ."

I went back out into the hall to Derek and Brianna's uncle. "What does she suffer from?"

"She's bipolar. She has depression and anxiety, they often go hand in hand. She's on medication, but . . . sometimes she doesn't take it. We help her through, take her to the doctor when we know she needs to go. Everyone's got their difficulties . . ." *Too fuckin' right. No arguments from me.* "This is hers. We do what we can." There was understanding in his face. I think.

I let my eyes linger a moment on his, my face expressionless. I wasn't a psychologist, but what I had seen was a woman who was scared. A woman who may know something about her daughter going missing, but scared nonetheless. I returned to the bedroom. Erin was talking. "Nicola, this is about your daughter. You've got nothing to fear from me, or from Matt here. We need to help, and we need your help."

She turned slightly, looked at us both through the matted hair. I took the opportunity. *She must know, right?* But if by some strange chance she didn't, we couldn't fuck about. "Nicola, there's no easy way to do this. I'm afraid your daughter Brianna is dead. Five days ago her body was found in the sand dunes north of Muriwai. You're probably aware of the news story. We've only just identified her. I'm so sorry." You couldn't beat about the bush with news like this. People needed to hear the words, hear the facts. No point drawing it out and risking ambiguity. Erin held Nicola's hand and she started crying. I had to explain a bit further though. "Brianna was murdered."

He'd been listening in the hallway with Derek, and at that, I heard Uncle David explode. "What the fuck!? Are you fucking kidding? I've seen the fucking news. The girl in the sand is Bree?" He came into the bedroom, followed swiftly by Derek. The colour had drained from the guy's face. He looked at Nicola and his face twisted. He gestured at her. "She's been like this for about a week, in bed the whole time. We've made an appointment for next week! Nicola, what the fuck . . ." he lunged past me ". . . did you do?" He screamed at her, pulled her off the bed onto the ground, started slapping her. "What the fuck did you do you crazy bitch!"

I grabbed him round the chest in a bear hug, pinning his arms at his sides, and Derek got him from behind in a headlock. We manhandled him like that from the room, out into the hallway and back toward the entrance. As soon as we let go of him though, he went charging back down toward the bedroom. Derek wasn't as big as David, but like I said, he enjoyed a good feed. He crash-tackled Kitson in the hall and I moved in and put some cuffs on him. "Fuck!" he screamed. "Fuck!" Dan and Derek marched him outside as other people came running in from somewhere. I returned to the bedroom and Nicola scrambled toward Erin and hugged her, sobbing into her stab vest. This job was getting weirder by the fucking second and I still didn't know what to think exactly.

Helen came in from outside and took everything in. "Let's clear the place and get this under control."

The team began a sweep of the property and gathered all the occupants in the lounge of the main house. As well as Nicola Darwen and her brother, David's teenage kids Jordan and Anna Kitson were also present, along with a flatmate-slash-farmhand. Helen explained to them all that Brianna was the girl on the news, and that this property was to be searched pursuant to a warrant issued by a judge. Everyone was given their rights, not because all were suspects . . . yet . . . but because their property was about to be sifted through. As the search began, Erin and I sat with Nicola in one of our unmarked cars. She needed some breathing space away from the others. We explained that Brianna obviously hadn't been reported missing, and that we suspected someone close to her was responsible for her death.

I hadn't got any further than that when Nicola started speaking. "I . . . I killed my baby. I killed Bree. She was my responsibility but I didn't . . . I wasn't able to do it."

Erin looked at me sideways, raising her eyebrows. I put my hand up to Nicola to stop her from continuing. "Nicola, look, I'd really like to talk to you about this, but I'm a bit concerned for you too at this stage. I think we'd better get you to see someone first. Because of what you've just told me though, I'm going to have to place you under arrest for murder." She nodded and sobbed as I presented her rights to her, but I explained we would be getting her assessed by a medical professional before anything more about Brianna was discussed. When the time came to leave, she had stopped crying and almost looked relieved. It had long fascinated me how telling another person something can unburden you. A heavy weight lifted.

I headed back into the house, looking for Helen to let her know we were off. She wasn't in the lounge and I moved down the hallway. I stopped at the first room on the right, looked in.

It had clearly been Brianna's. I stepped in and looked around. Small bed, bedside table with reading lamp. Desk with books. Clothes all over the show. *Normal kid's room.* There was a cork board on the wall beside the bed, covered in photos. I moved in closer. They were mostly of her. Brianna at school, laughing with friends. Celebrating her birthday, party hat on, laughing as she blew out the candles. At the beach with her mum. Nicola featured in quite a few. Brianna looked like she'd been a happy kid. She was smiling in every single one. I tried to memorise some of these. Burn them into my brain. This is who Brianna was. But I knew it wouldn't work. The only image I'd keep forever would be her dead body in those dunes.

I found Helen round the back of the house. She was surprised. "She admitted?"

"Yeah, but there are some complications here, and we'd better get a crisis team doctor before we interview her."

Helen nodded. "She's compliant?"

"Yeah, fully. If she wants to talk, I think she will regardless."

On the way back to the station, I drove and Erin sat in the back with Nicola. Derek accompanied us in the front seat. Nicola very much wanted to talk but I stopped her. "Look, we really want to sit down and talk with you, and I promise if that's what you want to do, it'll happen. But right now we have to be careful, because I really think you need to see a doctor first. You understand?" She looked at me in the rear-view and nodded. "We'll get a doctor to the station, and depending on what they say, we'll just go from there. You're in safe hands." Derek turned and smiled at her, and Erin was holding her hand. *Good work, B-Team.*

Nicola cleared her throat and spoke softly. "Will I have to go back home?"

I glanced at Derek. Then into the rear-view. Erin spoke. "Um, no, you won't be going home for quite a while, until we work though all of this." Nicola slumped back in her seat, and appeared to relax a bit more.

The car went quiet. "We can talk about other things if you like." So we began to chat, the four of us, about the rural property, sheep, grass, hay, dogs, anything we could think of to get her relaxed and comfortable. To get her mind off the murder of her daughter. Because we'd be returning to that soon enough.

SIXTEEN

Nicola was twenty-five and had been referred to mental health services on multiple occasions. She had attempted suicide once before but had been found by her half-brother David, the guy who had fired up back at the house. If Nicola had had Brianna at just sixteen then it appeared she'd had a lot to cope with from a pretty young age. She was seen by the crisis team who'd made it to the station. The doctor and nurse advised that she had come off her meds and would need ongoing treatment. But they also believed she was up to being interviewed. After speaking with Helen and Tim we decided to give it a crack.

Nicola smiled when Erin and I walked in to see her. Her hair was now back behind her ears. Her expression was warm, but something had died behind her eyes a long time ago. There was just no light there. Abuse was my guess – it was so under-reported. I was probably jumping to conclusions. I hadn't even been in her bedroom very long earlier that day and I'd felt the anger boiling inside me, at how people fucked each other up. Nearly every adult

I'd ever met in the course of my work who had serious anger, personality or drug issues had been abused as a kid. Physically, sexually, emotionally – or a combo. We talked generally for a bit, and she was a slow talker. She'd often glance behind me or behind Erin, or to the side of us, at the table or into her cup. She'd say something serious, then smile or laugh awkwardly. She paused and stirred her coffee about thirty times, saying nothing. *I mean, fuck, I did that. What was wrong with that?*

The semi-smart, evidential side of my brain – which isn't very big – was starting to tell me that even if this woman had something important to say, it probably wouldn't make it into a courtroom. But the court could go grab a giant spoon and kindly eat my arse. Even if the interview was argued out of evidence later, then at least Brianna's extended family would have more of the answers than if we just gave up.

Nicola slowly brought the cup up to her lips, stared into it. She spoke into the cup. "It's the same again, all the same. I watch the news every night . . ." she shook as she spoke.

I cut to the chase yet again. "Nicola, did you kill your daughter?"

She looked straight at me, tears now streaming out of her wide eyes. "Yep. Yeah, I did. Nothing I could do. Nothing. I deserve everything I get. She should've just done what she was told. I always had to."

She wouldn't tell us the course of events. Refused. That was pretty normal, it's difficult to revisit the moment. I changed tack.

I opened a folder I had in front of me. "Nicola, this is your cell-phone number, isn't it?" I pointed to a number on the first page and Nicola nodded. "Does anyone else ever use your phone?" She shook her head. "Not at all?"

"No."

"This is some data we've got from Vodafone for the period surrounding Brianna's disappearance and death. I'll go through it with you. We just need to ask some questions about it." I pointed to the first page of information I had, turning the folder so she could see. "This is polling data, it shows which cell-phone towers your cell-phone was working off at different times. See, that's the date, the time . . ." I traced my finger over the page. "This column here names the cell-phone tower by the area it's located. Now this isn't an exact science, okay? I'm no telecommunications engineer . . . I mean, I struggle with my nine times tables . . ." Nicola coughed through her nose and I couldn't tell if she'd laughed or simply needed to get some air out . . . "but I do know that cell-phones won't necessarily use the closest tower for lots of reasons. Weather, the amount of cell-phone traffic, geography . . . you understand?" Nicola nodded. I carried on. "But each line here represents a time your cell-phone connected with a tower somehow. That could have been a call, a text – or sometimes it's just the phone telling the tower it's around." Nicola nodded again. "So if you look at this . . ." I pointed again. "On the day Brianna was apparently missing, according to your brother, from 1 a.m. through to 4 a.m., your cell-phone polls in Puhoi, then Silverdale, then Helensville, then Muriwai. Moving, right? It polls in Muriwai again . . . one-and-a-half hours after it did the first time. Then after that in Helensville again. Then back in Puhoi. Now, sure, this doesn't necessarily mean you went to all these places at these times, like I said . . . but, Nicola, can you tell me about this journey?"

She frowned and then nodded. "Yeah, that's when I took Bree. Into the sand dunes. Buried her in the sand dunes. Buried her . . ." She started crying. Erin put a hand on her shoulder.

I changed my question line as Erin handed Nicola's mug to her. "Nicola, was Brianna ever abused?"

Nicola was startled, clearly, and dropped her cup onto the floor. "Sorry, sorry . . ." She tried to pick it up but I stopped her with a hand on her arm.

"It's okay, Nicola, it's okay . . . I've got it." Erin beat me to it and picked up the pieces, excusing herself and leaving the room.

There were deep-seated issues here and we weren't the solution. I couldn't get any more of a statement from her. Her thoughts were disjointed and nothing she said could be fully relied on. But she'd made some pretty heavy admissions, supported by some pretty solid evidence linking her to Brianna's body – pending DNA on a knife we found in the house, no alibi from her brother, and of course the polling information. She knew some things only the killer would know.

I turned the DVD unit off. I was getting ready to leave the room too, when Nicola grabbed my arm and looked right at me. I didn't see anything odd in there, all I saw was pain, hurt. Some of the light came back into her eyes, something was struggling back there. "This isn't . . . this isn't easy for you, Detective, I know. I know who you are. I've seen you on the news before. You've had your share of pain. Leave this, leave it for them . . ." she gestured toward the door ". . . or it'll be too late. Don't ruin your own life over me."

I didn't understand a word she was saying. "It's already over, Nicola."

She got focused on the table in front of her, dropping my arm. As I closed the door behind me, I heard her whisper to herself. "No . . ."

I didn't tell Erin I'd just had my brain rattled by a twenty-five-year-old murder suspect. Or that for the second time in the last year, someone had tried to tell me that I was a bit fucked in the head.

SEVENTEEN

We stood as far back as we could at the funeral. We weren't family, we were there out of respect, so we didn't need front-row seats. It was an emotional service, obviously, and Helen and Erin did enough crying for all of us. Derek and I did a good job with the face stretch, the yawn, whenever the eyes started filling up. I don't think we were fooling anyone though. Brianna's close and extended family took up the first few rows. As well as the Mahurangi clan, a few lived on the North Shore, and some had come up from Wellington. The eulogy was outstanding, delivered by a girl in her twenties. Maybe one of Brianna's cousins, or an aunt. Monarch butterflies were a bit of a theme at the service. Brianna had looked after a swan plant year in, year out, since she started school. There was a big board at the back of the room with a whole bunch of photos of her. Adventures, birthday parties, school, friends . . . and like the photos I'd seen in her room, she was smiling in them all. But even as I tried to imagine her in happier times, the memory of her body in the sand flooded my brain, and

I couldn't shake it. *Fuck this.* I moved outside, into the fresh air, and gazed out over the Schnapper Rock cemetery. *Back again.*

We all stayed for a little ceremony they did in the rose garden afterwards. They let a whole bunch of monarch butterflies out of a box. I watched them float about before they all fucked off in different directions. *A funeral for a nine year old.* I shook my head. Not even a car crash, an accident or a medical problem. *Murdered. Throat cut.*

My last brush with religion had been in primary school. No, no one fucked me. I was forced to go to church, that's all. But events since then had changed my mind, and I wasn't about to re-think my opinion on it. There was no light at the end of this tunnel. Still, I found myself saying a prayer for Brianna. Just in case it had all meant something for her.

I mouthed the words at the ground, and, looking up, I saw the girl that had delivered the eulogy smiling at me. She approached our group as we left. "Sorry, I don't mean to hold you up. I just wanted to thank you guys. I know how hard this is for everyone, but to do what you've had to do, I can't even think about it." She was visibly upset, and Erin stepped in to give her a hug. I smiled at her as they parted, and the girl handed me a business card. "I don't mean to create work, but, would you be able to let me know directly if there's progress? I'm Nicola's niece, my family are down in Wellington. We don't have much to do with our Auckland rellies."

I took the card and nodded. As we got to our car I slipped the card to Helen. "Good job for you I think, Sarge."

Nicola had been charged with murder and committed for trial, and it was looking like she was fit to stand. But a possible outcome was not guilty by reason of insanity – that would be up to the judge based on some reports by psychiatrists, and they'd carry out multiple assessments with her before concluding anything. But it was an awful series of events and I don't think anyone really wanted Nicola to face the full force of the law. That wasn't helping anyone. I think everyone thought she had probably suffered enough.

I watched out the car window and my eyes glazed over. I thought about where Brianna had been buried. *No, dumped.* Out in the dunes. A strange place to leave your daughter, even if you were mentally unwell. *Those dunes were where you hide a crime, stop people finding out about it . . . or to make it look random.* There were questions bouncing round in my head, but being in the job this long I knew better than to listen. This wasn't the movies. The so-called 'gut feel' was usually bullshit. The logical explanation, backed up by evidence, won every time.

Back at home, I was on the net looking at other famous cases, which is what I usually did to try and normalise it – convince myself Brianna hadn't been the first. The cases I found I'd heard about before, and they were mainly Australian.

Twelve-year-old Sian Kingi was abducted and murdered in Noosa, Queensland, in 1987. Riding her bike, she was lured into bushes by a couple, where she was raped, stabbed and strangled. Valmae Beck died in 2008, and Barrie Watts is still in prison.

Going even further back, I read up again on the spine-chilling unsolved murders of Marianne Schmidt and Christine Sharrock at Wanda Beach near Sydney in 1965. Their bodies were found buried in the sand dunes. They had both been stabbed, Marianne's throat slashed, and Christine's skull fractured. It remained one of Australia's most famous unsolved cases. There were suspects, some now dead. There was still hope for that case though – advances in DNA technology may eventually identify the killer.

I closed my eyes as Brianna's half-buried body came back into my head again. I tried to shake it. Failed. *Why did I do this?*

EIGHTEEN

I was kicking back with a beer at home when I got the call from Steve. "No biggie, mate. I'm at a lab fire in Dairy Flat. We've got it cos you guys are busy tidying up your shit. House is completely gutted. Remains of a lab in the garage, extraction gone wrong. No one here, but thought I'd call you because Gary Harding's linked to the place."

I spat my mouthful of beer back into the bottle. *Gary Harding?* Now he'd been laying low for a while. He'd only got three years for his part in murdering Gabby, and wounding her partner Warren Malcolm, back in '95. They'd placed him at the scene of the shooting but they couldn't prove he'd fired any of the shots, so he'd only gone as an accessory. His mate Thomas Calver was still inside. Calver had got a more-deserving twenty-one years for pulling the trigger.

I was surprised to hear this news from Steve. "Harding's a cook now?" He'd only been a dealer back in '95, far as I knew. And I hadn't heard anything about him since he'd got out years back.

"Is now, yeah. We've had info about him selling up here for a while. He's been up here for years. His vehicles have been seen near this address before. Chem Desk have him buying acetone at Hammer Hardware."

"You said linked to this fire . . . no idea where he is?"

"Nah. Done a runner. Nothing at any hospitals or A&E so looks like he got out in time, just as it went up."

"That's a fucking shame." I couldn't think of a nicer guy to go out in a ball of fire.

The extraction is the first phase when you cook meth. You mix a solvent with your precursor to pull the pure ephedrine out of the rest of the mixture. The solvent is flammable, obviously, and vaporises easily, so heat and flame aren't a good idea when you're doing this. But some of the fuckwits heat the mixture up to help it along. With all those fumes in the air, it doesn't take much to make it go boom. "Where was it?"

"Rural property, series of sheds out in the woods, off Kahikatea Flat. Been cooking rumours there for a while, nothing solid though, never enough for a warrant. But now this."

I started thinking. Pete Childs moved in these circles. "Time for a catch-up with our mate?"

"Exactly."

We caught up with Pete later that week. He'd only done nine months of the eighteen-month lag he'd got for the lab gear Steve's team had caught him with the previous year. He had no hard feelings, had pleaded guilty right from the start. He knew the game. He'd been meaning to catch up with us too, cos he'd jumped straight back into the mix.

He was looking older, less hair than last year. He was a bit gaunt in the face, looked like he might be back on the gear. He was licking his lips a bit, had that dry mouth thing going on. But he was still the same Pete. Likeable guy, bad choices. "Yeah the fire in Dairy Flat, it was that guy Gary. My mate introduced us. There's rumours about him, he was involved in that shooting . . . him and his mate, they shot that cop back in the '90s, up in Coatesville."

I corrected the location. "Riverhead. Yeah, I know a bit about it." Gabby's lifeless eyes stared up at me from the rain-splashed road. "What have you heard?"

Pete took a bite of the Snickers bar I'd got him. It wasn't bribery, fuck. Pete didn't do this for any reason other than he trusted us. Plus, Countdown had a three-for-one deal going. I'd already polished off the Moro and the Pinky. He washed the chocolate down with a swig of V. "Just that he was involved. Weird though. I always thought there was something fucked about that. No one shoots at the cops. No one. Unless you're fried off your face. The clubs dish it out if someone hurts a cop. Too much heat. It just isn't done. So what, they were moving a bit of gear? 'Fraid they'd get caught for that? Nah." Pete was shaking his head. "Nah, that was something else."

"Like what?"

"Well I keep hearing those rumours, you know, like before I went inside. The blue movies. Harding and this other fulla, this guy they call the Wizard. Long grey hair, creepy-looking cunt. Cooking, dealing, and fucking up girls. Hooking them on the shit, ticking it up, getting 'em to pay it back in other ways, you know. That Kahikatea Flat place, I went there to score. They weren't cooking there then. It was being cooked somewhere else, but they were selling outta that place. Went there, bought an ounce off him through my mate as soon as I got out. Him and the Wizard, always got a girl or two staying at their places. They've been churning the ounces out fast, always moving the labs. I'm not surprised one went up. Been meaning to catch up with you guys, didn't know how to get hold of ya's."

"What did you see when you scored the ounce?"

"'Bout a hundred K laid out on the couch. Few shooters. But they're cranking now, I hear, like eight ounces a fortnight. That's a cook every couple of days. They must have a lot of shit stashed ready to go." By "shit" he meant ingredients and equipment – everything you needed to cook. And it didn't matter what recipe you used, there were a few things you always needed. Ephedrine. Iodine. Acids. Bases. Volatile shit. But something wasn't adding up here. *They don't leave cash out so people can see it. That's how people get shot. People are greedy.*

Steve read my mind. "Why'd they have that sorta coin out when you went over to score, mate? Something you aren't telling us there."

Pete looked sheepish. "Not cos I don't want you to know, I just know you fullas don't *wanna* know." We both just looked at him. He put his hands up. "Okay, look, they've asked me to help out, they know I can cook, they needed another runaround and they said they'd share the profits. I've got a couple good ephedrine contacts."

Steve and I looked at each other and covered our arses. "Look mate, you can't do that, okay? You can't buy meth, can't source precursors, you can't cook. We can't look after you if you do that. Commit the crime, you're on your own. Don't do it." He knew the drill. We never sanction criminal activity. But the reality is, any decent source is gonna be committing crime, otherwise they wouldn't know fuck all about it. So, it's a fine line. I qualified our scolding. "But remember, mate, you do what you need to do to stay safe. If you can't call us, it's a 111 call, even for you." He looked at me and grinned. We knew he'd cook and deal because it kept him safe from his so-called mates. *But what can we do about that?* "Keep us in the loop. We want Gary Harding. And we want answers to that other shit, the films. Who, exactly what, and where. Soon as you know."

"No dramas, lads."

NINETEEN

Pete fed us more information on Harding's crew. Steve and the Organised Crime guys used it to knock over a few dealing houses in an effort to find him. They'd identified "the Wizard" as Damien Lendich. Steve's team had worked him up, identifying another lab out the back of Titirangi, a single-level place surrounded by bush off Huia Road. Orewa CIB were lending a hand for numbers, because these guys were from our area.

I was sitting in an unmarked car with Steve at the safe forward point on Godley Road, just outside Green Bay High. The house we were hitting was about a K up and through the other side of Titirangi village. But we didn't want to be too close as we got our shit sorted, or the jungle drums would ensure evidence got chucked long before the doors went in. And no, Steve and I weren't number one and two in the entry team like the detectives on TV. Our job was just to block the road once the Armed Offender's Squad convoy headed in. Exciting stuff.

I checked safety on the M4 rifle with my thumb, and adjusted the body armour so it sat lower at the front. It always rode up over the top of the stab vest. But tactical equipment never fitted quite right. Shit always moved around or came loose. You just made do with what you had. The AOS convoy headed in past us, a couple of dark four-wheel drives leading the way. Guys in grey chemical suits, gas masks, black tactical armour and all the other kit were standing on the sides holding on. A couple of marked patrol cars followed, also full of AOS. A dog handler's wagon brought up the rear. Steve pulled out and we joined the tail, following it left up onto Titirangi Road, through the village and down onto Huia Road. Bush on both sides, the road started to wind as we approached the target address coming up on our left. But instead of heading up the drive with the rest, we rolled past another thirty metres and blocked the road. Then we got out and stood around looking like dickheads.

Some guys from Steve's crew blocked the road on the other side of the driveway, back the way we'd come from. I could just see their car through the darkness. They seemed to be having as much fun as us. I listened for noise of the entry team going in. I could hear the vehicles roaring down the drive. The house wasn't that far away. I heard crunching of gravel under boots and swinging of metal gates as they disembarked and took up their positions. Seconds later I heard the loud hailer. I couldn't make out exact words but the message was clear. *Hi there. Please come out. Or we're coming in.* That was the gist anyway. Silence. And they didn't fuck about, this lot. Time to break something. I heard the smashing of windows, and then the front door must have gone in because the yelling kicked off and I heard more things breaking. A dog barked, more yelling, more glass breaking. This carried on for about forty seconds before it all went quiet.

The forward commander appeared at the top of the drive and waved me over. Stu had been my frontline Sergeant back on the Shore years ago, and had been AOS on the side for as long as I could remember. He was actually a Special Tactics Group Sergeant now. A short, stocky little Samoan bastard, he lived for this shit, and STG allowed him to do that full-time. "Hey Matt, all done and dusted. My guys have got three on the property, one's that long-haired guy, Lendich. There's a young guy and girl too, they're the tenants. Nobody else on the property. Lab set up in the garage so my guys and the three are going through the shower."

"Cheers mate, I'll get three ready to receive." The tactical guys are only there to make entry and secure the place. Once that happens their job is done. They'd take people into custody, of course, but then they'd hand them over to the investigation team so that they could clear off. But first it looked like all Stu's guys were going through the decontamination shower, along with the people found inside.

The Fire Service rolled up in their truck and started setting up the decon shower at the top of the driveway with the specialist Clandestine Laboratory Team. I started to see people walking up the drive. Lendich was first. He stuck out like dog's balls with his long grey hair. I couldn't tell who his AOS escort was, he still had his gas mask on. The guy had to yell so I could hear him properly. "Found him in the garage. Probably the most exposed. Nothing on him." The squad member patted Lendich's pockets to reinforce what he'd said.

Lendich was stripped almost naked and thrown into the shower. He doubled over. "Ahhhhh!" He sounded in pain. I didn't blame him, that shower wasn't a good time. High pressure jets of freezing water. It fucking hurts. Once he'd had his rinse, one of Steve's guys hauled him away to a car.

Steve and I were taking the other two coming down the drive. The young guy was skinny and pale, short hair, wide-eyed, and still reeling from the fact the Horsemen of the Apocalypse had just crashed into his bedroom and hauled him out. He screamed like a kid when he entered the shower. "Faaarrrk!"

The girl was red-eyed and shaking, trying to hold herself to-gether, looking suspicious of everything. Straight dark hair, she looked part-Maori. Someone had let her grab a duvet and she'd wrapped herself in it. She refused the shower totally though, started yelling and pushing back. After seeing her boyfriend's per-formance, she was having none of it. Until an AOS dude grabbed her in a bear hug and marched her into the shower, holding her there in the middle of the water jets. She stopped making noises, probably the shock of the high-pressure cold water. Even when it was over I heard nothing from her. The guys from the Clan Lab Team threw her some overalls to change into and I held up a big tarp to give her some privacy.

Steve and I drove the two back to Henderson for interviews. They didn't say a word on the way back. I'd fired up the warm aircon high as I could, but the girl was still shaking when we pulled into the station. I was a bit worried so left Steve to sort them into separate interview rooms while I made the hottest cups of coffee I could, throwing five sugars in for good measure. I grabbed a couple of gingernuts from the bench on my way back.

Tanya was her name. She still wasn't saying anything, just staring at the desk, hugging herself. I broke the silence. "Drink it, no rush. Look, I don't expect much from you at the moment, Tanya. As ridiculous as it sounds, that shower is only for your own good. That shit leeches into your hair and skin. I've been through that shower myself, several times. You did well, I didn't hear a thing. You should've heard me last time I had to go through it. Squealed like a little bitch." She finally couldn't hold back a grin. She took the mug and raised it with both hands, taking a sip. She put it back down and looked at me. She probably hadn't had the same fun most people her age had. She was nineteen but looked like she'd had enough of the world already. She would have been pretty, probably still was – maybe I was being harsh. But the drug had done its work. Once she'd tasted the pipe she would've been passed around from cook to dealer. No one can afford the habit. She'd obviously ended up with someone her own age now, but she was still using, clearly. And had to pay it back somehow. No way out. I carried on. "I'm not here to judge you, Tanya, for the world you've been thrown into. How can I? Sometimes we don't have a choice. I get that. I haven't walked in your shoes. Look, you and your boyfriend, you're just on the sidelines. It was Lendich we were after, and another guy who wasn't there, Gary Harding."

Her face creased up as she frowned. And she finally spoke. "That fuckin' cunt." She spoke my language. We had at least one thing in common now.

"Okay then, we'll talk about the lab in a minute. Tell me about Harding." She went on a rant about how he treated women, how he treated her and her boyfriend like shit. They were both users, couldn't pay their debts for all the meth they'd ticked up. They paid off some of it by letting Harding and Lendich cook in their garage. But there was something else going on too. She was tearing up. I let the silence sit between us for a while, let the emotion take her. Then I jumped on in. "He hurt you."

She didn't look at me. Bit her lip. *Was that a nod?* Her bottom lip was quivering. "No."

"Look I might look like just another cop, but believe me, Tanya, I actually give a shit. Harding and another guy, Thomas Calver, killed a friend of mine seventeen years ago, and I know he's done some messed-up shit over the last few years. I need to know what direction to go in. I'm not saying make a statement. I'm not even asking you to help the Police. I need you to help *me*. Because I can't piece this shit together on my own."

Then she started to cry. I wasn't expecting that. "I can't, not after . . . I can't . . ." she was shaking and looked away briefly. She looked back at me and her eyes were wide, the tears still pooling at the bottom of her lids. "Look, man, I'm sorry about your friend.

I am. I know what it's like to lose someone. But I can't help you. Please don't you fuckin' breathe a word to connect those guys with me. Fuck you, I swear, you do that, I'll . . ."

I interrupted her. "Fuck's sake, Tanya, I'm not asking you to go on the record here! I'm trying to help you. You and your boyfriend aren't going to go down for anything more than allowing premises. That's fuck all. That'll get you a rehab sentence. But what about when you get out? What happens? Straight back into it. And who are you going to go crawling to for a fix? We're going to do this again and again, you and me, and you aren't the people that it should be happening to. I want that fuck Harding, and whoever he's doing this with. So do you. Help me find them."

She wouldn't budge. I got a brief statement from her admitting use of the garage for Lendich, but that she had no idea what was happening in there. *Ah well. I tried.* It wouldn't get her off the charges but everyone would think she'd done her best not to nark everyone out to the cops. I didn't blame her – she was doing what she considered best for her, right now, with the limited information she had. But as I left the interview room, she grabbed my hand, and stared at me. "This is your job, right?"

I was a bit confused. "I don't do it for fun." *Well, sometimes I did. Less and less though.*

"No . . . I mean . . . you're not going to let this go. Your friend . . ."

"Of course not."

She stared at me, sussing me out. "You're not gonna like it."

I searched her face but there wasn't a hint she'd rolled over. She was giving me a heads-up about something. But it was all I'd be getting. When she didn't say anything else, I got up to leave the room. "I never do, Tanya."

Lendich was held in custody on manufacturing charges. I was helping Steve's crew sift through the electronic exhibits, because no doubt some of it would give up something. We searched what we could, unlocked phones and USB sticks. But all the password-protected shit, that all had to go to the Electronic Crime Lab to be opened. It was beyond our two-finger typing skills. I gave Steve the shortened version of what Tanya had said. He was interested. "So maybe Pete Childs is right? These guys are abusers – they coerce and get what they want."

"Yeah. But if this is the same group, then he reckoned they were making films, and with kids too. So, who are the kids? These guys are transient. All over the place."

"He seemed pretty disturbed by it. If he finds out, he'll tell us. He wants to fuck these people over as much as we do. If he's in cooking with them now, he's gonna get a better picture. We need to see him again."

TWENTY

Hailey enjoyed flying, but only on a nice day. Come to think of it, I was the same. Ian and his daughter Chloe were in the back seats. Ian was a mate from Army days, if you could call them that. Territorial Force. Part-timers. No gear and no idea. On a whim, we'd signed up at the same time, but I'd done it for eight years all up, dove-tailing with my Police career. I did get to Timor, but I was pretty shit at it, and decided now that I hadn't really enjoyed it that much. There's only so long I could be wet, cold, tired and hungry all at the same time before I got fucked off. Ian had reached the dizzying heights of Lance Corporal though. Over-achieving fuck. But ever since Waiouru we'd stayed in touch. Chloe was only twelve but she and Hailey got on pretty well. They didn't have a choice anyway, because their dads took any opportunity they could for a beer.

As I lifted off Runway 21, I checked the time and scrawled it on the log on my kneeboard. I made a climbing left-hand turn to vacate via downwind. We left the circuit and I made a right-hand turn, calling Whenuapai Traffic and crossing the Okura River mouth at fifteen hundred feet. It was a major reporting point, but my mind still wandered back to Operation Ariel and the skeleton we'd pulled out. *Would we ever ID the girl that had rotted down there? Forgotten for eighteen-odd years?* Hailey was watching me. I switched back on and made a call to Christchurch Information. As I picked up our track for Pauanui, I started grinning. The view up here on a nice day was ridiculous. In front of us, the sparkling blue of the Hauraki Gulf, the volcanic cone of Rangitoto, and Waiheke Island behind. The North Shore below us to our right. The tall buildings of the CBD further out to our half right. Ian piped up. My headset crackled, the sound of his voice distorted slightly by the comms set-up, competing with the constant drone of the engine in the background. "Can't this thing go faster? I'm feeling dangerous."

Already with the Top Gun references. "The only thing we've got in common with that movie is a dickhead in the rear seat." Hailey looked round at Chloe and they rolled their eyes. They hadn't said a word yet, they were too busy taking photos. "Can you two shut up as well? I can't hear myself think." Hailey punched my arm.

I made a position report and climbed to five and a half thousand. The flight across the blue expanse that was the Firth of Thames was smooth as. Views still brilliant. The weather was still good over the other side of the Coromandel. We descended on the eastern side of the ranges, the forests lit olive green by the morning sun. The waterways of Pauanui appeared in the middle distance, sandwiched between Shoe and Slipper Islands in the background. I joined overhead, checked the windsock and came in over the beach on finals. The touchdown was okay, which was a relief. I wouldn't have heard the end of it from fuck-knuckle behind me if it wasn't. It didn't stop him though. "Fuckin' hell, Guy Gibson, how many times you wanna bounce?" *Dick. The bombs bounced, not the aircraft.*

I taxied to the shutdown area on the south side of the grass strip, switched off and unbuckled. "Lunch?"

We ate at one of the cafés not far from the airfield. Hailey was on her phone most of the time, but to her credit, she put it away briefly once we left the café and checked out the beach. She actually started a conversation. "You're always happy flying." She then took her phone back out and started taking more photos. She held it in front of us and snapped a selfie.

I couldn't knock her really. A lot of teenagers wouldn't even have come with their dad on this trip. "What, I'm not happy much?"

"No, it's just, you know, your work isn't. I don't think I could do it. I can't imagine, you know. Caitlin, Taylor, Sarah – their parents don't do the stuff you do."

"I'm sure they work a lot harder than me." Hailey's best mates had awesome parents. Which was just as well, because we had a lot to do with them. And I couldn't stand fuckwits.

Hailey clarified. "Every time something bad's on the news, you're there. You can say it's hard sometimes. Mum wouldn't want you to put on a brave face. You don't have to keep it to yourself. There must be some stuff you can tell me."

I looked at her. She'd got most of her mother's genes – brains, I mean. "It's not that I don't *want* to talk to you about it. There's stuff you just don't need to know. Stuff no one should really know. But I actually struggle to describe it sometimes, can't put a label on it. So I just don't bother. That's why we hit the beers at work."

"We can work on it though, right? I mean, I tell you every-thing."

I laughed. "Bullshit."

"No, serious."

I looked at her. She did the shittest dead-pan-serious look possible. "Thought so."

"Well, we can both work on it."

"Deal."

My phone buzzed. It was Steve. "Matt, spoke with Pete just now. He sounds pretty stressed out, but he reckoned it could wait until tomorrow, he's tied up at the moment. Wants a face-to-face. Something pretty interesting, I think. You free?"

"Yeah mate, free tomorrow. Leave from your base?"

"Yep, sweet. See you round ten. We'll plan from there." I pocketed my phone and wondered what Pete had dug up for us.

Ian, Chloe and Hailey were ahead of me now. Ian turned and yelled. "Hurry up ball-sack!" *He should work on his language. You wouldn't catch me swearing like that.*

TWENTY-ONE

Pete was stressed. Wound up. That was out of the ordinary. He was so laid back with us usually that his heart rate couldn't have ever gone much over fifty beats a minute. But now we finally had him in the car, he was struggling to get his words out clearly. I tried to calm him down. "Pete, you're safe here. Take a breather, mate, we've got plenty of time. Everything's good here with us. What's the matter?"

"I always fuckin' wondered why they killed her, that cop . . . that other girl of yours . . ." He was almost hyperventilating. "It isn't just movies too, it's . . . fuck . . ." He was really losing his shit over something. But we didn't get the chance to talk it through.

I didn't even hear the first few rounds. Glass behind me exploded. Which window, I don't know. I was struck in the shoulder. Like a hard punch. Heat. Burning through my upper left arm. Glass fragments blown past my face. I left the car somehow. Falling sideways. Hard, out onto the ground. Searing pain in the left arm, and my ribs as I struck the ground. Moving. Across concrete.

Away. I was obeying a voice from the distant past, and it wasn't from my Police training. *Contact. Rear. Seek cover.*

The rest of my senses started to come back. I picked out the boom of rounds discharging above the pumping in my eardrums. I tried to focus on what the fuck was going on. I looked around. I was on my arse behind a concrete power pole. I poked my head out. I'd covered several metres from our vehicle. I went back into cover. Tried to work out what the fuck was going on. *C'mon. Regain some sort of fuckin' thought pattern.* My brain was churning round and round but I couldn't get it to stop and assess. My arm burned, I couldn't lift it properly. *Fuck you. Fuck you. Do something.*

I focused on my breathing, tried to slow my brain down. It was trying to work overtime, and was failing. I remembered I was armed. I reached under my hoodie with my right hand, felt for the pistol grip. Extending my trigger finger along the barrel, I depressed the release and lifted the Glock out of the belt holster. I heard more rounds kicking off from behind me, violent noise, my eardrums hurting, the ringing in them unrelenting. I finally made a choice and turned, on my knees, looking round the right side of the concrete pole, weapon in my right hand, up at eye level. There was a grey station wagon behind our car. Two guys, one out either side of it, putting rounds into our car and in my direction. One had a pistol, the other a rifle of some kind. Both had bandanas pulled up over their faces. *Both a good fifteen metres from me.*

All my training went out the window . . . *close one eye, relax your right hand, gently squeeze the trigger.* I was fucked and I only had the use of my right hand. This was taking the piss big time. I had the pistol roughly at eye level, looking for the sight picture, the three white dots. It was wobbling all over the place. I tried to bring up my left hand to cradle the pistol but pain just seared through me. *Fuck the sight picture.* I snatched at the trigger, sending seven or eight rounds toward the guy closest to me. I missed with most, but must have hit him somewhere low because his leg gave way and he went down with a yell, clutching at it.

I saw the second guy get back into the driver's seat and try to reverse their wagon up. I actually stepped out from cover, like a fuckin' idiot, and headed toward it. I fired, trying to put rounds through his windscreen. I must have missed though cos I got to the front wheel arch of our car and hunkered down, as more rounds came my way. There was a pause, and I peered out to see the first guy that I'd hit crawling into the front passenger seat of their wagon, still holding his leg. The car backed up and I peeked round, but couldn't see the rego. The sound of the wagon faded but the ringing in my ears was louder now, blood thumping around the inside of my head.

Where the fuck is Steve? Where's Pete?

I yelled out for both of them. Well, I think I did. I got nothing back. I scanned the car park we were in. *Where the hell are we again? Westgate.* A few people were looking out at me from behind cars, wide-eyed. Pale, disbelieving faces. A girl was looking at me, her mouth was moving, she was clearly yelling out at me but I couldn't hear anything. People were starting to make noises around the car park, but I couldn't see Pete or Steve. And then I heard the groan. *Oh fuck, no. Please.*

I ran around the front of our car and found Steve curled up on the ground beside the open driver's door. He'd taken a few rounds high through the back. It was bad, dark blood pooling behind his jacket, spread over the asphalt. He was clutching his chest, hands red and glistening as he tried to plug the exit wounds. I couldn't order myself, couldn't think of the right steps. But I knew I needed to plug the holes. I pulled my hoodie off, tried to use it to stem the flow. Then I saw the blood pumping from his right side too. I looked at his face and it was white. He was looking at me, and grabbed for my hand. He couldn't say anything. He looked like he was nodding at me. I watched the life drain from his body. I held his hand, watching his face, his blood leaking onto me.

I looked away, blinking, then looked up, looked around, couldn't see anything. *Blurry. What the fuck?* I wiped my face with my arm and blinked. *Better. Why the fuck wasn't anyone helping?* Then looking down at Steve I remembered we weren't kitted up as cops. We could have been anyone. I yelled out. "Police! We're Police!" I had my hands up now, covered in Steve's blood. "Call an ambulance! Call a fuckin' ambulance! I need help here!"

I got to work trying to do compressions on Steve but I knew the science didn't add up. Too many leaks. I needed fluids, blood expanders, proper shit to plug the holes, stabilise his system. People were running in now, trying to help with the bleeding, but I knew Steve was gone. I yelled out Pete's name again. "Pete! Where the fuck are you, Pete?"

A young guy stepped away from Steve and peered back into our car. I knew by his face it was bad. His hands went to his mouth and he backed away from it, paused, then dived back in and dragged Pete from the back of our car, out onto the ground. I could see from his eyes he was dead. He was covered in glass. He'd taken at least one round through the throat and blood had flowed across his chest and shoulders. I looked from him to Steve, Steve to him, and dropped back onto my arse, looking at my hands, stained red and sticky. My vision began to shut down and I had flashes of a dark, wet night in Riverhead seventeen years ago, leaning over the body of another friend. I saw stars glinting and put my head between my knees, squeezing my eyes shut.

I heard the sirens approaching then, through my aching eardrums.

PART TWO

"God is cruel.
Sometimes he makes
you live."

— STEPHEN KING

TWENTY-TWO

May, 2016

Ryan was pretty bloody good, to be fair. He was already three-quarters of the way toward getting his licence. At his age, I'd spent my school holidays hungover mostly, so good on him. We were doing steep turns today though, and he was struggling to keep the nose tracking the same line. I gave him the secret. "You'll smash this, mate. When you roll in, look for the mark on the indicator, and when you hit it, lock your elbow into the door. That's how I always do it. Then you can't move the ailerons. Hold it there, bit of back pressure, and you'll track the same line." I demonstrated the move with a steep right turn, highlighting my elbow against the door. Then I handed him control. He scanned the sky before rolling the wings left, applying a bit of rudder to keep everything in balance, and adding a bit more power with the throttle. He found the forty-five-degree mark on the indicator and I saw him jam his arm against the door. I watched the altimeter, and the needle didn't move much at all. "Told ya. Smashed it." He was grinning big time. He loved every minute of this.

And I loved this job. I'd been on the full-time instructor list for about three years now, with well over a thousand hours in my logbook. I earned fuck all but I didn't care. It was a rewarding job, and my office was the sky. I was happy.

Ryan maneuvered for an overhead join and I watched for other traffic. He talked through everything he did, verbalising all his down-wind checks. We rolled onto base and I looked for the runway. Another gentle roll and Ryan lined us up perfectly on final. I watched the airspeed indicator as we came in. He locked onto his landing spot. We were a bit high, so our speed was more than it needed to be with the now slightly sharper descent angle. He picked up on it straight away and reduced power. The speed washed back, and he kept the nose still. He was all over it. *Like a fat man on a Moro bar.* He killed the throttle completely as we crossed the fence, flared, and, like the textbook says, I heard the whine of the stall warning just before the wheels settled onto the runway. He cleaned up the aircraft and we taxied back to the apron.

He was my last student for the day. After our debrief, I checked in with Lisa on the front desk. No more aircraft bookings. I helped Mike, one of the other instructors, put the planes back in the hangar and then secured the office.

I sat in my car and checked my phone. *One missed call.* Unknown number. No message. I redialled it.

"Hello?" Female voice. *Student maybe?*

"Hi, sorry, I missed your call . . ."

A pause. Then: "Is that Detective Buchanan?"

That caught me off-guard. I sat up straighter. "Uh, it's Matt Buchanan, yeah, but I left that job a few years back. Can I help?"

"Oh." Long pause. I waited. "Look, I'm really sorry, you might not remember me, it was five years ago. It's Kelly Thornton, you helped me the day I was, um . . ."

"Kelly? Of course I remember. How are things? What can I

do for you?" I was surprised. You could brush something off as a passing job that you contributed little to, but someone else would remember it for a lifetime. We're pretty hard on ourselves, and overlook a lot of shit. I'd always hoped I'd done my best for Kelly. But I never thought she'd actually call me about anything again.

"There's some stuff . . ." she took a breath, ". . . happening with a few guys, uni parties. I have some friends that have had some shit happen to them. I just don't really know what to do, they don't know I'm calling you. Some of us reckon they should call the cops but they don't want to. It's hard. I thought you might like to know . . . no, sorry, what I mean . . . I mean, maybe you would know what to do?"

If Kelly was attending uni, I was pleased. Maybe her life hadn't turned to rat-shit after that trial after all. She didn't want to talk much on the phone, so we agreed to meet up the next day for coffee.

TWENTY-THREE

I was sipping a hot chocolate with extra marshmallows when Kelly walked in. She was the typical student – satchel, scarf and glasses. *Jesus, she's a hipster.* I stood up. "What will you have?"

I ordered her a trim latte, and another hot chocolate for me. I went back to our table and she was smiling. *Good.* I sat. "What are you studying?"

"Arts and commerce, commerce for the job, bit of literature and psych for fun. It's going really well."

I was glad. This was all new to me, catching up with a victim years later. It just wasn't something you did in the job – you moved on to the next thing. But I wasn't a cop anymore, and I could do whatever the fuck I wanted. This was a good thing, I thought. Someone I'd never in my life have met again was achieving, and after hauling herself out of a cesspit of shit too. I pointed to her glasses. "And your eyes?"

She grinned. "Eye test for my licence a while back, not up to scratch. I don't really need them to read. Just for distance."

We chatted a bit more about home and how her parents were doing. Then she asked about me. "You left the Police? I thought I saw you on the news a few years back, the—" She stopped mid-sentence, catching herself. "I can't believe what happened. Sorry, Matt, I'm sorry . . ."

I put a hand up. "It happened. No point ignoring it. Yeah, it was the shooting, and a few other things. It was time to go. For me, anyway. I didn't really have a choice."

"They made you leave?"

"No, nothing like that. I made myself. It wasn't really doing me much good. The shooting was sort of a wake-up call."

"You seem pretty good."

I looked out at the intersection of Queen and Victoria. The little man had just turned green and there were people every-where. And this conversation was going places I didn't want it to. 2012 had fucked me up – I knew that. But I didn't want to talk about it with Kelly. She followed my gaze out at the people crossing. She was waiting for me to say something.

"Well, I was anything but. Couldn't see it. Bottled it up. Some-thing was gonna give eventually. When Steve and Peter were killed, that was it. That was me done. In more than one sense of the word."

Kelly looked at me like she understood, but I hadn't trod anywhere near her path. I'd been a bystander for everything I'd experienced. It had always happened to someone else. She'd experienced her trauma directly. That was way different. It was part of her. I'd never be able to put myself in her shoes. But she was doing a good job of trying to stand in mine. "Have you been to a doctor?"

I shook my head. "Nah. I think things are better. This new job is pretty good."

She looked into her mug. "Until . . . until that night, the only experiences I'd had with the cops were parties getting shut down, and Dad getting pulled over. You know. The things everyone sees. I can't believe . . . the things we see on the news." She shook her head. "I used to turn the news off, you know, after the trial. I couldn't watch all that stuff. But then, in one of my psych papers, I read an article about PTSD in the emergency services. How they . . . they can't turn it off. Don't have a choice. So, I made a point of watching after that."

"Well, it wasn't every day for me. And besides, that's all behind me now. I had my daughter to think of – she couldn't lose me as well."

I hadn't meant to do it, but I'd fucked up. Kelly had been sipping her latte, and it took about ten seconds before she frowned, looked at me, then put her cup down. I had to spend the next five minutes explaining how my life had turned to shit nine years previously, when that truck had crossed the centreline on State Highway 2. When Kate had died on that road, and I hadn't even been there. *Yup. All downhill from there.*

"How old is Hailey now?"

"Nineteen. Second year at Otago."

"What's she studying?"

"Law, unfortunately. If she ends up doing criminal stuff, I'm cutting her off." Kelly laughed. "She's doing psych too. I think that's pretty interesting. Except she's always trying to get inside my head. She's having a tough time, hasn't found much yet."

She didn't laugh this time. "So what are you doing now?"

"I'm flying now, instructing up at Dairy Flat." She smiled and just shook her head. I probed. "What?"

"Couldn't you just do something boring? You could be a motivational speaker. Write a book."

Motivate others? I could barely motivate myself. I shared my thoughts. "Someone could eat a can of alphabet spaghetti and shit a more interesting read." Kelly frowned. *Okay, too far.*

We started talking about her friends, the reason for our catch-up. She had been at a party in Northcote Point the previous weekend, and there had been plenty of people there she didn't know. She'd had a bit to drink, but not as much as a few of her mates. She remembered one friend – sober one minute, passed out the next. And the girl came storming out of a bedroom a few hours later, disorientated and stumbling everywhere. Kelly had noticed several guys duck out after her and disappear.

Her eyes were wet. "It brought it all back. I think they drugged her, maybe, but she doesn't want anything to do with the Police. She reckons it was her fault, puts it down as a bad experience. Reckons she should have been more careful. It's not right."

I clenched a fist under the table, squeezed, relaxed. Considered Kelly's options. If her friend had been drugged, there wouldn't be anything left in her system to test now. But there'd be evidence others could give of how she presented before and after. "If she went to the Police, they'd investigate. Interview everyone. Other people at the party would provide context, you know, behaviour before and after, for her and the guys involved, her state, how much she'd had to drink, all that. If she's drunk or drugged, the law is clear. No consent. It's rape. The Crown would prosecute. She should go in and report it."

"Yeah, that's what I think. But I can't make her do it. And she'd lose her shit if she knew I was talking to you. Thing is, I think these guys have done this before. Some other guys there, I didn't know them, but they got pretty angry. I heard them talking about these guys sometimes preying on the younger girls, you know, high school parties. I'm scared for other girls."

"You know who these guys are?"

"Yeah, I found them on Facebook." She pulled out her phone and fucked about with it. I wasn't sure what to tell her. I could pass the information on to the Adult Sexual Assault Team or CPT, whichever it fell into. Get them to treat her as a source. That could work. Keep it confidential. But they'd just tuck it away as information, until another victim came forward. I could be wrong. They might pay them a visit, especially after that shocking Roast Busters saga several years back. Kelly turned her phone around and showed me the first guy. Some bearded fuckwit called Cam McCarthy. Kelly turned her phone back and fiddled with it, before showing me again. Jordan Kitson. *Finch from American Pie. Dead ringer.*

"Can you send me their Facebook IDs?"

She took screen-shots on her phone and sent them through to me.

"I'll pass your details on to someone I know who works in that district. She's really good. She'll talk through it with you, but they'll want to open an investigation. Don't worry, you won't get in the shit with your mate, that's not how they'll run it. And it's up to you."

Kelly liked the idea.

We parted on the corner outside Starbucks. "You've done right by your mate, getting advice I mean."

She smiled and nodded. "Thanks, Matt. Really. Thanks for seeing me. It's been good. You look pretty happy too. That's really good." She turned and walked off.

But as she headed up Queen Street, she turned back and called out. "Matt!"

I looked around. She was smiling, but her eyes were serious. "Don't go back to something just because you're good at it." She turned and continued on.

TWENTY-FOUR

The voice on the other end was familiar. "Hi Matt. Sorry to bother you." My brain pulled up a memory of some clothing on a beach, ruffled by wind and covered in black sand. Then a manufactured image of a blonde girl walking home from school deposited itself in my head. *But I've never seen Sam alive. Or dead.*

"No dramas, Karen. What's going on?" *How long had it been? Almost four years?*

"It's just . . . I dunno. I'm sorry, I could always do this with you and I know you were okay with it. Simon's got other cases. He's been great, I just can't talk about the same stuff with him."

Simon was a brilliant detective. He'd inherited the Samantha Coates file after I'd thrown in the towel. But he had a D's caseload, so probably had a lot more on his mind than small-talk with Karen on a monthly basis, as she had always done with me. It was what it was. "Well, I did say when I left you could always call. It's been a while."

"Three-and-a-half years since I last bothered you."

"Stop it. I would have cut you and got a new number."

She laughed. We started talking about Muriwai. Where Sam's clothes had been found. How brutal the cards were that life dealt out. She caught me off guard though. She'd been thinking harder about that stretch of coastline. "Brianna . . . that little girl . . . she was found on that same beach."

I looked out above the sink. The rain was still dropping in sheets, blown sideways by the wind before diving into the lawn. *Brianna?* I'd been through this in my own head before. "She was a lot further north." I didn't want to talk about other old cases. Not Brianna anyway. Fuck that. That was done. Even as I tried to prevent it, her half-buried body worked its way into my brain. Hair caked in black sand. C'*mon Matt. Sort your shit out.* I shut the memory down.

"Yeah I know. I just always think about it. A beautiful place. Unique."

"Yeah." The dark grey dunes. The smashing waves. The marram grass. The wind. I would have also said isolated. Bleak. Desolate.

"I hear you're flying for a living?"

"Just an instructor. You could hardly call the paycheck a living though. I do it for fun it. It's great."

"Just an instructor?"

I laughed. "I mean, I'm no airline pilot."

"You sound happy."

"Yeah, I am. I think it's been good for me. I mean, I fit here, in this place. It's a lot simpler." There was a pause, silence. I filled it. "I always think about her, Karen. I'll never stop throwing things around in my head. Simon's good, I know you don't know him well, but he's good. Better than I ever was. He's often on the phone to me, getting his head round it."

"It's great you've found something, Matt. You really needed it. You did too long, I think. Tortured yourself too long. I tortured you too long."

"Fuck, stop with the—"

She laughed again. "Yeah right. Sorry."

"I'm in the loop. I still hang out with some of the D's. I haven't vanished."

"I want you to, though, Matt, I really do. You deserve to be able to." She paused and I waited. "But please don't."

I considered Karen's thoughts. I didn't get anywhere though. All I got in was a good thirty minutes of staring out the window before my phone went off again. I looked at it. *Fuck. Can't I escape that fuckin' organisation?* I swiped to answer. "Hi Erin."

"Apparently CPT are already looking at those guys. Jordan Kitson lives in Millwater, and Cameron McCarthy's on the Shore. Sunnynook. They're the next Roast Busters. There's already a couple of complaints from other girls."

Good. If the child protection guys had the file, it'd be subject to some pretty high scrutiny. "Kelly will be pleased there's some work being done."

"Yeah, yeah, I've let her know. They're going to approach her friends in light of the other complaints. If all the girls have the strength to go through the process, and not all of them will, then hopefully these pieces of shit will be locked up for a while."

I took the phone away from my ear, looked at it in surprise. She was right in her description, I couldn't knock that. Even a bit too generous, if you asked me. But I hadn't heard Erin speak like that before.

I made myself a cuppa and resumed my task, checking out the window, making sure the fence hadn't moved. The little jolt Karen had given me down the phone lingered. *Nah.* Brianna Darwen, that was cut and dried. *Found on that same beach . . .*

Sam, however . . .

TWENTY-FIVE

It was time for a few brews at North Shore Aero Club. I'd decided to make the leap into a proper commercial job. I loved instructing, and would continue in a part-time capacity at the club, but I was on to the next thing. Barrier Air, as they now called themselves, had accepted me and I started my line training the following week. I wasn't sure where I wanted to go exactly, but multi-engine IFR, or instrument time, was valuable so I thought I'd give it a shot. They seemed to like me because of my Police background. I had chuckled during that part of the interview. *If only they knew.* But I was looking forward to the new role. It was one of the best entry-level IFR jobs in the country probably. So, I was shouting the bar. Most of the instructing staff were there, a few club members, and some of my students. But it wasn't all for me. It was Friday afternoon, it had been a good week of flying, and Steph and Joe – two good mates, and former students of mine in their early stages – had just completed their instructor ratings, so I was hoping to get a few beers out of them too.

I had gone for a leak and was checking my phone on the way back to the bar. *Four missed calls.* Could probably wait – I had piss to drink. But I checked the call log. *Erin.* I weighed up how much anything Police-related was worth to me anymore, and returned the phone to my pocket. But as I did that, it buzzed again. *Fuck it.* I went out on the deck and answered.

Erin's voice straight away, I didn't even say hello. "Matt. I'm doing a late. Do you want to come into Henderson? Something you should probably see." I didn't say a word. She hadn't convinced me. "Matt?"

I started guessing. "Kelly?"

"No, no. But that's getting traction. On a side note – one of the offenders, Jordan Kitson? Remember the Darwen case? He's David Kitson's son."

"David Kitson?"

"Brianna Darwen's uncle. Nicola's brother. Angry man."

Eh? I breathed out and started walking up and down the verandah. David had been pretty cut up that day at the Mahurangi house four years back. I hadn't spoken to him much, but he sure had let Nicola have it. "You're shitting me?"

"Interesting, yeah? But that's not the reason I've called . . ."

She spoke for another thirty seconds before I cut her off and headed for my car. Her words bouncing around my head, I left the verandah down the external stairs. It only took me twenty-five minutes to get to Henderson station. Straight down the motorway at Silverdale and out west on Constellation Drive. I wasn't exactly sticking to the limit. I parked outside the back gate. I called Erin as I climbed the stairs, and she opened the back door for me. I checked to make sure. "This is all good, right?" I knew the rules. It didn't matter who you were or what you had been, non-Police shouldn't really be fucking about in the CIB offices.

Erin shook her head. "Helen rang me first. Said I'd be able to convince you to have a look. She thinks you might have some idea what the hell has gone on. She's busy, they've just had a rape up in Waiwera, so she gave me a call, told me to get you in here and let you read it." I followed her to a computer in the General Squad office and she pulled up the intranet. I started reading. I had read news reports of a female fished out of the Tauranga harbour, but there hadn't been much detail and I hadn't given it too much thought. But now I was reading the inside word on the internal bulletin board. And I felt the ice crawl its way up my spine.

At 6:30AM on Thursday 19th July, a female identified as Tanya Redmond, PRN 90958876 was found by workers at Tauranga port. She had suffered severe head injuries and fractures to her arms and ribcage.
She is believed to have been sexually assaulted.
She was conscious when found and airlifted to hospital where she remains in critical condition.
Can staff view the attached images of vehicles and person(s) sourced from local CCTV in the area she was located?
Staff can contact either Detective Tim Broughton, File Manager – Operation Firth, or Detective Sergeant Greg Thurston, O/C.

I didn't click the images. I knew they'd be a collection of random service station patrons and vehicles crossing intersections surrounding the port and Tauranga harbour area. I looked at Erin. "What the fuck was she doing down there?" She shrugged.

I hadn't heard a thing about Tanya since the shooting. I'd only spoken to her once, after finding her at the Lendich-Harding lab back in 2012. That cold, shivering girl, chewed up and spat out by life. Harding had never been charged with that lab, far as I knew. Couldn't link him evidentially. Tanya and her partner . . . that skinny prick Schuster. Martin Schuster. They'd both been done for allowing premises and both got community service.

But it cut much deeper than that. Schuster had later confessed to killing Steve and Pete in 2012, to being one of the shooters. They'd executed a warrant at his address after the shooting, and found the rifle and pistol used in the killings. He'd given some pretty good detail, but had never dobbed in the second shooter. Not surprising. On the fringes of Harding's crew, there was no way Schuster would talk. If he had, he'd have gone the same way as Pete. Pretty good motivation to shut the fuck up. Apparently they did everything to try and link Harding to the shooting but couldn't. You needed more than motive. In fact, motive was probably the least important factor in proving murder. Schuster got life with fourteen years' non-parole and I'd quit the job. *And now Tanya had got her head stoved in, four years later. Who'd she fucked off?* I was trying to connect dots in my head, and was struggling.

Erin's phone rang. Helen. She put it on loudspeaker. "Erin, is Matt with you?"

I spoke up. "Yeah, I'm here. Have you heard anything more from Tauranga?"

"Only that she's in a coma, induced, they're trying to cool her down and save further brain damage. She'd been in the water a while but not too much water in the lungs – she was conscious when she was found. They may try to bring her out over the next few days. Thoughts?"

"Well, Schuster's inside, so perhaps she hooked up with the next best supplier. Harding himself even. Ticked something up, couldn't pay it back. Or she nicked something."

"I've told Greg, the O/C down there, about our previous involvement with her and the wider group. I've got Dan sending some files down and they're piecing it together. It may even become ours, this, if it looks like all the players are up here. Might be a chance to sink him."

Helen was trying to get me on board. I'll admit I was toying with it. Finally getting Gary Harding for something would be good. But my brain was heading in a different direction with this now. This wasn't clear cut. Karen and Kelly had both set something in motion in my head. *Too many questions.* And I was better off out of the loop. So, I didn't bite. Helen rang off and I was left with Erin. She looked up at me. "This isn't a deal gone wrong, Matt." She was looking for something from me. What I was thinking.

"No. Peter Childs. He was onto something for Steve and me. Abuse. Kids. Horrible shit, he said. He had something on these guys, on Harding, about that. Something had him spooked, physically shaking, in our car, soon as he got in. But the shots came before he got to the detail." This was news to Erin, I could tell. She hadn't been on that investigation. "And now someone else who had knowledge about that has been left for dead. When I interviewed Tanya about Harding in 2012, she shut down. I've never seen anything like it. Scared shitless. I mentioned abuse, and she just changed. Something far worse, and she wouldn't talk about it. But she told me to keep looking. I didn't."

"He won't go down for this."

"Probably not. Even if she wakes up."

Erin could read me like a book, one of the few people who could. But she wasn't getting the rest today. I left her to her shift and drove home through the rain. I got soaked in the short run from my car to the house. Flicking the lights on, I made for the kitchen and switched on the kettle. The rain lashed the windows and I pulled the curtains. I went to the closet in my room as the water boiled and searched under a pile of boxes for the shit I'd taken from my desk years ago. I found my dictaphone and took it back into the kitchen, grabbing my laptop from the study on the way. I fired it up and stuck the dictaphone into the USB port. Or tried to. *Fucking USBs. Fifty-fifty chance, wrong way round every fuckin' time.* I had a couple of files on there. But the one I was after was the recording I'd been making when Pete and Steve were killed. We'd recorded our meets with him, because we didn't want to miss anything. This one I'd kept, of course, because it had become evidence in the double-murder investigation. But I'd never deleted the recording from the dictaphone. I opened the file and listened to his voice from beyond the grave as he panted and tried to get the words out.

"I always fuckin' wondered why they killed her, that cop . . . that other girl of yours . . ."

Pete was killed because they had caught him meeting us. They always suspect everyone's an informant, but in this case, Harding and his crew were smart. Someone had installed a find-my-iPhone type of app on the whole crew's phones. They didn't suspect anyone in particular. Harding would have been covering all bases. But they tracked Pete right to us. Normally, if someone was caught talking to the Police, yeah it went bad, but murder was a big step. Often they just milked it. Took everything the source owned, and owned *them*, forever. They got more mileage that way. To kill, that was huge. High stakes shit. But the stakes must have been even higher than that. They'd decided to kill him while he was with *us*. They'd been forced to take Pete out then and there, killed Steve, and tried to kill me. Which meant more than just some meth and some labs. Pete was onto something dark. And Tanya must have put a foot wrong into the same shadows. I played it over and over as I sipped my coffee.

". . . that cop . . . [grunt] *. . . that other girl of yours . . ."*

There was something else he was saying, something I couldn't quite hear. I'd locked this away in my brain years ago, and now it was burning its way to the front again. I still thought I was mishearing it, making shit up. I turned the volume up even more, kept replaying the recording.

"I always fuckin' wondered why they killed her, that cop, and that other girl of yours . . ."

I frowned. He wasn't just talking about Gabby. He was linking

Harding with another murder, another murder he knew I'd had something to do with. There were a few. They were all pretty clear-cut. Domestic homicides mostly. And famous unsolved cases. Jane Furlong. Famous solved cases. Christie. Then there was the girl in the mangroves. And Brianna Darwen. *Both solved.* Karen's voice came back to me too. *That same beach.* Sam. I listened, re-listened, listened again.

"I always fuckin' wondered why they killed her, that cop . . ."

So Pete *had* found out. He'd found out exactly why Gabby had been killed. He'd banged on in the previous meet about how it can't have just been drugs. You don't want heat from the cops. You don't kill a cop over drugs. So why the fuck had Gabby been killed that night, back in '95? What had forced Calver and Harding to commit murder that night, make them kill her, and try to kill her partner?

Whatever Pete had found out, it had spooked him big time.

TWENTY-SIX

The new job was awesome. I flew some pretty spectacular routes – Great Barrier Island to Auckland International, to Ardmore, to Dairy Flat, Whangarei, and the Coromandel. Most of the flying crossed the Hauraki Gulf. It was the dream I'd been hunting. Like anything in GA, there was more money in delivering papers. But that wasn't why I was here. I probably would have done it for free. *Almost.* I'd just done a food run to the Barrier and was shutting down on the apron at Auckland International. Our aircraft were parked at the eastern end of the domestic terminal, near where you board the Air New Zealand regional turboprops. I jotted all the important shit down and re-checked everything was off. I packed up my bag and made for the crew office. Sara was in there, doing some post-flight shit. She looked up. "Good day?"

"Fuckin' windy, as usual."

She laughed. "Welcome to the fun." You get some horrendous cross-winds coming into the Barrier some days. Well, most days really. There was a ridge just above the airfield, and the wind would hit that and billow over it onto the runway. Either that, or a strong wind shear because of the ocean and the temperature differences that went with that. I'd been white-knuckled a few times now on approach, and aborting a landing wasn't uncommon. But I loved it. You couldn't call it a job. Some guys just wanted out – get the hours, fuck off to the airlines. But me, I was just enjoying the ride.

It was always better than the destination.

Turning my phone on as I walked to my car, I saw Helen had tried to ring me. I called her back.

"Matt, sorry, you've obviously been working. Are you free?"

"I am now, I'm just leaving the airport."

"Tauranga's sent some detail up about the scene for us. You may want to take a look. It's pretty bad. Tanya's come out of the coma, she's stable apparently. But she's refused to talk to Greg's team. Won't have a bar of it."

"Right. You working a late?"

"Yeah, come up to Orewa if you've nothing better to do."

I didn't. It was late enough for traffic to have eased but it still took me an hour and a half to get from Mangere to Orewa station. Helen met me at reception and took me through to the CIB office at the rear. Dan and a few others were tapping away at their keyboards and I gave Dan a wave. He stood up and came to shake my hand. "You coming back?"

"I'd rather cut my balls off. Earning nothing is too damn good. And I'm not kidding."

Dan didn't laugh. He must have known what Helen was about to show me, and his face said it all. It wasn't good. I followed Helen into her office. She picked up a ring-binder from her desk and passed it to me.

"A copy of the main scene and the victim file. Have a read. Sit down though. Coffee?" she was holding her mug up.

"Please."

She left for the kitchen and I took a seat, thumbing through the folder. I sometimes wondered if there was something wrong with me, mentally, or if everyone had it happen to them. I don't have anything to compare with, because I only have my own head to go on, obviously. People are pretty good at hiding their thoughts and feelings. You never know what's going on behind the scenes. *Everyone's got their shit.* But as I flicked through the file, I felt something go in my head. Like actually, break. Something switched on, or off, it was hard to describe. My thought patterns changed. That emotion I thought I'd been so good at containing all those years, it crashed into my head, breaking across it as I turned the pages.

I stared at each image. Photos of Tanya in the hospital. They didn't show much because she was bandaged and blanketed. But her head was wrapped in bloody dressings. Tubes in her mouth and nose. *Jesus.* I flicked further and got to the scene photos. A concrete slipway rising out of the water. Wooden pier towering alongside. *Close to the commercial docks.* There was dark blood on the slipway where she'd managed to haul herself out of the water before collapsing. I read the reports from the attending paramedics, the cop that had travelled in the ambulance with her to the hospital, and the doctor's notes. I didn't notice when Helen put the mug in front of me.

Tanya had had to be resuscitated in the ambulance. But they'd restarted her heart almost immediately, and she hadn't been without oxygen for too long. She was cold though, hypothermic. She'd taken in a bit of water, but getting herself to the slipway had saved her. She would have drowned otherwise as soon as she slipped into unconsciousness. She had a broken forearm, broken clavicle, broken ribs. Skull fracture. That wasn't even the worst of it. She'd needed reconstructive surgery to her pelvic area. She'd lost a lot of blood as a result of repeated penetration. Internally, congealed blood. Toxicity. I started to well up. But my eyes dried up as I felt that switch in my head move from *on* to *off*. Or the other way round. It turned the raw emotion into anger, and I channelled that into a plan. Helen was watching my reaction and spoke. "We're going to get that animal. Everyone in this office has read that, and we're about to take over the suspect phase from Tauranga because it's looking more and more like Harding's group."

"You won't get anywhere if she isn't talking."

"We might, it's been done before."

"Yeah, I guess."

She was watching me closely. "Erin's worried about you, Matt. Something about this has you worked up, I can tell. C'mon, this isn't the first case like this you've seen. You want to come back? We've got positions. Tim will have you back in a second."

I thought hard for a moment. Pieces of this jigsaw were clicking into place and I had to give this a nudge. Off the books ideally. I shook my head. "Just keep me in the loop. I'm good, just this takes me back to a pretty bad place, that's all."

"You need me, you ring."

I nodded.

TWENTY-SEVEN

The drive south took me two and a half hours. I hadn't asked for permission, or told anybody. Greg's Tauranga team were good at what they did, and really, she could have been dumped in the harbour for any number of reasons. But I didn't think so. They'd tried to kill her, and she'd got away. Barely. Otherwise I doubt anyone would have found her body. I needed answers, and only Tanya could fill in the blanks. She just needed reasons to do that.

I took State Highway 2 at the bottom of the Bombays, through pasture and farm blocks. I flew past the little white cross that marked where Kate had died. I was trying not to think about it, focus on the task ahead. But the tears started rolling and I wiped my face. *Get it together, dick.* The little wreath of purple flowers Hailey had made and brought on our last visit was still slung over the top. I concentrated on breathing and cranked the radio up. Crowded House. One of their first and best. I dunno if my voice had a truly sacred ring, but I sang along to it anyway, anything to keep my mind from the crash scene.

I fuelled up with gas and cheeseburgers at Matamata before heading east over the Kaimais. The weather was shit down here too, and I had the wipers on full the whole way over the hills. It was pitch black, and I almost went straight into the back of a truck turning out of Mclaren Falls Road. He hadn't looked, but then I was pushing the limits of my Mazda. I took several millimetres off my tires as they smoked up, and I shook my head, scaring myself into safer driving. *Get your shit together, mate.*

I came into the Tauranga city fringe, hitting the huge round-about and going straight through toward Greerton, then Gate Pa and the hospital. I pulled into the visitor car park and headed inside. There weren't many people about, and so, taking a guess, I headed for the recovery ward. I spoke to one of the nurses. "Hi, sorry to bother you. My niece is in here, Tanya Redmond?"

"Yes, she's here, room nine. But she's asleep. I'm really sorry but you'll probably have to come back tomorrow? It's pretty late . . ."

I checked my watch. 9 p.m. *Okay, you've got a point.* "Sorry, I lost track on the drive down."

"No problem, early tomorrow would be a safe bet. Sorry what was your name? I'll let Tanya know you're coming in."

I thought about that. *Fuck it.* "Matt. Can you give her this too?" I took a pen and paper from the desk and jotted a note down. If the nurse was going to give Tanya a heads-up, I'd better do my best at some damage control. Before Greg's team came asking questions of me.

> Tanya, we've got a place you can stay once you're out of here, better than that last one with that shitty cold shower. You were right, I'm not liking what I'm finding out. But we're getting there. See you in the morning. Matt.

I gave the note to the nurse, thanked her, and left. I found a passable motel nearby, checked myself into a room, and got my head down.

TWENTY-EIGHT

I wasn't sure what sort of reception Tanya would give me. Of the multiple options – pleased to see me; tipping off the Police; alerting the hospital staff that I wasn't her uncle – I wasn't holding out hope for the first. But she surprised me as I walked into her room. She was awake, but frightened. *Of me? Ah. The shooting. Schuster.*

"Matt . . ." She sat up. She started shaking her head. "I'm sorry, I didn't, I had no idea, but Martin didn't . . ."

I put my hands up in peace, tried to calm her down. "Tanya I'm not here because of the shooting. Well, sort of. You don't need to explain. I think I've worked it out, but I still need your help." She fell back onto her pillow, a weight off her shoulders. I continued. "Why won't you talk to the cops?"

She frowned. "Because. But aren't you on the same team?"

"No, I left the job after . . ." She knew what I meant. Her expression softened as she realised I was out of the game, but that I was out because of the world she'd been involved in. We had loss in common. She waited for me to continue. "Gary Harding. I know we missed something, missed a lot of things. I think you might have some of the answers . . ." She started shaking her head, but I kept on talking. "You've got some major issues here, Tanya. This wasn't just a hiding. They tried to kill you. You got away. I don't think there's much to gain if you don't cooperate with the CIB down here. Harding will find you." She looked like she knew I was about to try and sell her something. I didn't want to do that. I wanted her to buy. "I'm going out on a limb but I'm guessing Martin had no involvement in the shooting in 2012. He just took the rap. He's losing his shit in prison, and you thought you'd try and help him out by coming in from the cold. They got wind of it. Am I warm?"

She didn't move a muscle, just looked right into me. I kept going. "Wherever you go, they'll come. No doubts. You need to be protected, and you need Harding out of the picture. I can do both. But not without your help."

"If he ends up in jail, that won't change anything. So what, he goes inside for a fucking murder? Sorry, two murders? Big deal. He can pull strings from inside."

"I'm not just talking about the shooting. Yeah, that'd keep him in for a while. But I know there's more. I know there is. Kids. Girls. We need to talk about that. That's what will fuck things up for him. He'll have a huge target on his back in prison with that hanging over him." She thought hard, started listening. "You don't have any choices, Tanya, there's nothing to think about. We're running out of time. I'll protect you, get you into the programme and relocate you. Otherwise, next time you won't be in here, you'll be six feet under. Let's take care of you first, and then look at Harding. But I need to sell this to the guys in blue, the ones still in. I can't do that all by myself. I need the rest. The shit you really don't want to talk about. That's what we really need to—"

She cut me off. I had fired her up. "You can't take the normal approach, Matt. Fuckin' hell. You can't." She shook her head. "It won't work. I've seen people fall down around him, around Harding. Martin was just one more. Harding's clever. He's fuckin' evil. And he dodged the cops for years. Whatever you think you know, it's worse." She started shaking. *This has got to be pretty fuckin' bad.* "I know you suspected . . . I know that you know . . ." she was staring into me again, but her eyes were dull, something beaten down in there that was afraid to come to the surface. She wanted to tell me what he'd done to her, but she couldn't let herself.

I leant in close to her, so she got the message. "I've never seen anyone so scared, Tanya. Never. Not like I saw you after we raided that lab in 2012." She started to cry, passively. The tears just rolled out the bottom of her eyes, and her face remained still as she looked at me. "I need something, Tanya, something to kick this off. I can suspect all I want, but I need you to say something." She lay there, still. "I'm going to mention some things. You help me out where you can." *Was that a nod?* I started anyway. "Other women. Children. Kids." She was trembling more now, but she nodded. I pushed. "Where are they? Who are they?"

She started shaking her head, but she obviously knew more. She closed her eyes, squeezing them shut. I waited. When it came, I wasn't fully prepared for her answer.

"Dead."

Dead? I kept going. "The group, Harding's group. Who are the rest? Who visited your house when that lab was there? Lendich obviously. Who else?"

She nodded. I grabbed the box of tissues beside her bed. She struggled to raise her arm, so I dabbed at her face for her. She found her voice again. "There are others. I don't know who . . . ah fuck, you can't . . . don't fuck this up, Matt. Don't you fuck this up."

Her whole body was shaking now. *Dead women and children.*

I just needed confirmation. "Brianna. The little girl out on the beach . . ."

Tanya started crying fully then. She didn't have the energy to hold anything back. A nurse came in from the hallway and took in the scene. "Poor thing. You're safe here." She looked from Tanya to me as if to ask if everything was okay.

Tanya nodded at the nurse and she left. I spoke again. "I'm going to make some calls, okay?" I moved but Tanya grabbed my sleeve. I tried to put her at ease. "No, I'm not going anywhere. I'll make some calls, you'll be protected here, maybe even flown up to Auckland when they reckon you're able to. I'll stay with you as long as I can."

I went to move again but Tanya wouldn't let my arm go. "Matt . . ." She tried to pull me closer, but couldn't. I leant forward. Her voice had changed. Calmer. "I'm telling you, Matt, these aren't . . . these guys, you have no idea. Look what happened to Martin. He's in for that and he didn't even do it. That was Harding, and someone else. That's just the . . . the . . . not even the half of it. You can't do this your way. Do that, you'll lose."

I looked at her. *What then?*

She read my expression. Her face hardened again and she squeezed my hand hard enough to make me wince. She kept squeezing, and she dragged each word out slowly, her voice barely a whisper. Her words chilled me.

"Turn their fuckin' world upside down."

I frowned and stepped out to call Helen.

TWENTY-NINE

Tanya was under witness protection while Orewa CIB looked deeper into what she'd said. They were re-investigating Steve and Pete's murders, but that was all. Tanya and I had reached an understanding on the rest. *Not yet.* I had more digging to do, before I raised it with Helen. I was invited back to the job again by Helen and Tim, but again I turned them down. If I was back in the fold, I could be told what I could and couldn't do. I had a couple of things on my list before I wanted to toe the line again. I phoned Dan.

"Hey Matt."

"Got a request for you."

"Here we go. Which law do you want me to break this time?"

"Stop it. It's just shit I've seen before. Sort of. I need a copy of David Kitson's statement from the Darwen file. In fact, any jobsheets done regarding him as well."

"Okay, no rush hopefully? I'll dig it out of CID."

"There's something else." Dan waited. He didn't ask. "I'm after anything in NIA on the '95 shooting of Gabby. I need everything on Gary Harding, starting from way back then."

Dan breathed in. "Mate, I've got no problem giving you the Darwen stuff. You worked that, you've seen it. But I can't give you NIA shit, even though you attended that. You know how much oversight of NIA there is."

"Well, do it as part of your current work. It's related, mate. I know there's a link here. Give it to Helen and Tim if you need to, raise it with them. Just dig it out, and I'll explain when I see you. If you still don't want to hand it over, no dramas."

I met him in Orewa for a coffee two days later and he handed me a folder. "Everything on Kitson from the Brianna Darwen file. What are you thinking?"

"You remember Kelly Thornton, raped in 2011, trial 2012?"

"Of course. Poor girl." He dropped his head and studied his cup.

"A friend of hers was raped by Jordan Kitson and another guy. Didn't want to make a complaint. But it turns out there are plenty of other girls that have. They've connected them all. Mass complaint. CPT have it."

He joined the dots. "You're thinking it runs in the family?"

"Maybe. Dunno. I saw Tanya Redmond down in Tauranga. She thinks Brianna wasn't killed by her mother. I haven't passed this on to Helen yet, but—"

Dan frowned and cut in. "There was nothing to suggest anyone else was involved. There was nowhere else to go with it."

"Not then, anyway." I queried Dan on the other stuff. "What about anything on Harding from '95?"

"There was nothing in the NIA case, too old. But look, something that may get you somewhere, if it's the '95 shooting you're concerned with. Here's a number for Warren Malcolm. Gabby's partner that night." I nodded and took the piece of paper. "Get him to talk through the shooting with you. He's happy to do it. Knows you guys were close, in fact he's surprised you've never approached him over the years."

There was good reason for that. It hurt too much. But this was promising.

I looked through the David Kitson stuff back at my place. Another storm was smashing the roof and windows as I sipped from my mug. Nicola Darwen had always looked so scared when we executed that warrant. *Until she was in our car and told she wasn't going back home.* And a couple of things she'd said had always stuck in my head, burned in from that day four, nearly five, years ago now, haunting me.

She should've done what she was told. I always had to.

Ramblings, or was there some more to it? What did she actually mean? I swirled my cup and put the jug back on.

We'd had cell-phone data, forensics. And on top of that, Nicola had confessed. But Brianna had been brutally murdered and dumped in the dunes. On a deserted stretch of beach, near a cold, dark forest. An ill mother with no support, unable to cope? Possible. *But if it wasn't? The question mark over Brianna being sexually assaulted?* We'd never been able to take that further. Not enough to prove it from the post-mortem. I read the statements and jobsheets Dan had dug out for me. David had mentioned last seeing Brianna several days before her body was found. Everything was normal with her, according to him. Nicola was her normal up and down self too, she had good days, and she had "gone days". It was pretty generic stuff, nothing specific. Until I got to the paragraphs where the interviewer had clearly asked, "Do you think she could have done this . . .?"

These were interesting.

"Well, Nicola is hard to gauge, because of the depression, the paranoia. It's hard to tell one day to the next whether what she's experiencing is actually her, you know, or whether she's sick. I'd never have thought she could do this to Bree though. Not in a million years. She loved her. But have I seen Nicola violent? Absolutely. Lose

control? Absolutely. So I guess it's hard to answer."

David was pointing the finger directly at Nicola, without making it too obvious and dropping her right in it.

I sat back and thought. I was outside the rule book here. I wasn't a sworn officer. I could fuck up a lot of things. But fuck it. Whatever the truth was, she knew it.

THIRTY

Nicola was still a special patient with the Mason Clinic, but she was looking far better than she had four years ago. I didn't know what to expect. So, just as I'd been with Tanya, I was surprised when Nicola smiled and offered me the seat across from her.

"Not sure if you remember me, it's Matt. I was with the Police back in 2012. I'm not with them anymore."

"Matt Buchanan, of course. You want to know how it all happened? It's been part of the treatment here."

"Well, no, that's not why I've come. I was hoping to talk about your brother, David, and some of his mates."

It took her by surprise. Her eyes clouded a little, and she shivered. "How come?" She rubbed her face and looked at me, trying to suss me out, unsure of my motives. She wasn't going to open up to any old dickhead that wandered in. She had secrets buried deep, and had kept them hidden for decades. She'd try her best to keep them there.

I explained. "When I saw you back in 2012, you were a frightened solo mum, scared to even be in that house. When we took you away, you relaxed, calmed right down. I want to understand."

"Well, it was over, wasn't it? I didn't have to pretend. There was nothing else I could do."

"Except you *were* pretending."

She caught my eye again and I held her gaze, trying to work out what was happeneing behind her eyes. I hadn't given too much away. She might just think I thought she wasn't telling the full truth about Brianna's death. An ex-cop with a mixed motive. She ignored my last comment. "Tell me what you want, and I'll do my best."

"Nicola, I'm not here defending cops, or anyone. You've been failed by a whole bunch of people, not just your family and maybe your friends, but the state as well, on so many levels." I let her think about it, hoping she might start to see that I wasn't there to cause her grief. Then I cut to the chase. "I think we missed something back in 2012."

Her eyes widened a little but she regained control. "Like what?"

"Lots of things. Something you've hidden well most of your life. Dealt with on your own, in your own way. I had a feeling back then, but that's all it was. There was so much going on at once. So, I'm sorry. I really am. There's nothing I can do now, to turn the clock back, but I'm looking forwards. I think we missed just how much you loved Brianna. How much you still love her."

Nicola started to shake. I charged ahead. "I think the person that actually killed her is still out there."

She started crying and I knew the shutters were going to come down any minute. I had a very small window of time to shove them back up, or I was going to get marched out of here pretty soon for upsetting her. I grabbed her hand. "Nicola, I don't expect you to step up and tell your story to the cops. I understand why you can't do that. Look at me. I don't work for the Police any-more. I'm not playing by their rules. Help me understand what happened, because I don't think Brianna is the only victim here, or that she'll be the last." I put my other hand on top of hers. "Totally off the books. Confidential. I don't need all the details. All I'm asking is that you give me a little, point me in the right direction. I'll get the rest. Please, I understand this is bigger than I initially thought it was."

She didn't let my hand go, instead she squeezed. And whis-pered. "But I . . . you can't."

"I'd never do anything that's gonna hurt you. I'm going to ask some questions, mention some names. You just nod or shake. Brianna. It wasn't your fault."

"It was my fault."

"You didn't kill her."

Shake.

"Someone else did."

Nod.

"There's more than one person involved."

Nod.

"David and his mates."

Nod.

I was getting somewhere. Nothing to lose now. "Who took her to the beach? Was it you?"

Shake.

"David?"

She spoke. "I don't know."

"Who actually killed her, Nicola?"

"I don't know. I didn't see them." She started to shake, tears spilling out the sides of her eyes as she looked away from me.

I leaned forward, over our hands. "Nicola, I can do something with this, something that keeps you well clear of the whole situation. We'll take it slow, do this properly. But I might need to come back. You'll see that you can trust me." She nodded. "I won't do anything that makes things worse for you."

She nodded again. Then I thought of another question. "Did you ever meet a Gary Harding?"

She froze at the name. I took that as a yes. The shaking continued and I didn't push her.

She started crying again as I stood up, and as I tried to move off she hugged me, tightly. As I held her she whispered into my ear. And that familiar cold feeling found its way into my spine again. It was the way she so gently said the words. It just didn't fit. Her voice changed, dropped, and my flesh prickled.

"Do this once, Matt. Do it right." She paused.

"Or they'll kill you."

THIRTY-ONE

I needed more. I had theories, loose information, but I needed to understand the people I was dealing with. Gary Harding was top of that list. I'd called Warren Malcolm, who was very warm, welcoming and keen for a beer.

I met him at the Riverhead Tavern on a Saturday afternoon. The weather was actually okay, so we ordered a couple of pints and picked a table on the back deck looking out over the tidal inlet.

Warren had changed a lot in twenty-one years. *Hadn't we all*. He'd put a bit of weight on. Hair receding, cut short now, rather than the mop he'd had back then. Slightly pudgy face, wrinkles apparent. I'd noticed him limp to the table. "Still giving you trouble?"

He looked at his leg. "Oh, from '95? No, that healed up okay. I got full function back for years. This was up Cardrona, few years back now. Came off my skis and fell badly. Broke it just below the knee, but it's okay, just . . . yeah, I mean I won't be running a marathon anytime soon." We chuckled, and then he studied me, genuinely concerned. "Been a long time. We never really caught up after '95, except probably at the trial?"

I nodded. "Yeah, the trial would have been the only time afterward I think."

"How've things been?"

"Average, I guess. I still relive that night. Over and over."

Warren closed his eyes and sighed. He'd had it worse than me. He'd seen Gabby get shot, had almost been killed himself.

"You got caught up in the Westgate shooting too, didn't you? Steve Prentice?" I nodded. Warren kept talking. "Good bastard, he was. I'm not surprised you got out. Fuck, I would have after Gabby, but stuck around a few years, until I just couldn't do it anymore." He took a long sip of his beer. "You want some detail from the night?"

I breathed in. "Only if you're okay with it. I'm trying to get my head round it again. Around the players. Harding, Calver."

"How's that then?"

"Harding's cooking meth now, Orewa are after him." I considered telling him more, but thought there was probably plenty of time for that. "Also, I just need to get over this somehow. Probably should see someone."

He was nodding. "You definitely should. I did, but far too late." He looked out at the water. "Harding, that piece of shit. Didn't do nearly long enough. But his mate, Calver? He was a fucking piece of work. Real mean cunt. Glad he's still inside."

"Calver pulled the trigger, right?"

"Yeah. It was pretty dark, pissing down something shocking, as you know from when you and Andy got there. But I'll never forget it. Gabby saw their car racing along the Coatesville-Riverhead Highway, coming from the Coatesville end. We were parked up filling in a family violence report after a 1D in Riverhead. Flew past us. I wasn't that keen but she had a good point, they could've taken someone out. Fuck." He looked into his beer. "Should've gone with my gut and let it go."

"You weren't to know. And Gabby wanted to go after it."

"Yeah. 3T'd 'em on the bend of Riverhead Road near Deacon there. Right where you found us. Gabby got out, approached the driver. I called it in. Dark, pissing with rain. I can remember Gabby lit up by our headlights and red and blues. Then I saw her stumble back. Didn't really hear the shots. I started to get out, but the driver got out of their car. It was Calver. Pointed the shooter at me, let some rounds off. I remember them coming through the windscreen, didn't hit me then though. I knew the car was a death trap so I pushed the door, tried to get out. But he fired again, hit me high and low as I got out of the car. I went down, guess that was all they needed. Calver got back in their car, they took off. I moved toward Gabby, she was in a bad way. I got on the radio."

I felt sorry for him. I knew what it was like. Exactly what it was like. A mate killed in front of you, fuck all you could do about it. "You never saw Harding, right? If I recall from the trial?"

He shook his head. "Never saw him. Saw someone in the passenger seat. I couldn't ID them though. It was only later when the place got swarmed, they got 3T'd up near Helensville by AOS. It was Calver and Harding they got."

I nodded. This was cutting Warren up, I could tell, and I didn't want to put him out. I changed the subject, we chatted about how it was to have left the job behind. We agreed to catch up again at some stage.

We shook hands outside. "Take care, Matt. Look after yourself. I mean it."

He ducked into a blue Holden station wagon and started it up. I let him move off before reversing out and heading home.

I slept well that night, but I had a really vivid dream. Sam was in it. I relived the Westgate shooting, the moment I'd found Steve dying on the concrete. I looked up, and there was Sam, clearly screaming at me from across the car park. I couldn't hear what she was yelling. But something in my head was trying to tell me something.

THIRTY-TWO

I'd never met Thomas Calver. He'd murdered Gabby on that cold, wet night twenty-one years ago, but I'd only ever heard about him from other cops. The D's that interviewed him back then reckoned he was arrogant, self-important. A narcissist. He was a meth dealer in '95, but that was all I'd known about him really. I had only been a probationary Constable then. After his conviction I hadn't revisited information on the man responsible for the death of a good mate. I'd wanted to remember her, not him.

Gabby's death had played a large part in propelling me into the CIB. I'd struggled in the aftermath, seeing other people working hard on something so important to me. And there I was, a dickhead in a glow vest giving out tickets and dealing with drunks. I wanted involvement. But I didn't get it. Then, only five months after I'd been permanently appointed as a Constable in mid-'97, the country was brought to its knees. In the early hours of New Year's Day 1998, Olivia Hope and Ben Smart were murdered by Scott Watson in the pristine Marlborough Sounds. It gripped the nation. Shattered the illusion of the Kiwi Summer. My career path was confirmed. I didn't want to be on the sidelines when guys like that were being hunted. Watching the investigation into Gabby's killing happening around me, and later seeing the faces of Ben and Olivia every night on the telly, I'd felt helpless knowing that the next day I'd be pulling a uniform on and ruining someone's day. Oh, I wanted to ruin people's days all right. But they were a very select few.

Around that time I'd already been chewed out for giving too many traffic warnings. Once I'd even got a dude to tip his bag of weed out onto the curb and stomp on it. No arrest. That was something you did with a roach, but not an ounce. My Sergeant had reamed me in front of the whole section for that. But I was bored. There was more important shit to worry about. I got the study done. Put my head down, and got on the CIB selection and induction course. And that's how it happened. In hindsight, I probably should have just left. But here we are.

I sat waiting for him in the interview room. For some reason, he'd agreed to see me. White walls. Sterile. Table bolted to the floor. Presumably so he couldn't kill me with it. I had no idea what to expect. This would be interesting, however it went. After a small wait the door opened and a prison guard guided him in. He was dressed in a grey jumper and grey pants. His hair was the same colour as his clothes, down below his ears. He wasn't clean-shaven. He would have been in his fifties now. His face gave nothing away but his eyes were alert.

"Detective. It's been a long time. I remember you from the trial. 1996. Constable back then, wasn't it? You found your friend that night, didn't you? I'm sorry."

I'd decided I wouldn't let him work me up. I just kept my cool. "I'm not here about Gabby. And I'm not in the job anymore."

"Oh?" he looked surprised. "Gabby . . ." He breathed her

shortened name, already sussing me out. "Are you sure this isn't about her?" This was an intelligent man, probably knew a lot about me. Prison gives you a lot of time to trawl books, the news, and the internet if you could get access. I'd been in the news a bit over the years. He'd had five days between me making this appointment and my arrival to find out whatever he could.

I changed the subject. "You knew Gary Harding well, back in '95." He frowned. This wasn't where he thought this was going to go. He didn't answer. It was a statement I'd made, not a question. He knew the difference. I carried on. "Tell me about him."

"What would you like to know, Detective? I'm a bit out of touch . . ." he gestured at the walls.

"I don't want to know about him now. I want to know about him then."

He gazed at me, didn't move another muscle. His mind was working but his face didn't show it. He had all the time in the world to work me out. "I might be able to help if you were a bit more specific, Detective."

"Don't call me that, it's Matt. I'm not a cop anymore."

"But you're still investigating. Working."

"No."

"Ah. Personal." He smiled. "But you said it wasn't about her . . ."

Fuck it. "Okay, Mr Calver. Why. Why did you shoot Ga . . . Constable Gabrielle Stewart back in 1995?"

"Tom, please. Why did I? You didn't need to come here to find that out."

"Back then, you told them it was drug related. Several ounces in your car."

"So you know. So why are you really here?"

"Because I'm calling bullshit on your version. I've never known people to shoot cops in this country just because they've got drugs on them. Because they're *on drugs* maybe, but not just cos of some gear in their car." He didn't move a muscle. His eyes were still searching. I'd got him interested, but he wasn't yet sure of my motive. I needed to be honest. Shake this up. "You remember the young girl, Brianna Darwen? Found in the dunes, up from Muriwai, four years ago. David Kitson was her uncle. He lived with her. And he knows Harding quite well."

I let it hang, and didn't ask anything of him. I continued.

"In 2012, we found a meth lab, Harding's lab, out in Titirangi. We got Damien Lendich there, the Wizard. And two teenagers, Tanya Redmond and Martin Schuster."

I watched his face. He was keeping up. None of this was news to him.

"In late 2012 a good friend of mine, Detective Steven Prentice, and Peter Childs, one of Harding's crew, were both shot dead. You remember. That young guy, Schuster, took the rap."

Calver's brow furrowed at my choice of words. *He knows.*

"Thing is, Tom, there's more to Harding than cooking meth. I've heard rumours about child rape videos, dark movies, revolting shit. Making it. Pete was killed just after he found out."

Calver still didn't say anything. He was locking what I was saying away, piece by piece, so that he could recall it later. *Good. At least he hasn't walked out.* I was taking a gamble now. Helen, Tim, they would lose their shit if they knew I was here, talking to this guy. Mentioning this. But fuck it. I could do what I wanted. Tanya's words were ringing in my head. We had to get something moving.

"And you would have seen the news. Girl fished out of Tauranga harbour, by the Mount. Left for dead. That was Tanya Redmond, Tom. She was thinking about spilling on Harding. On what actually went down, why Steve and Pete were shot. Got her head caved in, tossed into the water." I leaned in to him. "But I spoke to her, Tom. A repeat of Pete's story."

He considered his words. "A big call, coming in here, Detective."

"Well, I'm going to take a stab in the dark, and say you aren't that close with Harding anymore. He did less than four, and twenty years later you're still in."

He sat back, staring at me, trying to work out what my gig was.

"Why are *you* here, Detective? Why do *you* care so much that you're here asking questions after giving up the game? Your friend, Steven? They could square that away without your help. If Harding was the one that actually killed him, then . . ." he threw his hands up, "well, I have all the faith in the world in the New Zealand Police Criminal Investigation Branch."

His disdain was clear. Not surprising. He was doing life for murder.

I clarified a few things. "You're right. They're looking at the double murder. But they aren't looking at the rest yet." I leaned toward him, hands on the table. I stared him down. "Dead kids." I looked into his eyes, looking for a glimmer of recognition, a touch of confirmation about anything I was saying. "Brianna, the girl in the dunes. Her mother didn't kill her. And Pete, just before he died, and Tanya . . . I've never seen two people so scared in my life. Harding is killing people, Tom. Give me something on him. Doesn't matter how old it is. I'll use it."

He leant toward me too, mirroring my action, and smiled. His face creased all over as he did it. He brushed a strand of white hair from his eyes. "When you're fully honest with me, Detective, I might be convinced to be fully honest with you. I mean, let's be clear – I am in here for murdering a good friend of yours. And you want information regarding an old associate of *mine*, who you think killed another friend of *yours*?" His smile faded and he clenched his jaw. He sat back, bored. "But you're attacking this wrong, regardless. You're going with the same old cops and robbers bullshit that you guys have been doing for a hundred years. You're feeling your way forward, piece by piece. 'This is bad' you're saying to yourself, 'this is different . . . I'm gonna change it up, do something outside the box . . .'. He waved his hands, doing a comic impression of me. "Well, Detective, you're fucked, because you're stuck in your box. You need to change the game."

I sat staring at him, waiting. I wasn't going to answer him. I wasn't hopeful for anything useful. I wasn't Dr Phil, but I was starting to think maybe prison hadn't been too good on him from a psychological perspective. But then, four walls for two decades would fuck anyone up. Calver didn't say anything else. *Ah well. Fuck this.* I got up to leave.

"You obviously need some convincing, Detective."

I turned. "What?"

"You want to play your little boys' game? Fine. Good for you. But when you want to get realistic, get back to me."

"What the fuck are you talking about?"

"He's got a unit out west, end of Keeling Road." He drew me a map on the desk with his fingers. I was familiar with Keeling from my Henderson days. "Down the end, on the right. Second place in. Container in the backyard. Fenced. Cameras. False name on the lease paperwork, Harding's got a contact in Land Transport. Fake licence."

I frowned. "He doesn't think you'd ever turn on him?"

Calver's face went cold. "No." I raised my eyebrows but his face didn't change. He carried on with more detail. "He doesn't cook there. Just stores materials. In and out. There'll be chemicals, equipment there, for sure. That'll distract the other cops. But it's electronic devices *you'll* be after." He was distancing me from the Police. Good. That's what I needed him to do. "Any drive, any disc, any storage device. That's what you want."

I nodded. But it shouldn't have been that easy. It wasn't possible. There was way more going on here than I could work out in my head right now. *This guy is intelligent. Dangerous.* He got up. It looked like our conversation was over. But as I reached for the buzzer that would bring the guard to let me out, he spoke again. "Detective, one more thing before you go. Nothing personal. To protect me in here. You'll understand."

I didn't even have a chance to reply, or enquire. He'd closed the gap between us by skirting the desk in less than a second. I didn't even manage to put any distance between us. I took three solid punches into my face before I got my guard up, all on and below my nose. I felt my teeth tearing my lips and I heard my nose go. I fell backwards into the wall, slid down onto my arse. I put my hands up over my face and head to try and give me some sort of protection. I kicked out at his legs, landing a good one just above his knee. He grunted and backed away, giving me time to get to my feet, guard up, moving in toward him. He backed off, but I kept going, getting in a few palm strikes to his face. He went for a haymaker which almost broke my arm as I blocked it. The force still knocked me off balance and he was on me as I hit the wall again. I yelled for the guards, and he started yelling back, spitting at me. "Fuck you, cunt!" he screamed. He was still swinging as the doors flew open and the guards ran in. "Try to stitch me up, cunt! Get fucked!" he was pulled off by two guards and a third pulled me up and out the door. As I was helped down the corridor to an office, I could hear Calver still nutting off on the other side of the interview room.

THIRTY-THREE

Things moved quickly after my prison visit. Tim and Helen asked me to come back yet again. This time I agreed. I needed in. They were pretty smart about the order they did things though. Once I'd signed on the dotted line, they both gave me a bollocking about visiting Calver in prison, and a warning about my conduct. I was supposed to sit there and take it. But I couldn't help myself. Out of the ordinary, I know.

Tim wasn't in the mood for jokes. "There isn't one fuckin' rule for you and one for everyone else. Who the fuck do you think you are?"

"Matthew Buch—"

"Shut the fuck up. Everything you do, Matt, comes through one of us. Everything. If you go off track, you fuck this up, this isn't just some minor shit. This is a multiple homicide investigation. We'll lose the public's trust for good."

I'd tried to take the advice onboard. So, unsure of the endgame, here I was, skulking through bush behind the Keeling Road factory in Henderson with Dan and two other guys – Dave from the Clan Lab team, and Marty from the Technical Support Unit, lock-picker extraordinaire. Sweating like pigs in chemical suits, with gas masks slung on our belts, we looked like we'd just escaped from a hardcore bondage dungeon. And being the dumb cunt most resembling a pack mule, I was carrying the foldable ladder in a pack strapped to my back. Dan and I were in the lead, Glocks out in the Sul position.

The risk warranted it. In 2008, Don Wilkinson had been murdered trying to fit a tracking device to a car outside a meth lab in Mangere. Since then, the red tape around covert searches had tripled, and rightly so. High risk meant take firearms. And breaking into a lab stockpile owned by a guy who'd been involved in killing Gabby, and had likely killed Steve, rated pretty high on the fucking scale. Dan and I would be giving evidence about this warrant one day, if we found anything. For now, though, the idea was no one would know we'd even been there. As well as noting any chemicals we found, I was also going to clone any electronic shit.

We obviously couldn't just pile out of a cop car and go in from the Keeling Road end. We had to do this unobserved. We had a friendly on a cul de sac off Spence Road, which was north of the factory and separated from the end of Keeling by a small stretch of bush. There was a public track through it, but we didn't want a bar of that. At 2 a.m. we'd driven into our friendly address in a plain van with all our kit. We'd got dressed up for our BDSM sesh and hopped the back fence into the bushline. With the night and bush canopy combo, we couldn't see a thing. Ideally you didn't want to be crashing about drawing attention to a covert Police operation, so it was slow going. With every step I'd keep my weight on the rear foot, then push my other one out slowly, feeling for obstacles, gently placing it down, only then shifting my weight forward before doing it again. I could just imagine tripping over a log or something, discharging my pistol as I arsed over. Probably wouldn't be getting any gold merit awards for that.

We picked our way like this through the bush, gorse and scrub until we sighted the white strip of public walkway that extended left and right, snaking behind the factory which was directly ahead of us. The factory was separated from the walkway by a tall wire fence. Marty had recce'd the area in the days prior, and we'd had surveillance on the factory for a week. We'd established routines not just for the target premises, but all the surrounding buildings as well. There were cameras covering the rear, which we'd sorted with a nice targeted power cut. During his recce, Marty had copied the expensive-looking lock system at the rear door and now had a brand new key to get us in. Our entry plan was sound, but getting over the wire fence was going to expose us the most. Dan took up a position covering the walkway left and right. I holstered my Glock, opened my pack and extended the ladder with Dave's help. I then rose and broke the bush line, moving carefully across the walkway to the wire fence. I placed the ladder and moved quickly up it, over the fence and onto the shipping container on the other side. I pulled my pistol out again and scanned the rear wall of the factory, before dropping to the ground and taking up a position beside the rear door. Marty followed me over, then Dave. Dan came over last, me covering the walkway in both directions for him. Once he was up on the container, Dan reached back over and pulled the ladder up. He collapsed it and dropped off the container to join us, bringing the ladder with him.

We stacked up on the door and Dave reminded us to mask up. We could be going into a contaminated environment. I pulled the gas mask from my belt and got a hand under the elasticated rubber that fitted around the back of your head. I stretched it out, slipped it over my head, and removed my hand, the rubber snapping into place. I adjusted the mask, then sucked air in and breathed out hard, listening and checking for any leaks, making sure the seal was good. Then we checked each other – wrist seals, boots, and the hood of our suits fitting around our masks. Marty got to work on the lock. He was in in seconds, but paused on the threshold, checking for secondary security. Dan and I were right up his arse, Glocks out. I was doing my best to listen out for threats but all you could hear in these fuckin' things was the sound of your own breathing. Marty moved to the alarm box and deactivated the connections to the sensors. I was breathing heavily in my mask, and there was already a little pool of water at the bottom of it. I could see fuck all. The diaphragm in the filter clicked every time I breathed in and out. It was like breathing through a towel, but the trick was long, slow breaths so you didn't hyperventilate. It was claustrophobic and you could panic quite easily, especially when you couldn't see.

Dave tested the air with this expensive-looking electronic thing. He gave a thumbs up, indicating we could take off our masks. *Thank fuck for that.* Not our gloves and suits though – the surfaces in here might still be contaminated. We broke out the NVGs and fixed them over our heads. The factory floor lit up. Tunnel vision though. No depth perception. And it's hard to describe, but because you're only working with shades of green, black and white, it's hard to identify objects because you're so used to real colours. You have to get a real close look sometimes to work out what the fuck you're looking at. Dan and I conducted a sweep of the factory just in case someone was playing hide and seek with us. We moved as a pair, Dan in front, me on his left shoulder, clockwise round the factory floor, checking obvious places like the rooms off to the sides and the toilet. The place was obviously clear of people though, and we started our evidential search. If we came across anything meth lab-related we'd photograph it, and that was about it. We had to leave everything as it was. If we needed to move anything, we'd snap a photo on our digital cameras first so we could re-create the scene before we left. We were looking for electronic storage devices for me to clone too. I moved toward an area on my left that had a series of drawers, cabinets and a desk. Dave and Dan went the other way towards the front roller door and a series of workbenches stacked with drums and containers.

I took a pic of the cabinets then pulled each door gently open. Not much in there. I checked the shelving, then searched the top of the desk. Papers, books, mechanic shit. There was a laptop, which I powered on. Password protected. No problem. I connected the neat little box the ECL guys had given me and in five minutes had cloned the drive. I unplugged the box and shut the laptop back down, replacing it where it was. I found a couple of USB sticks in the drawers, and cloned them too by sticking them in a USB slot on the side of the box of tricks. A wider search of this area revealed fuck all else. Dave, Dan and I met in the middle of the far wall and conferred. Nothing else my way, and they'd come across no other electronic shit their way. They had however found a stockpile of toluene under the workbench, and some large bags of caustic soda stashed near some tires. There were a few large pots and some heating elements too. It was a decent find, but like I said, we weren't taking anything today.

The four of us had a discussion. Marty took no time installing a covert camera covering the lab equipment and the roller door. A re-scan of the factory to ensure we hadn't left anything behind, that everything was back in its proper place. And we left the same way we'd come in.

THIRTY-FOUR

It was a rare day off. I'd spent the afternoon with Karen, Rob and Holly. I met them at Columbus Albany for a coffee. I talked through it with them. Yes, I was back in the Police. No, I didn't have the Operation Mist file, Simon still had it. How come? I didn't know. Not my decision. Yeah, I could still work on it.

They seemed pretty happy I was back. I'm not sure why. I'd made no progress for the last seventeen years, and it didn't look like I was about to dust off some leads and break open the case. *Fuck, this is hard.* I left them with nothing positive, except that I was back on board. *Some comfort.* I couldn't believe the time that had passed. Holly had been a kid when her sister had disappeared. Now she was twenty-seven, and an associate with one of the big law firms. I thought back over what I'd achieved in that same amount of time. *Not fucking much. Round and round, in the same bloody circles.* I wondered what Sam would have ended up doing if she were still here. I came away from the meeting feeling like the Coates were more worried about me than I was about them.

I was sitting back at home now, thinking through our initial actions after Sam was reported missing, like I had a thousand times when I got the call from Erin.

She was talking fast. "They've cleaned up some of the electronic stuff you cloned from Keeling. I'm coming to pick you up. Something you need to see."

She had to stop doing this. "Just fucking tell me this time, mate. This is a phone, not a pager."

"Sorry." She breathed out, and I could tell even just listening to her voice that something had thrown her off a bit. "But this, yeah, you definitely need to see this first. I . . . can't explain this on the phone. It speaks for itself."

"Erin?" Like a school teacher.

"Just…I'm nearly at yours. Just wait."

She drove me into Orewa and I got a brief from Helen first in her office. They'd found a pile of images on the cloned laptop drive. Child porn. I was having a rant about the phrase when Helen cut me off. "Matt, things have changed up. You were right about links. Among the rest, which OCEANZ have now, were almost a hundred images of Brianna Darwen."

What the fuck? It was what I'd wanted. Direct links between Brianna and Harding. But the anger started boiling inside me when I thought about what those cunts would have done to her. I picked up my empty mug, looked at it, squeezed it in my hand. It didn't break, of course. *Those fuckin'.* . . And I reacted, hurling it across Helen's office, where it smashed into the skirting below her window.

"Matt, fuck!"

I went and picked up the pieces, chucked them in her bin. "Sorry. Go on."

"Just . . . fucking sit there and listen. Not rape or naked images of her. Clothed, just photos. Probably couldn't even call them objectionable—"

I cut her off. "And that matters . . . why? That changes nothing. They were in Harding's fuckin' factory."

"I know. Tim's told us to re-open the Darwen murder case. Looking at Kitson and Harding."

I collapsed back in my chair, glad we'd got somewhere. I started thinking forward, on to the next step. But before I could ask any more questions Helen started talking again.

"There's something else." She called out past me into the CIB office. "Erin, Dan, can you come in here? The video."

Erin fucked about on the computer and brought up a movie file. She sat back next to Helen and watched me closely as I clicked the little play arrow on the screen. From the fuzziness and video dimensions it was pretty old. An analogue recording that had been converted to digital. I saw a dark-haired girl, a teenager, close-up of her face. She looked young. I frowned. She was screaming, clearly, but there wasn't any audio. The camera was being held by someone and it zoomed out a bit. She was tied to a bed and thrashing about. The camera panned. There was a guy fucking her, hard. You could only see his arse.

"What the fuck is this? Rape porn?"

I looked up at the three watching me, and their faces were grim. Erin shook her head. *No. Surely not.*

"Can you get this from the net?"

They all shook their heads and Dan pointed back at the video. I started to feel nauseous as I turned back to it. My world narrowed into that video playing in front of me. I closed off everything else. The view shook a bit, then zoomed in and out, then around. There was a glimpse of other people standing around, but you didn't get a good look at anyone. Until it showed the guy fucking the girl. *Harding.* Definitely. And then it focused on her again, on her face. I felt the blood drain from mine, and gripped my chair. That ice flowed through me again, prickling my flesh. The anger rose. The girl was screaming in agony, lips curled back, teeth showing. And the camera zoomed right in on the tears, the snot, the sweat, all reflected by the light from the ceiling in the room. And I realised. *This wasn't acting.*

THIRTY-FIVE

I was staring at Helen, Erin and Dan with my mouth open slightly. "Do we know who she is?"

Helen shook her head. "No. We're going to put a still image, the least upsetting one we can get, on the bulletin board. If that doesn't get us anywhere, we might have to release it to the media. There are a few bits in the video where you can screen-grab her face and not show what's actually going on."

"Tough call if word got out what that video actually was."

Helen said what I was thinking. "We don't really have a choice. We have to identify her. A rape on video. That alone would sink Harding. At least it would put him inside while we work on linking him to Brianna's murder."

I left with the USB and chucked it in my own computer out in the CIB office. I found the safest still image of the girl I could. I let Helen look over my bully board notice before I uploaded it. I followed Helen back to her office and glanced at Erin. She watched me the whole way, tiniest of frowns creasing the gap between her eyes. *What the fuck was her problem all of a sudden?* Helen sat down at her desk and I closed the office door, just to piss Erin off. But also, something was niggling at the back of my mind. Tanya had been hurt, but she was an exception. She was alive, I mean.

I queried Helen. "Is this the full video, or is there more?"

"That's the full file, that's all there is."

"There's more. Gotta be. It's like a clip from somewhere in the middle of everything. You've got to wonder why it's been cut . . ."

"I know what you're thinking Matt, but we can only work with what we've got. This is a rape, we've got to investigate it as such. But I hear you."

"What I mean is, the longer this cunt is out, and not in a cell, then people are at risk. We've got a video, let's just bin him first and ask questions later."

"You know we can't."

"Can't we? We're talking public safety here. Public interest. If Harding is what we think he is, he needs to be secured."

"We've got nothing, Matt. Some words from a Mason Clinic patient, a statement from a beaten-up meth user, and informant information from his own partner in crime – a convicted murderer rotting in Paremoremo prison. Some photos of Brianna. Until we find the girl in this video, or link Harding evidentially to Brianna, our hands are tied. I hear you, and we'll monitor. But the prosecution guidelines are clear."

I nodded and opened the door, walking out to see a frowning Erin who had probably heard every word. *Fuck the prosecution guidelines.* I sat back at my desk and re-watched the video, over and over. Something strong was building up inside, I could feel it, and I needed to do something. Erin came over and touched my shoulder.

"Matt, I know this is some heavy shit, but you aren't doing yourself any favours by—"

"Fuck's sake, Erin, I'm just trying to get some detail out of it."

She let go and drifted back to her desk, started clicking around and typing immediately. I closed my eyes and touched the bridge of my nose with thumb and forefinger. *What the fuck was happening to me?* I was looking for something, and I didn't even know what it was. Trying to make something out of nothing. But that cold spike had buried itself in my spine again, and it stayed there. Harding was dangerous. He'd been dangerous for a long time.

What have we missed over the years?

That image of Sam walking home from school pushed its way into my head. I shook myself, looked back at my computer screen, stared at it until it came back into focus.

But the goosebumps remained.

THIRTY-SIX

The internal bully board notice yielded nothing. But the media release did its job. She was in her forties. Sunken, broken. A wanderer that hadn't found what she was looking for. Brown hair to her shoulders, kind eyes. But sad. She'd thought about this hard before coming in. She was apologetic right from the start, but I wanted to get her comfortable. "Kerry, come through to one of our rooms. Coffee?"

"No, thank you." She followed me through from the reception area to one of the soft interview rooms. "It's always been my fault. I wasn't there for her." Her hand trembled as she reached into her bag and pulled out a photo frame. She placed it on the table in front of us. It was a school photo, a teenage girl, probably fifteen or sixteen. Brunette, like her mother, all straight hair and big smile. Happier times, sure. But there was no mistaking the girl from the horrific video. "That was form five, 1993."

I looked up at Kerry. Back at the photo. *1993? Jesus.* I knew she knew I'd heard her, but I sat there for what felt like minutes, looking at the girl in the photo. I said nothing.

"In form six, Anneke got into drugs. Started at parties, you know, but then carried on elsewhere. Some guys from her school had some mates that had dropped out – they had this new drug. Well, it was new back then. Speed. It took her." I knew what she was talking about. The homebake scene back then was quite a closed community. Needles weren't everyone's cup of tea. But speed, meth, P – whatever you wanted to call it – had made hard drugs accessible to the masses. Snort it, smoke it, inject it, you could do whatever the fuck you liked.

Kerry started to choke up and I reached out for her hand. *I was getting better at this shit. I was letting the robot go. But what good was it doing me?*

She continued. "I did what I thought I could. She'd left school, we couldn't get her to go. She left home when we grounded her, and when that didn't work, we got her into rehab. But that didn't last. She came back, we had to get the Police involved when she started hitting us. I'm not just talking slaps, right? I'm talking rolling pins, ironing boards, sometimes knives from the drawer. She'd come and go, float in, and it would be okay for a short time. Something would have gone sideways and she wanted her parents. Those were the good times, small moments of light. Then a switch would get flicked. Out she'd go. When I tried to stop her once, she knocked me back on the front step and I ended up with a broken wrist."

I looked back at the photo in front of me of the smiling schoolgirl. I knew the effects meth had, but it was hard to imagine this girl, Anneke, doing what her mother was describing. But then, meth just took away your individuality. You became a slave. If you became dependent, which didn't take much, it defined your actions and your personality.

"We had two other kids. Both younger than Anneke. We had to think of them. They were suffering. We trespassed her, and she came back once, but we called the Police. She would have been sixteen then, and we didn't see her for a few months. We heard about her, through friends. She'd float in, then be gone again. That drug just took our girl away. But I always hoped she'd make it back to us." She started crying gently.

"You never reported her missing?" I watched her, and could see the suffering she'd been through. That she'd dealt with in-house. Tried to bottle up. She reminded me of myself. But it had failed. *What did that mean for me?*

"We did, several times, when she was fifteen, and sixteen. Every time the Police made contact with her and, you know, she was okay, and then when she was almost seventeen, she said she didn't want to see us. So eventually, we stopped doing it. Stopped reporting." I just waited, listening, thinking things over. "The last time we saw her was in late '94. And after that, nothing. I heard things, but she just went off the map, not a sound. I assumed she was out there somewhere, but I didn't want to bring that all back."

My brain raced. *Late '94? No fuckin' way.*

She pleaded. "I really hoped you might have some answers for me. Can you tell me more about the video?"

Here I was again. What a position to be in. Kerry McBride needed someone to be honest with her and talk about the video. That was me. I couldn't duck shove it to someone else. And I had no idea how she was going to react. I had to choose my words carefully. I know she probably wouldn't care how I told her, she just want me to tell her. But in my head, I had to get this right. A lot of pressure, cops put on themselves. But recognising that doesn't make it any easier.

I explained the video to her, and the circumstances around how we'd found it. How it might be linked to other crimes. She listened, nodded, and sobbed through it all. I kept talking. "We've been trying to identify her because she'd be a crucial witness for us in an ongoing investigation. That was the purpose of the media release." I paused. But she needed to hear more. "Kerry, you said you hadn't heard from Anneke since 1994? We'll check our system. But there's a chance . . ."

She nodded. "I understand. Look, I'm realistic about all this. Whatever you need, I just want to help. I just want to know."

"Do you have anything of hers that may still have her DNA? It'll help. If we have anything of hers anywhere, it may help us establish what happened to her. And when."

"Um, probably not. I mean, I've thrown so much out. Still, there is a box that we keep in the attic, it's got all her old things. I just couldn't get rid of them."

"Anything like hair, a hairbrush, or a toothbrush?" As soon as I said that I felt a right fuckwit. *Who the fuck would keep a toothbrush? Twenty-two years after last seeing her? Dick.*

"Her hairbrush, that's in there, yeah."

"Perfect."

I followed Kerry home in an unmarked car. As I went through the front door after her, into the hall, I checked out the photos lining the walls. Three kids. Anneke, clearly, another girl and a boy. The other two kids had photos through the years. Looked like they were both married now. But Anneke had been locked out of that. A long time ago. Kerry dug out the box. I secured the hairbrush in an exhibit bag and made my apologies before heading for the car. I didn't quite make it.

"Mr Buchanan?" I turned. She was just standing there in the hallway, hands at her sides, tears down her cheeks. "It's not the answers that'll be the hardest. It's the not knowing."

I did my usual dickhead nod, didn't say a word, and opened the driver's door.

Back at the office, Dan had received all the relevant missing persons reports, and it all matched with what Kerry had been saying. Anneke McBride appeared in NIA on and off through '94 and '95, but the entries were so old there was little detail. Drugs, driving, alcohol. After June '95 there was nothing. I checked with immigration. No passport.

How does this happen? How does a girl drop off the face of the earth? I turned to Google. I searched a whole lot of different phrases, searching for stories about missing people unidentified for years. I was trying to make sense of this, get my head in the right space. I found the story of Swedish-born Reet Jurveston, who'd lived with her grandmother in Toronto but moved to LA in 1969. Her parents got a postcard, but when contact dropped away, they assumed she was just carving out a new life for herself. She had actually been murdered, her body dumped in the Hollywood Hills and found pretty quickly. But her body went unidentified for forty-seven years. Her family were alerted to a US Justice Department website just last year, and recognised a post-mortem photo posted on the site. She was then identified through DNA. So yeah, I guess it was possible.

And I was starting to glue the pieces together.

I didn't sleep that night. Not properly, anyway. All I saw was Anneke, bright-eyed and happy, before the meth took hold of her. Laughing, smiling. *More false memories. Why?* That drug had dragged her away and never gave her back. And I saw her face in that video. Over and over. But the timing was far too coincidental. 1995, the meth, the lack of contact since . . .

Anneke McBride was dead. I was certain of that.

Because I reckon they'd pulled what was left of her from a mangrove estuary back in 2011.

THIRTY-SEVEN

Operation Weave was a huge undertaking. Multiple homicide enquiry, stretching back to 1995. The cases were all merged. We'd had confirmation from ESR. The Operation Ariel body was Anneke McBride. I was sitting with Tim and Helen, discussing the way forward. Helen was starting to work on directionals. Tim had just got off the phone to his fellow Crime Manager at Auckland Central. We had more staff. He was relieved. "He's a serial killer."

"Not just any serial killer. He picks his so-called offenders to take the fall when he picks his victims. Brianna Darwen – he set up Nicola. She was sick. He knew she'd present that way. Pete and Steve – he set up Martin Schuster, who didn't have a choice. With Anneke McBride – Dylan Manning was the fall guy."

"We're re-opening Manning's suicide, but it's unlikely we'll ever prove it was murder."

"True." But there was another angle to work here though. Something had been knocking around in my head ever since I'd wondered back in 2011 why Anneke had ended up out on that highway. Now that we knew she had probably been running from Harding and his mates, I knew Manning had simply given them an opportunity. "The other people set up – they were all planned, chosen. But Manning? Wrong place, wrong time. For him and Anneke. But he still hit her. Ran her over. So, she came from somewhere nearby. Wherever Harding, and whoever else was in that video, was holding her."

Helen glanced across at me. "Pull the area search files from Operation Ariel. Go door to door."

I left Helen's office and brought up the video again. It didn't show much of the bedroom but you could make out two walls and a wooden-framed window behind the bed. I looked through CID and found all the area search photos from the Ariel investigation. Cops had looked through every house on Haigh Access Road and some along the highway, not invasively, but with the consent of the owners, both to inform them of the body and see if there was anything obvious. They'd all been pretty helpful. I went through the photos from every property. It was needle-in-a-haystack stuff, but as always, someone had to do it. *She had to have come from somewhere*. I looked at all the bedrooms and windows. There were about twelve properties that had a similar set-up in one of the rooms. I couldn't narrow it down further from the photos alone. They were all too similar. And they weren't making it into National Geographic anytime soon for their clarity. I had to get on the road.

By midday I'd spoken with seven people who'd been living in their houses back in '95 so I ruled them out. I pulled into the driveway of the eighth house. A few hundred down Haigh Access, on the right. Long driveway, stopping just before the ground rose to the south. I knocked on the door. I was greeted by a girl of about eleven or twelve who went and found her dad. They both came back, along with another kid, a boy of about ten. I introduced myself. "Matt Buchanan, Orewa Police."

The dad shook my hand. "Andy. What can we do for you?"

"Did you live here back in 2011?"

"Yeah, how could we forget?" He turned to his kids. "Guys, to your rooms please. This isn't for you to hear." That was like a red rag to a couple of bulls. They'd have their ears to the door without a doubt.

Once they'd disappeared I went on. "What about in 1995?"

"1995? Hell, no. I was in Torbay back then."

I knew already. "We've identified the body, from 2011. She was Anneke McBride, sixteen. We'll be doing a media release shortly. It looks like she may have been killed somewhere close by, before she was taken to the estuary. Murdered after she was run over."

"Oh my god." he brought his hands up to his face. "Somewhere on this road?"

"Yeah, probably. There's a video . . ." I was mindful of the kids, probably listening in. "Andy, sorry, you're right, they definitely don't need to hear this. Nothing to concern you yet, it's just the content, you know . . ." I heard footsteps sneaking back down the hall.

"Ashley." Andy called out, then got up and went and saw her. He made her sit out on the deck with her brother, where he could see them, but they couldn't hear.

I carried on. "We found a video. A video of Anneke being raped. Probably from 1995, because we think she would have been killed shortly afterwards. Tried to escape, but was hit by the car driven by Dylan Manning, the guy who supposedly hanged himself back in 2011. The room in the video . . ." I fought for words, doing my best to explain ". . . we're trying to find the house from the room in the video. It's probably the murder scene."

He took a breath in and breathed out through his teeth. "Righto, you just want to look around?"

"Please."

"I'll get out of your way. Have you done a few of these?"

"This is the eighth. I had narrowed it to twelve, from photos taken back in 2011, when everyone was letting us into their homes."

He nodded. His face was grim. "Take your time, please. This is important." He went out onto the deck and put his arms around his kids. I hoped he was giving them the short version.

I went down the hall and into the first room on the left. *Nope.* I knew the set-up I was looking for. The room across the hall from it wasn't right either. I carried on down the hall into the next room on the left. I stared at the window spanning the exterior wall. The join of the exterior and adjacent walls. *Yeah, definitely.* Looking around, it was a study, no one's bedroom. I held up the photos I had. The same. Then I pulled out the stills I had from the video, and held them up. Yeah. No doubt. The same space. I looked out the window. It faced south-east, into the hill that rose up south of Haigh Access Road. I wandered back out onto the deck, past Andy and the kids, and onto their back lawn. I looked around. The nearest house was a good five hundred metres away. And a lot of these houses had been built on subdivided land. In '95, the nearest house could have been even further away. I looked west. *The direction Anneke would have run. Toward the highway.* Straight through a couple of fields, neighbouring properties. If it was dark and wet, she would have missed the other houses. Straight out onto the road. I put my hand up to my face, felt the stubble. *Twenty-one years. Twenty-one?* I got a chill.

I went back to the deck. "Andy, sorry, we might need a little time here. To take a better look. Get some forensic teams. It's been a long time, but it might be the key we need. I'm sorry to disrupt your family. It's the study, but probably best if we lock the whole house down, at least just for a day or so." Andy got the message. The kids were still clearly wondering what was going on. "You can tell them whatever you think you need to, mate."

I went back out onto the driveway and got in my car. I got on the phone and called Helen.

"I've found the scene. Where the video was made. The owner's really pro. Was here in 2011 when she was found. Yeah, I'll get hold of ESR, and photography. Is there anyone spare?"

Derek met me about half an hour later. We taped off the house, and I thanked Andy again. His wife had arrived home, and I assured her we'd be finished with the main house in a couple of days. Nice family, these guys. They really just wanted to help, even though we were uprooting their lives for a few days. They'd packed several bags and were going to spend the time with some other family on the Shore.

It was a long process. While waiting for dark so we could luminol the house, Derek and I examined the exterior, and searched the route from the point Dylan Manning had indicated he'd run her over on the highway, back to the house. It wasn't very far, and there was obviously nothing evidential along this line more than two decades on.

After night fell the scientists started their luminol testing. The study first. They didn't get anything, so we lifted the carpet. They got some results with the wooden floor beneath. We then ripped the whole carpet up, and the luminol showed up a large area of staining. No drag marks though. She would have been lifted into the tarp here, probably.

After they cut her up.

THIRTY-EIGHT

We needed to stir up some activity, get them talking, get them meeting up. It started with the CPT squad under DS Scott McKay. They were terminating today on Jordan Kitson, Cameron McCarthy, and their mates. We weren't involved in that, but I was sitting with the headphones on, monitoring our intercepted lines. It didn't take long. Scott's team arrived at Jordan's address in Millwater at 6 a.m. They completed their search and then binned him, taking him away. By six-thirty David was on the phone to somebody. My screen flashed up showing his phone was dialling an unknown number. I double-clicked the line and my headphones crackled.

"Yeah, me. Cops just turned up at Jordan's. Locked him up. Rape. Those fuckin' sluts."

Long pause. Breathing. "You're fuckin' joking." *Harding.*

"No. Rocked up an hour ago. Search warrant. They took his phone, laptop, some of his clothes and shit. There were a lot of them apparently."

"You know I don't like using this thing. I'll come over."

"Good. See you soon."

I called everyone over and replayed the conversation with the speakers on. Helen called the surveillance Sergeant. His team was on Harding. "Sean, he's leaving in a minute to head to David Kitson's address, Mahurangi West. Yeah. Yeah, we don't want to spook him. Yeah. Yeah, if you can eyeball him leaving, great, but don't get your guys following him up there. We'll get Eagle to fly over later, confirm he's there, to give you a start point later if you like. Yep, sounds good. Thanks, Sean."

Everyone headed to the kitchen for a cuppa. We all wanted to catch the next conversation live. The surveillance team had Harding at his Riverhead address so we knew it would be at least half an hour before he arrived. I sipped my coffee and looked out the meal room windows. Bit grey today. Rain due later.

Erin came up to me at the window. We were out of earshot of the rest of the team. "Are you okay, Matt?" I frowned, but she didn't wait for me to say anything. "I've never seen you like this. Never. You're quiet. Withdrawn. It's been a lot all at once."

I looked at her and shook my head. I wanted to fob her off, so I was trying to think of something to redirect her. A joke, to throw her off the scent. But I was all out of jokes. *Fuck, something really was wrong.* I looked into my cup. "I'm sorry, mate. I'm fucked up. This has fucked me up. Twenty-one years. The murders. And we got it wrong more than once."

"You aren't the only one. No one talks about it. I've been going to a psych for years . . ." I started to open my mouth, seeing the golden opportunity she'd just given me. But when I looked at her face, I stopped myself. I couldn't make a joke about it. "It's survival, Matt. You're good at it physically. But you've had more than ten lifetimes of shit. You've managed to raise Hailey through it all. But you need to fight your mental fight too. You've left it for too long."

We returned to my monitor with Dan and Helen. We had the audio line into the bug in the house open and on speaker. They were never the clearest, these things. Picked up everything. There was a lot of shuffling and banging as David moved about the house. But it was obvious when Harding turned up. I couldn't make out the front door opening, but you could make out voices and then the front door banged shut as they entered the lounge.

Harding was straight into it with Kitson. "How many charges?"

"Don't know yet. Haven't heard. I'm just hearing from his flatmates. He got arrested for rape. Apparently the Sergeant was saying there's been a series of complaints, schoolgirls mainly, some older. Drunk and drugged."

"Stupid cunt. You can't trust straight bitches. Thought he was smarter than that? Those chicks will always go running to the pigs. Hook them, then fuck them. What else did they say?"

"Not much. Said they'd be in touch."

"No other agenda?"

"No. Why?"

"Orewa feds have been sniffing around. Heard from a few people. Buchanan visited Tom inside. Came out with a broken nose." Laughter from them both.

The others looked at me. Helen raised her eyebrows. *I know. They know me. That's not good.*

Kitson's voice continued through the speaker. "What did he want?"

"Apparently he was asking about the shooting in '95. Wanted to know the reason behind it. Tom fucked him off with the drug story, said he didn't talk to pigs, blah blah. Buchanan kept at him. So he hooked him."

"Well, nothing lost?"

"Nah, apart from the fact this cunt is still sniffing round. And I wanna know why. All these years later. I thought we'd sorted it all with that snitch."

Pete Childs? Was that an admission?

"He was first there, wasn't he? Buchanan? The shooting of the girl cop?"

"Yep. And bought it all. Hook, line and sinker."

"So it's the young girl then. Gotta be. Worked it out."

"Yeah that's the only fuckin' thing I can think of, you know. They put her in the news just recently. They'll know who she is now. He's sniffing cos he's not thick. We just gotta shut it down when it comes."

"Yeah, yeah. Well you know how hard it is for those cunts to make something stick. He's gonna have to work his arse off."

More laughter. They had clearly started drinking. They didn't talk about much else, just shit. Fucking girls. How Jordan better toughen up if he's going inside. Eventually I turned the speaker off. It was all recorded anyway. The four of us were thinking hard. Dan spoke first. "Calver narked you out?"

"Nah, he knows I wasn't there to talk about Gabby's death. I went there to find out about Harding. He gave up the factory. Calver didn't tell Lendich that obviously. He's still on board."

Helen was surprised. "I didn't know Lendich was in Paremoremo too?"

"Yeah."

Erin chipped in. "But they know you're looking at something. They spoke about Anneke."

"Yeah, some good circumstantial talk that."

Dan switched the news on. Tim had just fronted the media. It was the headlining story. Four males arrested on a range of sexual offences, including rape, unlawful sexual connection, and stupefying. There wasn't much other detail. Never was, with sexual offences, to protect the victims. Then the story dragged up Roast Busters and made comparisons. Dan switched it back off.

I headed home through the rain. I'd zoned out. Harding and Kitson had made a link that my subconscious probably had, but

I hadn't. Twenty-one years? Gabby. Anneke. *Late '95. Anneke. The reason they killed Gabby.*

My phone buzzed. Text message. I read it. *That doesn't make sense.* My brain ticked over slowly. I rid my head of thoughts on Gabby's murder. It was a good few seconds before I panicked.

THIRTY-NINE

I dialled her number, but it rang and rang. No answer. I then phoned Tim directly. He'd just come out of the media scrum. "Boss? Tanya, where do Witpro have her?"

"Why?"

"Just got a text from her. Thanking me but saying it's all too much. Telling me to keep going."

"Fuck."

Tim had to hang up but said he'd call me back. He was back on in two minutes. Two minutes that I spent in the car. The rain was falling in waves again, battering the windows. I answered.

"Matt, ambos and section are heading there now. You gonna go? I'll get hold of Dan too. You just drive."

He gave me the address. *Fuck, that's miles away.*

I knew I'd be well behind the ball, but I did a hundred and thirty most of the way. I got off at Highbrook and took a left, winding through Cryers Road and past Botany Centre. I passed the ice-skating rink and McDonald's on my left, and kept going, left at the next lights onto Chapel Road. North to a roundabout, then right, heading east. Beachlands was a quiet, sleepy settlement on the coast, separated from the edge of the Auckland suburbs by a lot of rural land. Well, it had been sleepy, but it was becoming more popular as Auckland house prices fucked everyone over and people went looking further out on the fringes. But as good a place as any I guess to secrete a witness. I overtook a few trucks on the double yellows. *Not good*. But I wasn't exactly thinking straight. I had my phone balanced on my thigh, waiting for it to go off with some good news. But every minute that ticked by it remained silent, and I started to lose hope. My heart rate was high, and I could feel the pressure in my head.

At the Beachlands–Maraetai roundabout I went left, following the road all the way, round the right-hand bend into Beachlands proper, through the shops toward the water. Another right and I saw the lights up ahead of me. A patrol car on the grass verge and an ambulance in the driveway. I stopped short. Out of my car, didn't even lock it. Stumbling through the rain, up the drive. Two paramedics standing at the front door. *This isn't good*. It meant there was nothing for them to do. A uniformed Constable turned as I came in, holding both hands up, doing his job.

"Sir! Sir!"

I apologised, pulled my ID out. "Orewa, she's a protected witness for us. Where is she?"

He went white. A frown, then apologetic. His face said it all. "Far bedroom. Sorry mate."

I looked right, down the hall. Nobody was down there. Looking left into the lounge, I saw the Constable's partner on the phone. "CIB are coming from Howick." He nodded at his partner in the lounge. "Cat's just on the phone to the Sergeant. He'll be along soon too."

It wasn't like the movies or TV when detectives show up. You can't throw your weight around and do whatever you want. That would destroy the integrity of a scene. And it branded you a giant horse's cock. So, I asked permission. "Do you mind if I take a look?"

He looked surprised. "Go ahead, you know what you're doing."

"Anything obvious I'll fuck up?"

"Don't think so, it's all contained in there. We cut her down. She was in the wardrobe. Left of the door. Ambos tried to resuscitate, but there wasn't anything they could do. There's a note on the desk."

I borrowed some rubber gloves from him and pulled them on, heading for the room at the end of the hall. It was weird – despite talking to that cop, my heart was still elevated, in suspense, as if I wouldn't believe it until I saw it. I looked into the room. The door opened against the wall on the right. A double bed ahead of me, and to the left a large window and desk.

She looked more at peace than any time I'd seen her. Pale. Eyes shut. At rest. The knot was still around her neck, trailing about twenty centimetres of rope. I glanced behind me to the left, into the wardrobe. The rest of the rope trailed down. I looked back at Tanya. I just knelt there. I didn't touch her, or move anything. I didn't want a kick up the arse from Howick CIB when they arrived. Both times I'd seen her, at the meth lab in 2012, and then in the hospital, she was tormented. Broken. A girl who'd been sucked in and chewed up by the scene. Trying to survive her demons, battling through every day. I couldn't imagine what life had been like for her. But it wouldn't have been a comfortable place, living with her thoughts and memories. I could see exactly why. It was totally out of her hands. A product of her mind and everything in it. Not really her decision. Another victim, unsupported, alone, afraid. I moved to the desk and saw the pad. I read the note. It was brief.

I'm sorry.

I whispered a promise and left the room, moving back under the overhang outside the front door.

FORTY

It had been twenty years since I'd spoken with him properly, at our wedding. I can't remember talking to him at Kate's funeral, but I must have. I'm not even sure why I'd come here. Sounding board, I guess. I kicked it off without any pleasantries.

"Someone I know died two days ago. Suicide. But not her choice. I was supposed to be helping her."

He raised his eyebrow. He knew my line of work. "You can't protect everyone, Matt."

"I fucking understand that. Where should we start? Best mate in Police College, dies in front of me, murdered a couple of months into the job. I watched her blood drain through my fingers. Then Kate. Maramarua. I wasn't even there for that. But I can draw every inch of that roadside, opposite the community hall. Another good workmate of mine, murdered almost five years back. Shot dead while I cowered behind a power pole. Another mate killed in the same event, took one through the throat. I didn't even notice him right away, someone else did."

He shook his head. "And that's not even counting the cases you've had over the years. It's too much for one person, Matt. This tragedy, this girl who has just died. You can't blame yourself. You need to talk about it."

"Yeah, well, I haven't exactly got the head for that. I don't talk about shit. It hurts less if I box it up and shove it to the side."

"Does it? That might have worked for the last twenty years. But how's it working now?" I nodded. He was right. I could see little things, I had some self-awareness. Cracks starting to form. Thoughts. Ideas. False memories. The victims, coming back. Again and again. "That could have been you who was killed, quite easily, in most of those events. You realise that, don't you, Matt? You didn't survive because you're a coward. It was the dice, nothing more."

"Thought you'd attribute it to something else."

"Well that wouldn't get me anywhere fast with you, would it?" He smiled.

"Right."

"You'll be in my prayers, Matt. Always have been, you and Hailey."

I opened my mouth to make some anti-religious quip but he held his hand up.

"Yeah, yeah, God doesn't exist and all that. You're like a broken record even though I haven't even seen you for two decades." He was grinning. "But you're not asking. I'm just doing it." He knew I'd rejected pretty much everything after the car crash. No, before that probably. But I'm sure he was reading much into the fact I was here, now. It wasn't for the drinks and nibbles, that's for sure. It didn't stop him having a crack though. "Why do you think you feel so much loss? If it all means nothing, why bother? Why so much effort? When you know it's doing you harm? You keep going anyway. Why? There must be a reason."

I got up to leave. I was here to vent, not to be recruited. And I couldn't resist a parting shot. I turned back. "Something I heard once, can't remember who said it. But the walls of the hospitals have heard far more prayers than the walls of the churches."

I'd meant it to be a dig, to show how pointless this place seemed to me, but Father John just smiled.

FORTY-ONE

I felt like I'd been slapped in the face. It was burning. I stared at all the degrees and diplomas behind her, tunnel vision again. I thought about Hailey, my future, my job, how I'd continue with this case.

I had been summoned to a meeting with Helen and Tim a few days ago. Erin was concerned. Could see things starting to go. I hadn't taken Tanya's suicide well. Helen would have mentioned the mug thing, probably, too. I should have been grateful, in hindsight. Erin was one of a handful of people that really gave a shit. Tim asked me to see a psych. Framed it around Tanya's suicide, how I'd reacted, and then went into everything else I'd been through. Gabby, Kate, Steve, Pete. Brianna. Anneke. Tanya. And then something that had really fucked me off. He'd introduced Sam to the equation.

"Erin's seen you going through the Mist file, Matt. Simon's got it now, leave it with him. We've got other shit on our plate. Look, you can have it back eventually, but I need you on this.

I need you on Harding. Let Samantha Coates go for a while. It isn't your fucking fault mate. Never was. But I need your head in the game here. You're a better D than you credit yourself with."

I'd thought about launching into him, but instead just put a cap on it and took the roasting. Looking back on it he was actually complimenting me. I'd agreed to see a psych. And I went full noise. Psychiatrist. Let's hear it from the fucking best. I don't know if Laura was the best, but she was highly recommended. And now I was staring at the wall behind her, regretting even coming. Deliberately not looking at her. Her words still ringing in my head. I sought clarification.

"PTSD?"

Something I knew was becoming better diagnosed, that it wasn't just combat veterans and crime victims that suffered it. Kelly had mentioned it to me, how emergency services suffered too. Still, veterans and victims was how I saw PTSD. And I wasn't either of those. My deployment to Timor with the army had hardly been Mogadishu or Fallujah.

She tried to calm me down. "Your whole life, from your late teens on, has been filled with experiences most other people never encounter. But your responses are normal, Matt, so don't beat yourself up about it."

She had gone over in detail the majority of my life, both inside and outside the job. Apparently not only was I suffering from PTSD, but this had gone undiagnosed for so long that I was also heavily suffering from depression. I wanted a quick answer. "Short version. Can I keep working?"

"Of course. In fact, I think your job gives you some daily structure, which is important. So, I don't think taking that away would be beneficial. But look, you might have to screen the cases you're working on. Is that possible in the area you work?"

I lied through my teeth. "No problem. The bosses are really good like that. I'll stick to drugs, fraud, that sort of thing."

"Perfect. I think while we work on your health it'd be best to keep you from some of the more traumatic cases."

I grinned and nodded like an idiot, trying to say and show what she obviously wanted to hear. I received a prescription for Fluoxetine. I paid up, headed for my car. During the drive I worked on my lines so I could bullshit Helen and Tim when I got back to the office.

FORTY-TWO

Op Weave had come a long way while I'd been off. They had more intercepted conversations between Harding and Kitson. They had trawled the historic Operation Ariel and Brianna Darwen files, digging through everything that they could tie to Kitson and Harding. They pulled all the historic organised crime investigations into Harding and Lendich. In total, with what we had recently gathered, we had plenty of evidence, direct and circumstantial. We also had the polling data that we'd dumped from the west and north-west Auckland cell-phone towers back when we'd found Brianna in the dunes. With some extreme luck we'd find some phones from that list at their houses when the doors went in.

But the targets knew something was in the wind. And they'd dropped their cell-phones. The ones we knew about anyway.

Surveillance had been busy on both of them. Caught them meeting up at various public places. They were keeping conversation out of their houses and cars now. It was frustrating. We had these two well sunk, but we wanted a clear admission on the wire. That would save a lot of work down the track. I found myself working nineteen-, twenty-hour days trying to figure something out. I wasn't taking my meds. I kept them at home, and I was never there. I found myself sitting in the office sometimes, alone, staring at the board, looking at the faces, thinking of an answer. I didn't want to fuck this up. This had been too long in the making.

Then a bit of luck came our way. Surveillance caught both Harding and Kitson buying new burner cell-phones. Harding went into a Henderson 2 Degrees store. Kitson bought one in Warkworth. They were smart, these guys, but not smart enough. They set their phones up in their cars. Harding took his packaging with him, but what did Kitson do? Binned his.

When the surveillance Sergeant called, Dan and I raced out. We made it to the bin they had propped on. We both reached in like we were mental, rummaging around, hauling garbage out until we found the SIM packet and little box the phone had come in. *Gold*. We now had a number we could intercept.

And just like that, we were back listening live, and more confident. We'd pick up Harding too when Kitson called him, or the other way round. We just had to instigate some chatter.

The media release went out at 2 p.m. to stir it all up. It was on all the news sites immediately. We had the Stuff article up and the *Herald*. It was all in there:

Police re-investigate historic murder.
Police have identified the body found in the Okura estuary in 2011 as missing sixteen-year-old Anneke McBride, believed killed twenty-one years ago in late 1995. Dylan Manning was charged with the murder but died in prison prior to the trial . . .

I skipped the old stuff.

. . . after identifying her, Police are now re-investigating links between McBride and other persons of interest. In an explosive twist, Police have revealed they are revisiting Manning's involvement, and are looking again at the circumstances surrounding his death in Mount Eden Prison.

If that didn't set them off, nothing would. And we were right. Within an hour of the story going online, a call went in to Kitson's burner phone.

Erin cranked the volume.

"Yep. Probably figured out Damo was inside with Manning back then. But it's the same story, mate, they've got fuck all solid shit on us. We say nothing, they can't touch us. But we'd better prep ourselves. They'll come, pretty soon I reckon. Me and you. Maybe Calver. Damo. There's fuck all we can do for those two. But fuck them. We're the ones on the outside."

"Yup."

"We've gotta sort this. That fuck Buchanan, he's way too thick into this. If anyone's gonna fuck us it's him. I know he worked on Anneke's case when they found her. He worked on Brianna. He was with Childs when that went down. Still dunno what was said in that car. But that cunt is popping up everywhere."

"We need a plan. This is getting out of hand, Gaz."

"Lawyer, silence, yeah? Nothing on those girls. Manning ran Anneke over. He hung himself. That's it."

"Yeah."

"This ain't nothing we haven't been through before, Dave. Same cops. Same fuckin' story."

"And Buchanan?"

"Tonight. We talk."

And like that, we started preparing for termination. We were all in front of our computers and Helen was throwing out tasks. "Dan, can you start working up a document for the Crown?

We're getting close, and we may need to move pretty quick on this shortly."

If only I'd listened properly to what Harding had hinted at during the conversation.

FORTY-THREE

I was sleeping like a baby, and had no idea what was going on outside. The surveillance teams on Harding and Kitson had tailed them to Harding's place, then away again. They were reporting to Helen, but it all happened far too quick.

I didn't wake when the first one came through the lounge ranchslider. It was the second, smashing through my bedroom window and bursting into a ball of flame that had me falling out of bed onto the floor.

Disorientated. Heat. *Where the fuck am I?* Home. That's where. I got my shit together and looked for the door. The flames crackled and burst, igniting the carpet, curtains, bedding. I pulled myself over the floor and out into the hall, spluttering as I went. I remembered Hailey was home on her uni break. "Hailey!" I got a lungful of smoke and coughed it back up, starting to retch. "Hailey!"

I saw the flames in the lounge, heard the crackling. Smelled the smoke that was now billowing around the ceiling and getting ever lower. Thick dark clouds swirling throughout the house.

I stumbled out into the lounge and tripped over something, flying face first into the table and chairs. They were on fire and I felt the heat, burning my arms as I covered my face. *Roll. Roll, you dumb cunt.* I couldn't see, just needed to get away from the burning. *Where's Hailey?* I still couldn't see. I thrashed about on the floor just trying to get clear.

I felt hands on me, grabbing a foot, dragging me somewhere. "Dad! Dad!"

"Hailey!"

She disappeared, came back, and I received a burst of pressure and white powder in my face. Sight left me again. I had snot pouring out of me and was in shit state. I realised she must have given me a dose of the fire extinguisher.

More dragging by the feet, and I managed to roll onto my arse, and get one of my legs underneath me. Hands under my arms, trying to lift me up. We made it out the front door, me right behind her, pushing her out onto the driveway.

I still didn't really know what the fuck had happened.

Hailey stood there, bent over at the waist, hands on her knees, dragging in air. I grabbed her and hugged her. We moved further down the drive to the road, where some of the neighbours had come racing out.

I heard sirens, and just held Hailey as we waited. Our house was well on its way to being fully gutted. We both just watched it, totally helpless.

It wasn't until later that I found out.

If it hadn't been for the surveillance teams, Hailey and I would have been shot dead as we came out our front door.

FORTY-FOUR

That was the end of Op Weave. We terminated that night. Surveillance had confronted Harding and Kitson as they threw the
firebombs through our windows. Brave work from those guys –
they weren't armed, and had saved our lives. Harding and Kitson
had jumped in their wagon and gapped it, but were tailed. They
fired shots at the surveillance teams, but they'd stayed on them.
Within thirty minutes Harding and Kitson were forced off the
road by non-compliant vehicle stop and taken into custody at
gunpoint by AOS.

They'd found two rifles in the car.

I was told to worry about my house, but what the fuck could
I do about that? I needed to be at work. Hailey came into the
station after the ambos checked us out. Erin set her up in the
cafeteria and I told her to call if she needed me. She'd just saved
my fucking life, but I needed to be here.

I looked across the interview desk at Gary Harding. His hands
were closed, not fidgeting. His small eyes were cold. His short,

thinning hair was plastered flat across his forehead. The scars stood out on his sweat-drenched face. I had nothing but pure hatred for this man. He'd killed people close to me. He'd almost killed my daughter. And I very much wanted to kill him. That was no exaggeration.

He sat across from me, staring me out. I outlined the case to him.

"You were arrested tonight for arson. But you're sitting in front of me for murder, got that? You've exercised your right to silence. Fine. Up to you. You've had legal advice. And you've done yourself no favours. You're going to be charged with some serious shit, and you might change your mind. We're laying ten representative charges for objectionable material. The child abuse and child rape images found on your personal devices and in your Keeling Road factory."

He smiled at me then. His whole face creased into a horrible grin. It was all I could do not to launch myself across the desk and rip his throat out. But he'd be doing decades for this once convicted. *Was that enough?* I looked back at my notes. He'd noticed my anger. He smiled even more.

"Multiple charges relating to equipment, materials, and precursors involved in the manufacture of methamphetamine."

Nothing. And on we went.

"That's the minor shit, Gary. But it gets better. You're charged together with David Kitson for the murder of Brianna Darwen."

He didn't move a muscle. His grin widened. "She wouldn't have been the best I've had."

I kept it together. "And charged together with David Kitson and Thomas Calver for the murder of Anneke McBride."

He just sat there and watched me, confident. Then he spoke slowly, examining me with every word. "And, I assume, two attempted murder charges? You and your daughter?"

They'd be coming all right. "There's also a charge of sexual violation, and one of fucking with human remains." He frowned. *He doesn't know how we know. Good.* I'd unsettled him. I couldn't resist and leant in close. My voice wasn't much above a whisper. "We found the video of Anneke, you cunt. And we know which house." His eyes widened briefly but he caught himself, went back to his poker face.

I locked him in the interview room and met with the others out in the office. Something was up. Erin was talking to Helen. Her eyes were wet. Dan was looking white. They all looked at me as I approached. *What?*

Helen spoke. "ECL have trawled Kitson's devices. There were images on his computer, Matt. Encrypted, but they broke through it . . ."

"Abuse?" I was distracted by the look on Erin's face. She looked like she was going to pass out. I frowned and looked back at Helen.

"Worse. Pictures of Brianna. And Anneke . . . after they were killed."

"Jesus Christ." I actually stepped back. "Snuff pics? I thought that was an urban legend."

"Nope. Not just Eastern Europe and Mexico, Matt. Here. But these sick fucks are going away."

I nodded. "Do their lawyers know yet?"

"No, we'll talk to them shortly. We can advise Kitson and Harding. Then let's get them to Henderson and into the cells."

Harding stared at the desk when I told him. He then shook his head, blaming Kitson. "Stupid cunt. Stupid, stupid cunt." Then he looked up and stared me down. "I'll take comfort from the fact your whole soul is permanently damaged, Buchanan. And I'm not talking any of the charges you've mentioned. You'll never find her." *What the fuck's he on about?*

"You've tortured yourself over her, and that's good enough for me."

I'd had enough of this cunt. I leaned in close. "You're not gonna make it back out. You're gonna die in there, Gary. But before that happens, enjoy getting fucked in the arse, you piece of shit. If you killed yourself, you'd be doing yourself a favour."

I spat in his face and walked out.

FORTY-FIVE

Present Day

Laura's office hadn't changed a bit. The certificates still hung behind her.

"You're a high-functioning depressant, Matt. People like you are the part of the iceberg below the water. Society is all over mental and psychological illness now. Because we've realised that everyone's struggling with something."

I smiled. "Wait till I tell the office. There are some odd fuckers there."

She suppressed a grin. "Because we're so open with our understanding now, we've formed this image of how certain illnesses should manifest. Depression, for example. Most people think you should be curled up in a corner, unable to function. But that isn't the case. With you, and a lot of others, you can still function perfectly well, perform every task, and nobody is the wiser."

So, is this a good thing or a bad thing?

"This is one of the most serious, high-risk forms of depression . . ."

Oh, good.

". . . because even you'll fail to recognise it most of the time. All those post-suicide comments you read in the news, or in your case, you've probably actually heard them direct from people when you've attended those deaths – you know – how no one had any idea? Surely not him? Surely not her? Being at the mercy of your brain in that high-functioning state, well, that's a dangerous thing for you, Matt."

"What's the solution?"

"Medication. Time. Working through the events in your life. We've made some progress. Kate's death, I think we've thrashed that one. It's your work I'm concerned about now. How it inter-twines with your personal life. Those are the things we need to focus on. Gabrielle. Steven. Those deaths had a big effect on you. Not just professionally, personally. And rightly so. But you got a double blow with those. If we work on them, the rest we shouldn't have too much of an issue with."

"The rest?"

"Your cases. Repeated exposure to things people shouldn't see. The murders. The deaths. Cissy. Christie. Jane. Anneke. Brianna. Tanya. I've been sitting here listening to people's trauma for two decades, and I can't believe the weight you're operating under, the things you've seen. You've had to deal with it all, box it up, push it aside, and continue on. It's been too much."

I looked up from the floor. "It's no different from any other cop. Any other detective. Everyone's seen what I've seen. Of one kind or another. Where are they?"

She explained. "More of your colleagues see people like me than you probably think. And the ones that don't, well, they probably should. But it's not just the murders, Matt. It's the personal cost. Gabrielle, Steven, Kate, they were personal. And there's the other work cards you keep close to your chest. The ones you haven't let go, the ones you beat yourself up about.

Tanya. Samantha. Sam in particular you've been beating yourself up about for eighteen years. We need to work through those."

"How?"

"Cognitive therapy. We'll revisit them, talk them through. How you felt then, how you feel now. What the issues are. What most people feel, objectively, versus how you do, subjectively."

"Right." I rubbed my chin, checked out the floor again. I sucked my lip. She then mentioned what I hoped she wouldn't.

"Work, Matt. You need to take a break."

"I can't, we've got the trial in a week. Erin, Dan, Helen, they're working their arses off. I need to be there. And I'll be on the stand anyway giving evidence once it starts."

"Okay, we can't avoid that. But after. We talk. We come up with a solution. We need to, Matt. Or this isn't going to end well for you. We've got the ability to turn this around. You can. After the trial, we talk, okay?"

"Done." I thanked her and left with a repeat prescription. I picked it up from the pharmacy and drove home.

I took the dosage and then poured a bourbon. *What the fuck am I doing?* But it numbed my brain. That felt good these days.

FORTY-SIX

The trial started off well. They always do. You go in with the highest of expectations. The Crown are positive. You've reviewed the case with them, gone over every witness, their evidence, the exhibits, the full picture. Anticipate defences. But once it starts playing out, things often go downhill rather quick. I'd learnt this the hard way, after twenty-two years. I never went into court positively anymore. The legal system was set up for one purpose and one purpose only. To ensure that innocent people were not convicted of something they didn't do. Fair enough. But today, "not guilty" in a courtroom verdict, and "didn't do it" are two very, very different things.

There are so many hurdles, loopholes, technicalities, and established cases swirling around the legal system that convicting someone for something is actually a pretty difficult task. Jurors don't think the Police did a good enough job? Acquittal. Jurors believe the accused did it, but think the accused wasn't cross-examined properly by the Crown? Acquittal. Jury didn't hear a crucial piece of evidence, because it was thrown out at a pre-trial argument for being too prejudicial against the accused? Acquittal. These things happened all the time. I knew. Those emails I'd got over the years were proof. But the system wouldn't change, so fuck it – I cared nothing for the system. I only cared about the victims. And as an extension of that, protecting the public. I had no interest in anything else. So far I'd been positive most of the way through. The Crown evidence was solid. It was mostly cops, ESR staff, forensic experts, analysts from the telco's talking about cell-phone data. It painted a good picture. It was a sequence of events, of logical inferences. We played all the audio interceptions, from the Kitson house, and the phones. Coupled with some witness testimony, it had been looking good.

But there was always a cunt-factor. In a pre-trial argument, we'd lost Tanya Redmond's evidence. The judge ruled that what she'd said couldn't be taken for granted just because she was dead. Her motive to say what she had was unknown, given the world she moved in. And since she wasn't here, her evidence couldn't be cross-examined. So, the jury would never hear it.

The defence case began. Kitson didn't take the stand. But Harding did, much to everyone's surprise. And there began the downhill slide. He pointed the finger squarely at Kitson, Calver, Lendich. For everything. He muddied the waters, sowed doubt into the jurors' minds. And his defence lawyer kept coming back to the images found on Kitson's computer. They were the strongest evidence now. Images of Anneke and Brianna. Dead. On Kitson's computer. Not Harding's. We'd found nothing on his. The jury sucked all this up. It confused them. Made them question the totality of evidence.

And so I sat at the back of the court with Helen, after both prosecution and defence had concluded, eight weeks after the trial had begun. More than a hundred witnesses had given evidence. Listening to the Judge deliver his direction to the jury on what reasonable doubt meant. *You must be sure.* But there will always be doubt. *Because we can't take the jury back to the fucking crime and let them watch it being committed.*

They filed out to deliberate and we went out for a beer.

Six days later, I felt my chest tighten as the jury walked back into the courtroom. Not all of them looked sure of themselves. A few carried the look of defeat. Like they'd been shouted down. An older guy, he looked old school, locked eyes with me as they filed in. His face was apologetic. *Fuck. No fucking way. What?* A few looked pleased with themselves. Like they took this legal business seriously. A few looked relieved. Like they hadn't burdened themselves unnecessarily. The most telling thing was a repeat of what had happened after Kelly's trial. The forewoman glanced at me, saw me looking at her, and looked immediately at the floor.

You're fucking kidding. Is this happening?

I didn't even hear the judge address them. I didn't focus until the registrar started reading out the charges. Until then I was watching the dock. Kitson looked worried. He watched the jury intently. Lendich stared daggers at them. Harding just sat there, staring straight ahead. I felt the anger rise up from somewhere inside. *No prison time is long enough. No punishment good enough for you cunts.* I stared at the backs of their heads. And then Tom Calver turned in his seat, looked directly at me. No emotion on his face, but his eyes said it all.

You wanted this, Detective? Here you go. You got it wrong. The curtain is about to fall on this fucking debacle.

It started off okay. Kitson, Harding and Lendich all were found guilty for large amounts of objectionable material. Kitson was convicted on the clan lab equipment from the factory. Not Harding though.

Kitson was convicted of Brianna Darwen's murder. Harding's main link were the images found in the factory. But apparently we hadn't proved it beyond reasonable doubt. They'd believed him when he'd fingered Kitson, and they found him not guilty.

I stared at Harding as each verdict was read out. He settled further back into the bench with each one.

All three were acquitted of Dylan Manning's murder, and the planning of it.

By the time it came to Anneke McBride, I was ready to walk out. But I forced myself to listen. Calver. Guilty of murder, and misconduct in respect of human remains. That's the way the Crimes Act phrases chopping her to bits. Kitson. Guilty of murder and chopping her to bits. Harding. Not guilty.

I sat there in a daze. Things happened around me, I didn't hear any of it. Nobody had been found guilty of raping Anneke. *Of course. You need the victim to speak to you, right? Well she can't. She's dead. Did she look like she was consenting in that video, you fuckwits?*

Kitson and Harding were both acquitted of attempted murder on Hailey and myself. Not clear enough, obviously. But they both went for arson.

As they were led from the dock to the cells, Calver was the last to file out. He turned again, and we came eye to eye. Again, that emotionless face, but his eyes were alive.

Happy, dickhead? They said. *You fucked up. You won't live with this.*

He could have been the only person in the court that had nailed the truth that day.

FORTY-SEVEN

Oddly, the prison granted the visit. Even more strange, it was Calver who had arranged it. His lawyer had advised him against it, but he'd gone and requested my presence anyway.

"You, Detective. Me. We're two sides of the same coin. Similar, but different."

He was calm. Accepting of his fate. He'd be inside this prison for the next two decades at least.

"We aren't that different, Tom. You're there, I'm here, but through nothing more than circumstance, and a bit of luck. If I'd lived the life you've lived, experienced the things you have . . . fuck, maybe I'd be sitting exactly where you are now. And if you'd had mine, you might be working for us."

He liked that. "Let's not get too fucking carried away." He chuckled to himself. He looked up at the ceiling, and raised his arms up in jest. "Here, but for the grace of God, goes Detective Matthew Buchanan . . ." he laughed again. "As if. But we're probably more similar than we both think." I let him speak.

"You think I don't have a moral compass? Course you do. You get people. Most cops don't." He leaned forward, looked into me with those piercing eyes. "I know the difference between right and wrong, Detective. Of course I do. That's why we're similar. We both understand the difference. I'm not saying I'm an angel. Never fucking have been. What I'm saying is, every time I've done wrong, I've *known* it was wrong." He let that hang. And he had a point. Everyone fucked up. Everyone did bad things. *Everyone. No exceptions.* The difference was whether you knew if you were doing it or not.

"Harding's gonna be out shortly, Tom. Time served. I need to stop him. He's killing people."

Calver sat forward and his face changed. It wasn't jovial, or in agreement. It was colder. Harder. "Forgive my French, but fuck me, Detective, he's been killing people a long fucking time. We've had this conversation before. You sat there, I was here. I told you. The system isn't set up for these men. I told you, and you went and did it your way anyway. You fucked it up. Or don't you remember?"

I held up my hands, palms up. He shook his head as if to bat my gesture away. "What, you've done what you could, Detective? Played by the rules? Help me, Tom, please, I can't do any more?" He spat onto the floor. "You think the system will ever catch up to him?" he kept shaking his head. "Detective, he picks his killers, he picks his victims, always someone placed to take the fall. Always."

I understood what he was getting at. "Are you going to sit there, look me in the face, and tell me you didn't shoot Gabby?"

"Yes, I am."

"You're saying Harding pulled the trigger?"

He paused. Breathed in and out slowly. "Detective, I'm not going to send you down this path without a warning. Because I know what makes you tick."

"What the fuck are you on about now, Doctor Seuss?"

"I've never murdered anyone in my life, Detective. But before you dribble on, I asked you here for a reason. I'm not here to make deals. I've accepted my bed, and I'm lying in it. I've accepted the hand I've been dealt. There were things I tried to stop, but I didn't try hard enough. I tried to prevent Anneke's death. I failed. It would've been my end too. But selfish isn't good enough. I've got things I need to fix. And so do you."

I laughed. "You don't know me as well as you think."

He smiled and leaned in. I stayed where I was, but he actually reached forward and grabbed my shoulder. His eyes burned into mine. "Oh, *I know you*, Detective. I know that Gabrielle and you were close. I know about your wife, about Kate. I am truly sorry. I hope Hailey is doing okay." I frowned, but didn't say anything, didn't move a muscle. He carried on. "Personal losses. Would've broken anyone. But you picked yourself up and continued . . ."

My fists started to clench. *What does he know?*

"Detective, the human psyche is a fragile, fragile thing. It is not equipped, nor can it ever be truly trained, for what people like you see." He let the words hang, and we watched each other. I'd read that before, or something similar. Former cop from Australia had said it. Article about PTSD that I'd read. But I don't think Calver expected a response. He knew the statement was correct. Which worried me about where this was going. "You stayed in, all that time. Then, almost five years ago. Detective Steven Prentice. You left the job after that. Understandable." He was still examining me, watching me, reading my brain. Then he asked the question. "What I don't understand, Detective, is why you came back. No, that's not true. I do understand, but do you?"

"Dead kids."

"Right." He sat back in his chair, crossed his fingers. "But your colleagues could have done it without you. You needed in. Why?"

I still said nothing. He'd go where he wanted to go.

"Because you left something unfinished, Detective. And I'm

not talking about getting the wrong people. You've got suspicions, you've got thoughts, circling about inside your head and maybe you don't even fully understand them. But they're there. '95 was tough for you, but you put your head down and kept going forward . . . something bigger has carved you apart since."

He was building me up. I waited. He was going to hit me with something, and I felt my stomach muscles tighten as I waited.

"You've dealt with the dead, Detective. Many times. It's the unknown you struggle with. The missing. You smashed headfirst into a psychological brick wall seventeen years and six months ago. Operation Mist. Samantha Coates. Your greatest failure. In your own eyes, if not anyone else's. And that . . ."

He paused. I'd been staring at the desk, just listening to him. But my eyes flicked up now to see him pointing a finger at me –

". . . has well and truly *fucked you up*."

My eyes started to water. *He wasn't out in '99. He was inside then. Can't have been Calver. What would he know?*

"Samantha's dead, Detective."

I couldn't hide my reaction. I was starting to lose it.

"She isn't coming home. She didn't go to a friend's house. She didn't run away. She didn't have an accident. You may have had time, early on. You may have been able to save her. But your leads ran out. You ran out of time. *You* did." Those eyes just burned into mine. "She was abducted. And then she was murdered."

I launched myself out of my chair, over the desk, and grabbed him by the collar. I got an arm under his armpit and hauled him over the desk toward me. We both went down, but he was underneath. I started striking him in the face, palm strikes, both hands, hard and fast. He got to his knees but slumped backwards, and I delivered a fist to his face, knocking him back into the wall. He covered up and got two good ones on me before I did the same. We got into a wrestle again and both went back down onto the floor. He was gritting his teeth, bleeding through his split lips, spitting. I put a choker hold on and spoke into his ear. "What the fuck do you know, Tom?" I squeezed tighter. "What the fuck do you know?"

He spoke fast. "She's dead, Detective. But no one took the fall. No offender to stitch up. He fucked up. That's your window, that's your opening. Harding's arrogant. Got away with it. But it's the one thing he fucked up."

I kept hold of him but stopped trying to beat his head in. He was breathing hard, sucking air in and out between words.

"Get . . . out of your little fucking box . . . Detective. The . . . the only thing that's gonna work. You've got . . . both hands tied behind your fucking back. You're . . . fucking yourself over . . . and you know it . . ."

I hauled him up and put him back in his chair. He coughed blood across the desk, but just sat there, looking at me. I said nothing. He got his breath back. He looked at me with those grey eyes, always searching. He wasn't done. "When you drift off to sleep at night, when you're about to cross that threshold, and everything's well, what do you fear, Detective?"

"In that moment? Not much."

He didn't believe me. He looked around the room. "There's no one else listening. Just you and me. I want to know. Tell me, Detective."

"Probably our kids not being safe anymore."

He jumped on it immediately. "Well, you should be scared shitless. Especially after everything else. I thought you'd get it."

I got up to leave. "Go fuck yourself, Tom."

"You'll get there, you know."

I turned. I couldn't help it. "Get where?"

"To where you'll justify it. Where you'll fall over the edge. You'll remember this conversation."

"For achieving fuck all. You haven't told me a thing. Fuck you."

"I can't convince you, clearly. Convince yourself then. The false name, Detective. The factory. Have you explored that? Other properties? Storage? Safe deposit box? Find his other hiding places. Because there's more. Much more. Find it, and maybe then you'll do your actual fuckin' job. The job you needed to do in the first place."

"Actual job." I repeated the words and laughed, stepping toward the door.

He continued talking to the back of my head, raised his voice. "When your time comes, Detective . . . could be on your drive back to the station. Could be a low-level engine failure in your Cessna. Could be a truck, head-on collision on a State Highway. Could be another shooting, I don't know. But when death finally stares you in the face, where will your thoughts wander?"

I paused at the door.

"Will you burn out peacefully, in the knowledge you did all you could for a dead fourteen-year-old girl? Future girls . . .?"

My hand was about to knock for the guard.

". . . or will you go out with total contempt for yourself? Sickened that you followed all your neat little laws and protocols, but got nowhere? That an animal continued to kill and you had the ability to stop it?"

I knocked hard on the door. The guard swung it open.

"Detective . . ." I turned again and locked eyes with him.

"Do not go gentle."

FORTY-EIGHT

I was stood down while they investigated. There was no hiding the injuries to Calver's face. But we'd both said nothing, which fucked them a bit. I did get banned from Paremoremo Prison though. Corrections had served a notice on me. So here I was, sitting in the D-Sergeant's office. She wasn't here. But though Helen's vagina may have been elsewhere, there was still a cunt present. The professional standards investigator was a uniform Sergeant, and I knew for a fact he had spent his career doing three-fifths of fuck all. He was angling for promotion. And he didn't like me.

"You're lucky you're not losing your job and going to court."

Fair one. I couldn't help myself. "And you're lucky there's a career path for fuckwits."

He didn't bite, just sat back. "Take your warning, smart-arse. Otherwise we keep looking, and you know what? There's always a way to get rid of someone like you."

I thought about my psych sessions and bit my tongue. "Give

me the letter." He passed it over and I signed it.

I walked out into the CIB office. Everyone had clearly been listening, but now they were pretending to work, staring hard at their screens. "Fuck me, crime doesn't stand a chance, does it?"

I saw Erin grin. Dan looked up. "Warning?"

"Yeah. . . ." The Sergeant walked out of the office behind me, heading for the back door. I thumbed over my shoulder. "Lord Farquaad here put me in my place." The guy kept walking, didn't look back.

Helen came from the other direction, from the kitchen. "You don't know when you've been dealt a good hand, do you?"

"What? Fuck them."

She sighed and waved me away. "Take some time. Couple weeks. Tim will work something out for your return date. I'll call you."

I already knew what I'd be doing in my spare time. Calver had hit home. I was going to find whatever it was he thought I needed to.

FORTY-NINE

I'd spent a week fucking about near the Westhaven Marina before I'd spotted the *Transient*. Calver had been right. Harding did have other shit in the same name as the factory. I couldn't take the official route and go through the Marina company, not for what I was about to do. But I'd finally located it, third pier in from the western side.

I parked my car on Sarsfield Street, up by the Point Erin pools. I grabbed the sports bag off the back seat and walked back up to Shelly Beach Road, turning left toward the Harbour Bridge off-ramp. It was getting dark, and there were a few people about. I'd tossed around plenty of ideas. But decided the straight in, overt approach was the safest. I'd try and bullshit my way out if things went bad. I crossed over the off-ramp bridge running over the motorway. It was fucked underneath me, chocka going both directions. I'd always liked the sound of flowing traffic, on nights like this that was. When I didn't have to hear it for too long. Not to live near though. *That'd do my fucking head in.* I made a right after crossing over the motorway and dropped down the pathway that angled steeply from the over-bridge down onto Westhaven Drive, toward the marina. I headed straight across into the car-parking area, heading for the third pier in. It was about fifty metres past Sails restaurant.

I opened my bag and gloved up, then keyed the code into the pad and pushed the door. *No problems.* I'd watched people do it often enough over the last several days. I was dressed in shit clothes and boat shoes, and I stopped and pulled the mop from my bag too. As long as it looked like I was heading somewhere to do something, no one would bat an eyelid. Hopefully. I started walking down the pier, passing quite a few people working on their boats. One guy was hauling a chest-freezer off his yacht onto the pier.

"Hey mate." I greeted him as I wandered past, and he gave me a wave. *Friendly bunch. I could get used to life on the ocean wave.*

The *Transient* was about a hundred metres down the pier, right-hand side. I dropped down onto the back of the launch. A walkway extended left and right around to the bow. In front of me was the main cabin, and just to the left of that a series of steps lead up to the top level and open deck. I paused. It struck me that this boat was probably the scene of Tanya's torture and beating on the Tauranga harbour. I went straight ahead into the cabin, like I knew where I was going, trying not to look suss. Seating, tables, a small room to the left which had cooking facilities. On the right, toilet. Ahead of me to the right was the driver's seat. To the left of that, straight in front of me, the door to the living quarters. Padlocked. *Of course.* I removed the bolt cutters from my bag and made quick work of it, then slid the bolt out. I opened the door and slipped in, closing it behind me. No point drawing attention to myself. There were two windows in front, left and right. The floodlights outside were giving it heaps, it was pretty dark now.

I wasn't sure where to begin, so I started a systematic search, clockwise from where I was, left to right. I moved around the living space, feeling with my hands, lifting and moving everything. There was no hiding the fact I'd been here. This was going to look like exactly what it was. A burglary. I found sleeping gear and pillows. Lifejackets. A few books and DVDs. I checked the disc in each. They seemed legit. I moved around the small space, and stopped at a small cabinet on the ground on the right side of the cabin. Another padlock. The bolt cutters did their thing, and I pulled open the cabinet door. There was a safe inside, a small grey one, bolted into the cabinet on two sides. I couldn't pull it out. I checked the front. Hinged on the outside. Combination lock. *Fuck it.* I knew I'd have to break lots of different shit so I'd come prepared. I pulled the mallet and chisel from my bag. I got the chisel onto the hinge and lined up the rubber headed mallet. I gave it a few test taps to check the noise. Ah, fuck it. People whacked things on their boats all the time, right? A few dozen hard hits got me through the first hinge. I was halfway through the second when I heard footsteps out on the pier. They stopped. Didn't carry on. *Fuck.* Then I heard him.

"Hello?"

Deep voice. Middle-aged. But unsure of something. I didn't move a muscle. I heard him drop onto the back of the boat. *Ah, for fuck's sake.*

He called out again. "Excuse me? Just security. You working for the owner?"

I pulled my cap a bit lower. *Nah, that won't do.* I grabbed a cloth and wrapped it round my face. *I can't go down for this.* I opened the door and called from where I was. "Yeah mate, just tidying some things up. All good?"

It should have been, but he wandered in, following my voice. As he poked his head in, he saw a fuckwit with a cloth wrapped around his face. And the broken padlock. And the safe. His face changed. *Cunt.*

I'd come too far to fuck this all up now. I grabbed him around the head and pulled him right into the cabin. I didn't pause and rained blows on his face and nose, which dropped him cowering onto the floor, hands up, trying to cover his head. I kept going. I needed control. The hits were quick, a series of strikes to disorientate. That's all I wanted. He started moaning and I leaned over by his ear. "Shut the fuck up. Shut the fuck up, no noise, I'm leaving soon. Let me do that. This ain't worth your time and effort, mate. I'm going to tie you up. Then I'm leaving. Let me do that, or the fuckin' mallet comes out."

I held it up in the light through the windows. He got the message and nodded. I looked for something to tie him with and decided on the bedding. I made a rope out of a sheet by rolling it. Wrapped it tight round him and double knotted it to the rear. I repeated the process with four more sheets. I reminded him every few minutes with a slap to the head. *No noise.* I found a couple of pillowcases and some electrical tape. I stuffed half a pillowcase into his mouth, leaving the rest hanging out. Then I taped around his mouth and lower jaw, round and round, leaving his nose clear.

Once done, I gave him a big, exaggerated thumbs up. "All good mate?" He nodded. *Good.* Poor bastard. But he'd be okay. Then I pulled the other pillowcase over his head. I pulled the door again and got back to work on the second safe hinge. By the time it broke loose my hands and fingers were fucked from the odd angle. I lifted the door off toward me and checked inside. There were some documents in a plastic sleeve, several USB drives, and a portable hard drive. I took them all and stuffed them into my bag. I looked round the room. *Burglary.* I had to make this look like what it was. I stuffed some of the DVD's into my bag, and took some alcohol sitting on the floor for good measure. I then made a bit more of a general mess and, grabbing my bag and opening the door, slipped back out into the main cabin. I paused at the rear of the boat, listening, and then climbed up onto the pier. I headed for the gate, casual as I could.

FIFTY

I don't know what I expected. I had got here on Calver's direction alone. He'd been right about everything so far. That's what scared me a little. He'd said something about tipping the scales, sending me over the edge or some such shit. I was mindful of that.

But I still wasn't prepared for what I was about to see.

I double-clicked one of the last videos. There'd been a few already. The majority of stuff on the drive so far had been horrific. But, if I thought I could stomach it all, I was wrong.

God, was I wrong.

The video started playing. This camera was still. It must have been on a tripod. It showed a room, a bed in the centre. A ripple was going through it all the time, that old fucked-VHS-tape ripple that travels annoyingly slowly from the bottom of the screen to the top.

Someone from off camera brought her in. I saw a mess of blonde hair, and it was pulled aside. I gripped the legs of the chair as I recognised her. My body went cold. *No, not cold.* I couldn't feel anything at all. Numb. Nothing. Her face. Distress. Fear. She started crying and then screaming. Begging them not to do it again. One of them punched her in the face. She started whimpering. I looked at the volume control, considered turning it off. *No.* The psych's advice rang in my ears, ordering me to turn this off, but I shut it out. I kept watching.

She was tied to the bed, slowly, methodically, firmly overpowered. I couldn't see their faces. But I knew one of them was Harding.

I watched as two of them raped her, one after the other. The camera came off the tripod and changed hands. Never showed any of their faces. But it showed Sam's. They moved it closer. And I watched every second she endured. I watched as they each had their turn again, throwing in more punches and slaps as they did it. I watched as they paused, and moved off camera, leaving her alone. She lay there, broken, sobbing. Snot running down from her nose, over her mouth. Dark stains down her legs. She rolled her head from side to side. Sobbing gently, not fighting anymore. The fight had long gone.

My head was trying to protect me, and superimposed over what I was seeing, came that false memory of her walking home from school. It lingered around behind my eyes, but didn't win.

I kept watching the video as one of the men came back into the room, dumping a duffel bag on the bed. He removed a white cloth, tied it round the lower part of her face.

I grabbed hold of the desk in front of me as he removed the knife. *No. Fuck, no . . . not like this . . .*

I watched her face as it twisted up. Pure terror. She started shrieking, begging. Her eyes were white, no pupils, rolled back in raw fear, the most horrific thing I've ever witnessed. She started convulsing a little, chest rising, and I realised she was starting to vomit a little into the cloth across her mouth as the reality set in and she lost control completely.

I forced myself to watch as the man gripped the knife with his right hand, holding it up for a second near her face. He continued to rape her, and then drew the knife across her throat, hard. Back and forth, sawing, not a single cut. Her eyes. *Her face.* The dark stain spread, down across Sam's neck and chest, and onto the bed.

FIFTY-ONE

I'd taken a few moments. I'd been physically sick, took a while to get my shit together. But I was in control now. Well, not really. But I wasn't throwing up anymore.

I found a Silver Mazda parked in Browns Bay, same year as mine. I knew there were no cameras round here. And this time of night, no one was about. I got to work and removed the plates. I drove up to Hooten Reserve in Albany, fixed them to mine. *Little things.* You didn't have to explain everything. You just had to cut the evidential chain. Like putting a river between you and a dog.

I was on autopilot. I didn't think about the end game. I don't remember making choices. On some level I knew something had cracked inside my head, but it didn't register as a problem. It all made sense. Tanya's words rattled around inside my head. *Turn their fuckin' world upside down.* Nicola was in there too. *Do this once, Matt . . .*

But it was Calver that I found myself repeating. I could still feel the words just before I'd walked out on him.

Do not go gentle.

I headed up the Albany hill and took a left at the top, heading west on the Coatesville–Riverhead Highway. I took a turnoff, parked up on Boundary Road, just before it became Cobblers Lane. The other side of the forest from his place. I was wearing jeans and a hoodie, but before I stepped out I slipped the forensic booties over my shoes. I pulled the backpack over my shoulder and put my head down into the rain. I was soaked in seconds. I trudged in under the canopy, large drops still hitting me as I checked the glowing arms of the compass and started my walk south. I was aiming for the Rangitopuni Stream. It was about six hundred metres away, and I counted my paces to give me a rough idea. In the army I'd learned that a hundred and fifty of my steps was a hundred metres. I was a little bit out, but it was slow going through the trees, and my paces were short. I couldn't see fuck all, had one hand out in front to deflect branches, the other holding the compass. I just trusted that compass. I'd walked for about twenty minutes when, even at this time of night, I could see the glint of the water ahead of me as I approached the treeline on the stream bank. I then turned right, staying under the trees but keeping the water visible on my left.

Images drifted up as I walked. I smelled the acrid mangroves as I pulled the tarp aside, seeing Anneke McBride's bones protruding. I felt the stepping plate beneath my shoes, smelled the ocean spray, as I examined the pale body of Brianna Darwen in the dunes. I felt the rounds punch through our rear windscreen. Steve and Pete took the hits while I scrambled behind a pole like a bitch. Tanya's dead body on that bedroom floor. And I saw Sam's face as that knife came out.

I moved with purpose. With rage. I'd never wanted to do anything more in my life. *At least Martin Schuster and Nicola Darwen have been pardoned.* I didn't want to think of poor Dylan Manning. I trudged on. I followed the stream bank until it made a sharp turn directly south, away from me. I checked my compass briefly, and struck out away from the stream in a south-westerly direction. Same deal. Dark. Arm out in front to stop me losing an eye. Other hand holding the compass. One foot in front of the other. Soaked. Cold. I hit the boundary of a property and skirted it, coming out on a road. I took a breather, getting my head around where exactly I was. I looked left, then right. I tried to remember. Yeah, his place must be down there further, to my left. I started walking again.

I saw the lights from his place ahead of me, filtering through the cold, wet dark. I could see several cars in the drive. I left the road, ducked back into the bush, coming around and in from the north again. I propped myself on a small ridge behind his house. On my stomach, under the trees, beside a low fern. I watched and waited, as the rain splashed down around me and the fern fronds jumped around as they were struck by the drops.

I stayed for about two hours, listening. No loud voices. Nothing. Not that I could be sure with the falling rain. But he had strict parole conditions and maybe he wasn't taking chances with being recalled. I backed up further into the trees, pulled the tarp from my backpack and spread it on the ground. Then I stripped. The rain pouring through the canopy covered all sound. I pulled the forensic overalls on, pulled on the gloves and put the hair net and mask on. I then pulled a second pair of gloves over the first. I bundled my clothes up in the tarp, and stuffed it all back into the pack. I pulled out the Glock from the side pocket. I locked the top-slide back and checked the chamber with my finger. I was doing it all by feel, because I couldn't see shit in the darkness. I felt for the mag in the backpack, gripped it, used my thumb to feel for the holes that would usually let you see how many rounds you had. Getting the mag the right way round, I pushed it into the mag well, listening for the click and giving it a tug to make sure I wouldn't lose it. Then I released the slide by pulling it back and letting it snap forward. I put the pack on over both arms and headed down the slope for his back door.

I approached it from the side, listening, hearing nothing. There was a camera to my right, but covering the driveway at the front. Nothing back here. *Too fucking late now, even if there was.*

I reached for the handle and turned it. It gave. I slowly pushed it open to its full extent. I then quartered the doorway, stepping carefully, slowly, purposefully. Glock in front of me in both hands, up at eye level, but held in close. I didn't want to extend my arms. I wanted to be as small as possible. I slowly cleared the door space from right to left, then moved into what looked like the laundry. I stopped and listened again. Nothing. I closed the door softly behind me and crept toward the hall. It went left and right. Right? Lounge. Left? Rooms. *Left it is.* I followed the hall, past a room on my left with a closed door. I listened. Nothing. I kept the weapon up in my eye-line, about twenty centimetres from my face. The hall went straight ahead to another bedroom, but it also branched to the right. To the garage probably. I took that option. I moved along the hallway, a door at the end. Light spilling out into the hall from the gap underneath. I approached it and listened. Movement. Shuffling. Someone walking around on a concrete floor. No voices. I waited there for probably ten minutes. My legs ached. My feet burned. No voices at all. Things getting moved and shifted. He was busy with something. Hopefully it was just him. *Fuck it. Time to do something.*

I pushed the door open and quartered the garage, starting right and moving left. Instantly I picked up Harding, standing at a bench at my half left. I needed instant compliance.

"Armed Police! Search warrant! Hands on your head! Do it now!"

He turned and threw his hands up as he faced the pistol. His eyes widened, but I didn't let him get a word in. I threw him the cuffs.

"Put them on. Now!"

He complied, cuffing himself to the front. Then he stood there, smiling at me in recognition, despite my face mask and hair net. He looked around.

"Where's ya mates, Buchanan? Or are you the cannon fodder? All you'd be good for, if our last trip to court's anything to go by." He laughed.

I walked forward and face palmed him, putting him on his arse. Then I gripped his hair with my left, and smashed his head into the concrete garage floor.

"Fuck! Faarrk! Ughh!"

By the third one he was just groaning. I dragged him by the neck to a chair in front of the bench he'd been at. I hauled him into it. He sat there dazed. I opened my bag and pulled out the rope. He started squirming but I got it round his chest and knotted it behind. Then I pulled out the cable ties. I secured his hands better, and secured his feet to the chair. Then I got in front of him and slapped him hard across the face. He came around and looked at me. He spat blood between each word.

"You fuckin' stupid cunt. You're finished. Fucked." He looked around again and sneered. "Where's ya mates?"

"Does this look like a warrant?" Calm. Didn't raise my voice.

His face changed. He looked around again and started to assess the situation. Uncertainty now. I wanted to enjoy it, but I wasn't here to fuck about and I cut to the chase. "Samantha Coates. Where is her body." No question. Just a demand. He frowned.

"What the fuck's this? I want a phone. Lawyer. Now. I'm not answering your fuckin' questions."

I found a piece of four by two, strolled back to him, and smashed it into his face. He wasn't ready for it and his head bounced around on his neck as he took the blow.

"Yeah, you fucking will. Sam. '99. Where did you put her?"

I kept my voice calm, low, controlled. The rain hammered the garage roof.

He sneered again. "Get fucked. I'm gonna fuckin' have you. You're over. You're fucked. Going to prison." He spat at me.

I slapped him in the face, hard. His eyes watered. "Look at me, Gary. Look at how I'm dressed, you dumb fuck. This ain't an official visit." I needed him to understand the stakes. I got eye contact by gripping his hair again. I leaned close, breathing onto him through my face mask. "I know what you did to her. I fuckin' know. I broke onto your boat." His eyes went wider. Processing. Thinking. Working it out. "I watched it, you fuckin' cunt. I know."

His eyes gave him away. Panic spread over his face. He knew I'd seen it. No other way to explain it.

"I watched the whole thing. She was a kid, Gary. How the *fuck* . . ." I looked away as I closed my eyes and thought of some way to describe him, but failed. There was no describing him. Sub-human.

The video played back in my head. Sam's face. The terror. I tried to focus, shook my head.

Harding didn't understand the struggle I was having with myself. He laughed at my head shake. "Burgled my boat? Well there goes that evidence. Good work. You got nothing."

I slapped him hard again. "You're not getting it, Gary. This isn't a fuckin' interview. I'm not asking. Get it? I'm not *asking*. Tell me where you buried her. And who else was in that room."

"Get fucked."

I kicked his chest and he went over onto his back, still tied to the chair. I checked the bench, and stopped dead when I saw what he'd been fucking about with. *Fuck me*. Couple of parcels of pseudo. No mistaking the pink and yellow granules. I looked around further and found the urns, the heat plate, the solvents. *Fuckin' clan lab*. He was a bit out of date on his technique – it was mainly pure ephedrine everyone used now, not pseudo – you cut a stage of the process out by using the pure stuff. But this suited me fine. An idea was forming. An unforgivable idea. But the wheels were turning too fast to stop. *First things first though*. I grabbed a couple of leather chamois from the bench and a bucket from a corner by the garden tools. I filled the bucket with water from the sink. I soaked both cloths in it. Autopilot was on. I could see Tanya getting pulled out of Tauranga harbour, the photos of her injuries. I stuffed one of the cloths into Harding's mouth. He tried to yell but I shoved it all the way down his throat. I then laid the other over his mouth and nose. He struggled against the cable ties, trying to twist his body, but he couldn't move much. Not on his back, tied to the chair. I tipped the bucket of water over his face. He coughed, spluttered, screamed into the cloth. I kept pouring. He started whimpering as the water swelled both rags, and he struggled to get air in. Every time he sucked in through his nose the chamois clamped to his face. And I kept pouring. He started thrashing in the chair, trying to roll over, but I kept it where it was with my legs, standing over him. When I thought he was almost gone from lack of air, I ripped the chamois off his face and pulled the other out of his mouth.

He spat. And started hyperventilating, sucking air in madly. "Fuck! Faaarrrk you!" more spitting. His eyes were like saucers.

"Two things Gary. Easy as. No drama. Just relax. This ain't an exam. And you know the answers. Where is she? And who was with you? It ain't hard."

"Fuck you, you cunt. I'll fuckin' destroy you. Fuckin' destroy you. You've fucked up big time. I've got people inside. They'll fuckin' kill you after this."

"Nah. I don't reckon."

I jammed the cloth back in and laid the other on top. I tipped the bucket. Water splashed over his face, over the concrete floor. He writhed, spluttered, couldn't cough. To him, it felt like he was drowning. But really, he was just getting no air. I gave him twenty more seconds, then pulled everything off him again.

"I could keep this up all night, Gary. And you look pretty fuckin' uncomfortable, I must say."

Before he could reply I stuffed the cloth in again, dropped the other over his face, and kept pouring. This time I went for a good minute. He passed out. I pulled the cloths away, slapped him a little, turned his head to the side. I listened for breathing and heard low, shallow breaths. He coughed. Choking, spitting. Opened his eyes. Disbelief. Panic.

"Look at me, Gary. I'm playing for keeps. This ain't optional. Don't answer me, you're done. But I'm offering you a way out. Take it."

He stared at me through watering eyes. "What the fuck are you doing? What do you think I'll do after this? Let it go?" He went back to his grin. His sneer. "You don't have the fuckin' stones, Buchanan."

"You're not hearing me, cunt. You haven't told me anything. Where is she."

"Fuck you, Buchanan. You're a pussy. You're fucked, and I ain't saying shit."

I looked around the garage. I found a red petrol container and poured some of it into an empty paint tin. I looked around for smokes. Nothing. I went back into the house, into the lounge. Smokes and lighter, on the kitchen bench. Back to the garage. I lit a piece of wood, dropped it into the paint tin. Faint flame. No smoke. I found some more bits of wood and paper and chucked them on. It all started burning. I used my leg and kicked it toward Harding. Then I sat him up over it, gripping him again so he got a face full of smoke.

"What the fuck . . .?"

He spluttered and choked as the dark plumes rose and hit him. I left him to it and sorted out my next task. I looked around. I pulled a large aluminium pot out from under the bench, along with the heating element. I plugged that in, and sat the pot on top. I checked the range of solvents and popped the lid on a drum of tolly. I poured a couple of litres into the pot. Then I ripped one of the bags of pseudo open and poured the granules in.

"What the fuck are you doing?!" He was confused. I must have seemed insane. Maybe I was. No. *I definitely was.* How many people had this guy killed? I was sure of three. Anneke. Brianna. Sam. And more convinced by the hour that Calver was doing Harding's time for Gabby. *But how many others?* The images I'd found on his drive flooded my head. *Those kids. Who the fuck are they? Are they alive? Dead? Overseas?* The images of Brianna we'd found on Kitson's computer took over in my head. Then the videos. Anneke. Sam. Finally, I was listening. *Turn their fuckin' world upside down. Do this right, Matt. Or they'll kill you. The system isn't set up for these men, Detective. Do not go gentle.*

I let Harding breathe the smoke for a bit longer, then I poured some tolly into the wood fire. That sparked a bit more than I was expecting, but I needed some of it in his lungs for the pathologist's benefit. He was in a bad way now, constantly coughing and spluttering.

I found another two aluminium pots, larger than the first. I emptied the other packets of pseudo into them, lifted the drum of tolly and poured a few litres into each. I left the pots on the garage floor. I let his brain tick over and switched the heat plate on below the extraction on the bench. Then I kicked the burning paint tin away. I took out the Marlborough packet I'd found in his kitchen. I removed one, stuffing the packet into his shirt pocket. He watched me, totally confused. I stuffed the ciggie into his mouth. Then I picked up the drum of tolly and started splashing it over the benches, onto the floor, then over anything in the garage that would burn. He still didn't get it. Still thought I was working inside the box.

I went in and gripped him by the collar. "This is it, you get that, you fuck? You tell me, or you're fucked. You slit her throat. You fuckin' pig." I screamed into his face, but it was muffled by my face mask. "Where is she?!"

And then he fucked up. He spat the ciggie out, staring at me with that grin. "She was the best, Coates was. Tightest of the lot. You should've felt it, when I cut her." He relived the memory, fucking with me. I closed my eyes, breathed. But something cracked. There was no pulling it back together.

Fuck this. And fuck him. I pulled the lighter out of my pocket. His lighter.

"You should be more careful with these pseudo extractions."

I must have looked fucking mental, cos it was at that moment that Harding dropped his nuts. He started to realise maybe I wasn't fully in control. He was frowning now, concluding I wasn't so full of shit after all, and that he was in trouble. The panic had returned to his eyes and it stayed there. "You . . . you fuckin' need me, Buchanan. You'll never find her without me."

I was done. He didn't know it yet though. And I had to make this all look right. "Stay still. One move, I shoot you." I had the Glock out, and moved in, cutting the plasticuffs and the rope, removing them and putting them back in my pack, all with my left hand. I had to keep the Glock on him. "Stay in the chair."

A rational person could have stopped there, paused, called a halt. Thought it through. But that wasn't me. The rage, the fractured memories, the damage. It had spilled over, and something else was in control. I picked up the ciggie from the floor. Then I picked up the drum and splashed the last of the tolly over him. He looked confused as he spat out some that had gone into his mouth. "What the . . . I'll help! There's another . . . not just me . . . you gotta deal?"

I saw Hailey, gasping out on our driveway, having just saved my life. And if the surveillance teams hadn't been on, she would have been killed right then by this cunt. And I saw Sam's blood spreading over that bed again.

I smiled. "Yeah, I've made a deal."

He relaxed. Closed his eyes.

I stepped back. "Just not with you."

I flicked the lighter, lit the ciggie. As I tossed it onto him he screamed at the top of his lungs. I legged it for the hallway. I heard the crack and roar behind me as the tolly went up, spreading across Harding, the floor, to the bench. His piercing screams followed me. I heard him crash to the ground as he tried to move away from the inferno. More screams, then the sound of the fire took over.

I needed out before the pots went up. I could feel the heat behind me as I raced into the hall, left, then right into the laundry. Out the back door, pause. *Check the ground.* Plenty of prints in the mud. *Shouldn't be too many issues with sign.* The first pot went up. I heard the *cruuump* and flames burst out the front of the garage door, lighting up the dark behind me. I turned briefly, looking back. Then I struck out north through the bush, heading for the road. I took my time, hand in front again, bending branches, not breaking them. I had time. When I eventually hit the road where I'd left my car, I stayed in the trees and dropped my pack. I pulled the tarp out and placed it down. Clothes out and down to the side. Overalls off, mask off, hairnet off, booties off. Onto the tarp. Tarp wrapped. Back in the pack. Clothing back on. *Get to the car.* I headed east along the road. At my car I pulled the door, sat my arse in, and pulled off the gloves. Into the pack they went.

I started the car and moved off.

FIFTY-TWO

This was one of the best views of the Auckland city skyline at night. I liked it because it was right in the heart. If you stop halfway along the Hopetoun Street bridge, which connects Ponsonby with Pitt Street, the city opens up. Spaghetti junction flows underneath you. The whole thing is just smack right in front, Harbour Bridge to the left, the Sky Tower taking centre stage. Whatever the time, people were travelling, moving, heading places. The city was alive here.

It had been one of Kate's favourite spots. It had reminded her that whatever was going down, people worked, played, carried on. Thousands of people moving through their own lives, their schedules, jobs, families, loved ones, plans and problems. All with their own minds, feelings, thoughts, emotions, stories. She'd thrived on that collective heartbeat. I didn't think Father John had it a hundred per cent correct. I mean, I couldn't write my notebook up exactly the ways things had happened, minutes after they did. So, I was confident a two-thousand-year-old book probably wasn't spot on. But I wasn't arrogant enough to think there was nothing after this, things we couldn't comprehend with our primitive heads. So, call it what you will, but for whatever reason, I'd always chatted with Kate.

I've lost it, Katie. Things have fucked me up. Couldn't hold onto it. The worst part? Saw it all coming. Saw it coming, didn't do a thing about it. Can't pull it all together. I'm afraid for Hailey. I should have quit. Back in '95, I should have quit.

I talked *to* Kate obviously, rather than *with* her. But here, it seemed like more of a two-way conversation. I thought about my daughter and her promising future. She'd been through a lot. Too much. Losing her mum wasn't fair. Being raised by me wasn't much of a consolation prize.

Out of the blue Sam's face flashed up in front of me. She was smiling, laughing away, looking at something on a cell-phone with one of her mates. It was another scene I had made up, created in my head. Don't think cell-phones were big back in 1999. *What the fuck had happened to me?*

Hell was a folk story spun by communities of old, to scare kids into telling the truth and prevent husbands fucking the neighbour's wife. It didn't exist, not somewhere else anyway. There was enough horror here. Things that had bent my head, warped my psyche, altered my views on life. There was quite the camera reel. Gang members pushing their way into the house of a guy who had fucked up. Brandishing the crowbar and baseball bat, throwing him a rope as a less painful way out. Forced him to hang himself. An addict of a mother, angry with the world and the lack of support. Beating her kid with a broom handle, breaking her arm, pouring boiling water on her, ripping her toenails out. A girl stabbed in the chest with a screwdriver multiple times, driven around while she bled out, and dumped behind a warehouse to decompose in the soil and scrub. A mother, run over as she walked home, dragged into a car, raped, and her throat slit. An angel of a daughter, killed in her own home by her stalker. A stalker released on bail after kidnapping her. I just couldn't shake any of it.

I looked out at the city. I envied the accountants, the teachers, the courier drivers – those who earned money from their jobs, enjoyed their jobs even, and went home to spend it. That's how it should be. *Not this*. It didn't matter how many good things you did, or saw. It was the horrors that always floated back. Good memories? Few. When I was frontline, a mother and her teenage daughter had brought a bottle of wine into the station for me. I'd helped shut down the daughter's party when it got out of control. They had no idea who I was, but while they were at the front desk describing me, I strolled on past and the daughter recognised me, grabbing her mum and stopping me. They thanked me. For some very minor shit. Minor to me maybe. Not to them. The good was there, but I struggled to remember the moments. I'm sure there were more. Yeah. Guy run over in his driveway. Not good. Internal bleeding. Bad injuries. Ambos had taken him to Auckland Hospital. It was looking like he wouldn't make it. I'd picked up both his kids from somewhere nearby, couldn't remember where. They hadn't been home. I turned the lights and sirens on, against policy, just to get them through peak traffic so that maybe they could see their dad before he went. I'd driven like a lunatic. I was chewed out after that. For blue-lighting with two kids in the car. Not going to an actual job. But fuck it. I did what I thought was right. I got the kids to the hospital, to their mum. The dad made it. I was glad.

I'd joined up to challenge myself, do something for other people. Find lost kids, save people who couldn't swim, do something worthwhile. To give something back. But after everything to the contrary, I'd still stuck with it. Why? To prove something to myself? To everyone else? That I was hard enough?

Well, now I knew. *I wasn't.*

FIFTY-THREE

Sam was probably buried out here somewhere. Maybe. The clothing down at the surf zone, Harding's last words. But it was a big area. I breathed in. I'd never get the truth. Of the two people who knew where she was, one was dead. The other could have been Kitson, could have been Lendich. Both in prison with no reason to talk. I'd lasted twenty-two years. It was always going to catch up with me. Each nail into my coffin. I'd known. Felt them all. My life had been a slow-moving train crash. I could see it. Could see the end-game coming from a long way away. But I'd boxed it up, set it aside. Tried to ignore it. Dealt with the present. I'd never attempted to change my future. It was like I'd accepted it, ever since those first few months on the job. Harding was the last nail. I couldn't reconcile any of this. And I didn't expect any help from Kate this time.

I listened to the surf in the darkness, breaking in front of me, down on the beach. I felt the sand shifting around my shoes. The wind blew through the dunes, strong, rustling the marram. Smell of salt. Nobody about for several kilometres probably. Maybe at the surf club down the beach. Who knows.

My world was dark. Black. I couldn't see anything. My mind had fractured after that video, and I couldn't pull the pieces together. Killing Harding hadn't helped. I knew he couldn't hurt anyone again. But it hadn't helped *me*. I'd considered calling someone, but there was no point. I knew they'd be better off if I didn't. Everyone would. I couldn't lumber my shit onto anyone else. It was mine to deal with. *And I was going to deal with it.* Hailey was winning, she was carving her own path. The last thing she needed was me, a thorn in her side, trying to offload. No one needs a dad like that. No one should be a burden to their kid. That's what I reckoned, anyway. Even though I wasn't in control of my head. But she'd get over it. She was stronger than me.

I smelt the ocean, heard the wind. Shivered. Who would find me? Didn't matter. Yeah, someone I knew would probably do the scene. They wouldn't let anyone real close to me do it. But it would be someone. My mates, my colleagues . . . Dan, Derek, Erin, Simon . . . yeah, they all might find it hard. But they'd get past it too. Deal with the job. Deal with the funeral. Shut it out. Move on. The bosses . . . Helen, Tim . . . they'd probably say they saw it coming.

My brain couldn't isolate a single positive thought. Subconsciously, it must have been trying fucking hard, but I wasn't aware of it. All I saw was the darkness in front. Real and perceived.

I thought I could tell the difference between an image in my head, and something I actually saw. Sam. Laughing, happy. Smiling. Reading. Doing homework. At a birthday party. With family. A series of images that had never happened. Well, they might have. But I'd never seen them.

And then I saw Kate. *Matt, you don't need to do this.*

My phone buzzed and I looked down at it. Hailey. *What the*

fuck did I bring my phone for? I didn't want to answer it, but my thumb swiped across it anyway.

"Hailey?"

"Hey, Dad. Last exam's done, I'm flying up on Friday."

"How'd it go?"

"Good, I think. You never know though."

"Well, I wouldn't even have been able to read the questions."

"Dad, I'm not ten. You aren't thick. Stop saying you are."

"Just ask a few other people I know."

"I love you, Dad. Can't wait to see you. At the airport, right?"

Pause. No. *Breathe.* Okay. "Course. Text me your flight. I love you, too. See you then."

A promise. The images had gone. Faded. But I could make out the dunes now, the surf zone, lights down the south end of the beach. Coming into focus.

I returned to the work car I'd nicked, parked back on the forestry road. I got in and thumbed the mag release, ripped the mag from the Glock I'd been holding. I held the pistol grip with my right, and locked the receiver back gently with my left hand, letting the round drop into my palm. I looked at it, the casing, the primer, the projectile. Then I replaced the round in the mag, pushing it down onto the other sixteen. I let the slide go forward on the pistol, and dropped both items back in the lock box. I started the car.

FIFTY-FOUR

Why was it always fuckin' raining? The weather hammered my iron roof. Spat against the windows. The TV was on but I wasn't watching. Some shit morning show. I checked my coffee cup. Empty. *Cunt.* I moved to the kettle and filled it again, flicking the switch on. *Gotta wash this fuckin cup now.* Cold water. *No good.* Hot water. *Better.* Dishwashing liquid. *Yep, off you fuck, coffee stains.* I made another cup once the jug had boiled itself stupid. *Need a new jug.* I moved back to the couch and flicked through the channels till I found some news. I checked the time. 7:07 a.m. I found TV3. Newshub. *Why the hell did they change that again? Let's hear it then, Newshub.*

I froze. Felt around for the remote to turn it up. Knocked the mug off the coffee table, sending it across the floor. I didn't really notice. I was drawn to the TV screen. My hand closed around the remote and I turned the noise up.

"*. . . occupants are currently assisting Police with their enquiries. There is a huge Police presence here, ambulances in attendance. But* *we do know the children are alive, they've been taken for medical treatment but they're all in a stable condition."* Cut back to the anchor. *"And we'll bring you more shortly as soon as there are developments. Overseas now and . . ."*

I grabbed my phone and went to the news there. First article. *Helensville horror house raided.* I skim read it. CYFS involved. With Police, searched a home in the North Auckland suburb of Helensville. Six children found living in poor conditions. Varying ages between five and twelve. Adult occupants are a male and a female. De facto. Children weren't schooled. Rural address. Unsure of relationship between children and adults. Someone reported their concern for the kids after visiting the property. *Jesus. And most people think all this shit happens overseas.*

It was six hours later when I got the call from Erin. I'd headed out to Okura for a jog through the rain. I'd just got back to the car and jumped inside to escape the downpour.

"Hi."

"Matt."

"I'm not interested."

"Probably not. But I had to let you know."

"I don't want to know. Sorry." I hit the red button. *What a cock.* Erin had probably been in touch the most since I'd left for the second time. She probably thought it was only temporary again. That it would only take another pull on the strings to get me back on board. But I was done with it all. My new job kept my mind off other shit. When the flight planning job had come up, Air New Zealand took a look at my CV and wondered if I was serious. But I was. I was learning to ignore it all, shut it all out. It was a desk job, problem solving, something I had an interest in. It seemed to be working out okay. I'd always been a curious fucker, except I knew how it affected me now. And I knew that if I went back, I'd end up back on that beach. The phone rang again. I ignored it. I found *Crime Investigation Australia.* Watched it for five minutes. Something on Ivan Milat. *Nah. Don't need that.* I changed over to Comedy Central.

But it must have been pretty important. I was kicking back after a delicious plastic-and-water-flavoured microwave macaroni dinner when there was a loud knock at the ranch-slider. I looked up and Erin was standing there, soaked. I jumped up and slid the door open.

I couldn't believe it. "What the fuck are you doing?" She was drenched. "What's wrong with the front door? It's covered, you know."

"I knocked, Matt. You didn't answer."

"Right. Sorry. Been busy." She looked at the TV. Then back at me. She was proper soaked. I stated the obvious. "Do you want a towel?"

"It's okay."

"Nah, I'll get you a towel. You're dripping all over my carpet." She looked at the coffee stain I still hadn't sorted from this morning and she actually laughed. Shook her head.

I returned with the towel and she patted herself dry. She remained standing. I put her out of her misery. "I'm joking, mate. Take a seat. Coffee?"

"Please." I moved to the kitchen. She spoke across the bench top. "You've seen the news obviously. The kids."

"Yep. Sexual abuse?"

"Worse. Half the kids are his, half hers. All getting abused. But they were filming it, Matt. Or had been. We found a few cameras."

I stopped dead and looked at her. "Filming it?" She nodded. My mind turned over, for the first time in a while. "Others involved?"

"We're working on that, yeah. The . . . I don't want to say 'parents', but the *parents*, they're sort of the gatekeepers. There were definitely others involved. Hard to tell how recently."

"The images of the other kids we got out of Harding's factory. The ones we found on Kitson's computer . . ." I could tell from Erin's face already. "Fuck!" I smashed my cup into the sink, ceramic fragments going everywhere. Erin's eyes went wide and she stood up. I apologised. "Sorry. I'm okay. No, actually, you know what? I thought this was all done."

"It is. Harding's dead. The others are inside. These two, they're on neglect charges at the moment, the sexual charges are coming, once the kids have been EVI'd. We can't tell if there's been anything recently. But yeah, some of the kids have been identified in the material we found before. It could be the last part of that group, Matt. We're just closing off the loop."

I fetched another mug from the cupboard. I made two cups and poured the boiling water in. *Dickhead. Milk first.* I took both cups to Erin, handing her one. "Well, you guys better close it. Cos we never had any other suspects." I took a sip. *Burnt.* I knocked back a few of the prescription for good measure.

Yeah, I was a fucking mess all right.

FIFTY-FIVE

I picked up the phone and rang Hailey, left a message. I was onto my second cup when she rang back.

"Hey, Dad. Sorry, was still in bed."

I laughed. "Good night last night? It's fuckin' cold up here. How's the snow?"

"Slippery. Makes walking home from a night on the piss difficult. Excess wines. You know how it is." She'd meant to make it a joke. But it was definitely the truth. I could smell her hangover breath through the phone. She kept talking. "I've been stuck to the news the last few weeks. Have they got you involved yet? Those kids?"

"Nah, they're all over it, I think. Looks like the parents continued the abuse, but we got the ringleaders last year. This is more about the safety of those kids, I think, going forward. No disclosures of anything recent, but from what Erin and Dan have told me, the kids are going to need a lot of help before they can talk fully about everything. It'll be a slow process."

I heard Hailey breathe in. "Nothing to do with Sam?"

She knew Sam was dead now, and that her killers were either in prison, or had died in a P-lab fire. But she knew the body thing still bugged me. I wasn't supposed to let it. That's what the psych said anyway. I was working through it. "No, they knew the same people, but this was a bit separate from what I hear. They've dug up the whole place, nothing."

"You still reckon the beach?"

"Yeah. Well, fuck, Hailey, this is a morbid conversation. Plans for the weekend?"

She got the message. "Flat party at Sarah's. Well, party . . . more like sit around freezing our arses off watching the Highlanders. The heater's broken. Ah well. Should be a good game."

"They'll thump us."

Hailey remained an avid Blues supporter despite rules to the contrary when you went to Otago.

"You gotta have some faith, Dad." She laughed again.

"Well, I won't keep you. You've got some sleeping in to do."

"Thanks. Dad?"

"Yeah?"

"Ring me if you need anything."

Even my daughter knows I'm a mess.

FIFTY-SIX

I was hoping my Google searches weren't about to get me an official visit from my old workmates. I'm sure some alarms would be going off at Vodafone or Internal Affairs. But I was trying to understand. Trying to put this latest shit, and previous shit, into some sort of context with cases overseas. I found out about Lee Kaplan, who'd lived with a husband and wife in Pennsylvania with twelve children. Nine of the kids were theirs. But they "gifted" Kaplan one of their daughters when she was fourteen. The remaining kids were hers. It had been abuse and neglect on a major scale. Intervention only came after several years, neighbours and Police putting clues together here and there but never suspecting the worst. Kaplan, and the husband and wife went for a series of abuse, neglect and child sex offences. But the kids themselves? How did they carry on? No sentence could ever be enough.

Closer to home I read about Matthew Graham, convicted in a Melbourne court and given fifteen years inside. A judge described his acts as "pure evil". He'd been involved with a series of websites specialising in the torture, rape and abuse of children. He apparently had encouraged the rape and murder of a child in Russia. He'd had a series of videos depicting the torture of infants. He had images of dead children. So this – the Helensville house, Harding, Kitson, the whole lot – they weren't exceptions. This wasn't fiction. This was all too real, too often. I sat back in my chair. *Was the world always like this? Probably. Technology just means we hear about it now. Five hundred years ago, who would know if this was going on? No one.*

Calver's words came back to me. *What do you fear?* He was right. That man, for whatever he'd done, had been right. Every time. I'd always known he never told me the full story, but what he had told me had been spot on. He was right. Harding had to die. I agreed with Calver on that. Nobody else would. But I did. Yeah, it hadn't helped me. *But it wasn't about me, was it?* I found it had been getting harder and harder for me to consider consequences.

Which didn't help when the call came at about 1 a.m. "Ian? What's happening mate?"

Ian didn't drunk-call his mates. Something was wrong. I could hear road noise in the background, he was driving, pretty fast. "It's Chloe. Are you on the Shore tonight?"

"Yep."

"She's been taken to hospital, drug overdose they reckon, or, nah, a reaction to something. I dunno . . ."

"She's at North Shore Hospital?"

"Yeah."

Ian and his wife Emma lived in Bucklands Beach, so a bit of a drive. I was already looking for my keys. "Heading there now. Call you as soon as I know more."

I pulled on a puffer jacket and went out to the car. I took East Coast Road and then Forrest Hill Road, straight down to the hospital. The nurse on the emergency desk looked at me strangely.

"Family?"

"Pretty much."

"Pretty much?"

"Family friends. Her dad's on his way. Look . . ." Two uniformed Constables walked out through the doors leading into the emergency wards. I recognised Paul. "Mate, Chloe Donaldson . . ."

"Yeah, Matt, she's going to be okay they reckon, pumping her stomach although it was already in her system. Her heart rate went through the roof but they've got it under control."

"Cheers." They walked out to their car. I started to get worked up. I called Ian. "Just heard from two cops who followed the ambulance in mate. They've pumped her stomach and stabilised her, reckon she's going to be okay."

"Fuck . . ."

"I'm going to find out a bit more."

There were a group of teenagers in a corner of the waiting room, looking a bit worried. I approached them. "You guys Chloe's mates?"

One of the girls answered. "Yeah . . . you know her dad?" *They overheard my call.*

"Yup. Where was she?"

"When she took it? Well she didn't even take it, someone put it in her drink—"

"What?"

"Yeah, this guy, he had a few e's but they weren't, they're like that fake stuff—"

Are you fuckin' with me? Had I heard her right? "Someone put it in her drink?"

"Yeah he's a fuckin' dick—"

I kept cutting her off. "Who?"

"Tony—"

"Where's Tony?"

The two girls looked at each other, and the guy with them opened his mouth. "Still at the party probably—"

"Where was the party." They looked hesitant. As you probably would when some random old fuck starts interrogating you. But I was starting to lose my cool and I didn't want it to burst here in the hospital waiting room. I tried to calm myself down. "Your friend is in ICU because of this Tony fuckwit and you're here because you're worried. So am I. I know the family. But there's fuck all I can do here. Where's Tony?"

One of the girls pulled out her phone. "I've got his number if you—"

"Can you call him?" She looked up at me, confused. I explained. "Look mate, I need to find this guy. I want to figure out what Chloe took exactly, that's it. No one's in the shit here. I just need to know where he is."

She dialled a number. "Tony, it's Kylie . . . What? . . . Yeah, she's . . . yeah, she's still here . . . What . . .? What . . .? No, you fuckin' dick, she's not fine . . . Where are you . . .? Where? Ah 'kay . . . yeah, I think she will." Kylie looked up at me. "They left the party, but they're heading to Mairangi Bay, drinking at the surf club."

"What's he look like?"

She brought up Facebook and showed me a picture. "Are you going to . . .?"

But I was already on my way out the door.

I took Shakespeare, then left onto East Coast and up the hill. Right onto Castor Bay Road, down to Beach Road, and left. Dropping down the hill toward the Mairangi Bay roundabout, I turned right, heading for the surf club. It was dark, but the streetlights ahead of me lit up the beachfront reserve area. I slowed at the corner but couldn't see anyone, so turned left following the road around. My headlights lit up the playground and there were a bunch of people sitting around. I saw a couple of cars parked up beneath the pines. I pulled in next to them and switched off.

I kept the image of Tony in my head and I walked up to the group. I didn't bother looking around, I knew he was here somewhere. I tried the fishing approach. I couldn't see anyone that clearly.

"Tony, mate. Matt Buchanan, Police, just got to cover off something about Chloe Donaldson. No dramas. Should be quick." *Bullshit works wonders sometimes*. I listened and watched the group, and they all glanced toward one guy who started talking.

"Oh yeah, sweet. This gonna take long . . .?"

Took the bait. No threat, and he outs himself right away.

"Nah, this won't take long, mate." I walked up to him and delivered a single punch to his face, connecting somewhere above his nose.

"Aahh fuck . . .!" He went sideways off the wooden seat and onto his back. He started whimpering. His mates started making noises, getting up off their seats.

"Fuck! Fuck! Fuck!"

I needed some distance so I got my arm under Tony's neck and dragged him about ten metres into the dark toward the surf club. A couple of the group started moving toward me so I dropped Tony and headed back toward them. One guy was wearing chinos, a fancy shirt. His mate had a big white hoodie pulled up and over his head. Chinos took a step toward me.

"What the fuck do you want, Harry Styles?"

He paused. His mate in the hoodie piped up. "You can't swear, officer. It's . . ."

"And where the fuck does it say that?"

"You wanna go, cunt?"

Oh good. I was no martial artist. I knew fuck all about fighting, really. You only got the basics down in training, and it was all self-defence. You made the rest up as you experienced it. These guys were both young skinny pricks, but I couldn't take both on. One punch in the right place and I'd be down, and in trouble. I needed to take control. I stepped forward and dropped

Harry with a palm underneath the nose, helping him on his way by giving him a shove in the small of the back as I stepped past him. He went over and down, clutching his face. I covered up and went for the guy in the hoodie, but he was already legging it back to his mates. Harry was getting up but I bent and struck him again to the side of the head. He covered up, tried to crawl away. I called out to the group. "Now fuck off. Tony and I got some shit to sort out."

Tony had been crawling slowly toward the road and gave a groan as I grabbed him by the collar and dragged him back toward the playground.

"You fuckin' piece of shit. Chloe's getting her stomach pumped . . . they had to stabilise her, control her heart rate . . . could've died if they didn't get her to an ambulance . . ." I kept dragging him toward the playground, trying to find what I was looking for. "Did you give anyone else one of those pills, Tony? Drop any into anyone else's drink?" One slap. Hard. "Did you?" Another slap.

"Fuck! Nah, ahh, nah . . ."

The group had moved back toward their cars, leaving their alcohol in the playground. I found a bottle of wine. I dropped Tony, picked up the bottle, opened it. I held his jaw, poured the wine over his nose and mouth, kept on pouring. He choked, spluttered, tried to turn his face. I got my knee onto his chest, gave another punch to his head, and held the bottle there, still pouring. He started gasping, coughing up wine, trying to spit but not able to suck any air in.

"Faark . . . stop . . . Fuck!"

I heard the sirens and picked up the next bottle. Tony was dragging in air, coughing, chest working hard. I wasn't even threatening Tony with anything. I wasn't warning him to sharpen up his act, or change his ways. Fuck no. I just wanted to keep hurting him. I elbowed him in the nose again and then got pouring. He couldn't open his eyes now and was blind, trying to breathe, probably feeling pretty claustrophobic. *Pussy.* He wasn't going to die. Well, he probably didn't know that.

I was almost finished the second bottle when the I-car raced up, slamming on the brakes. I heard doors open, feet running. I dropped the bottle and put my hands on my head. They pushed me into the ground beside Tony, pulling my arms into the small of my back.

"Don't move! You're under arrest!"

I just let them do it. Fuck it. Yeah, I'd done wrong. But so had Tony. Fuck him.

The cuffs went on and the two of them dragged me up and toward the car, opening the back door and pushing me in. One came round the other side to belt me in.

"Matt? Fuck!" *Paul.* "Fuck, I can't . . ."

I stopped him. "It's all right, mate, it is what it is. No harm done. Just do what you need to do, all these kids will make a complaint otherwise . . ." I grinned at him.

Paul rolled his eyes. "Fuck, Matt . . ."

"You should probably give me my rights though if you want this to stick."

He started laughing. "Stay here, I've got to check on this dude."

Paul left me with his partner who rattled my rights off to me, while Paul went out to Tony, knelt by him. They waited for the ambulance before taking me away.

FIFTY-SEVEN

I was in a bit of a downward spiral, I guess, to put it mildly. But even then, life still had a few more fistings hidden up its sleeve specially reserved for my arsehole. A few months after getting binned and discharged in court, everything I thought I'd known was about to change.

I'd gone into the kitchen and boiled the jug early. I'd pulled my phone out and checked Stuff news.

Nah. No way. Not fuckin' possible.

I was fucking about now with my phone in my right hand, driving with my left. Heading west on State 17, making for Henderson. I was doing about thirty over the limit. I dialled Erin and she didn't answer. I dialled Derek.

"Hey bro. All hands to the pump here. You'd be welcome. Murray's running it and I think he wants to pick your brains anyway. Erin's got the Operation Mist file here, they've just found clothing, dumped on the side of State 16. Call me when you're here and I'll let you through the back gate, all good."

The right people were on it. Murray was a long-serving Detective Sergeant at Henderson. Methodical, but practical. On his watch, shit got done.

I pulled in and parked in the usual spot to the left of the driveway at the rear of Hendo station. I called Derek again and he met me at the door. We headed past the general CIB office and took the familiar left into the serious crime room. Nothing had changed in this building. It was all the same. Except for the people. Murray was writing on the whiteboard and a couple of D's or DC's I didn't know were putting photos up. A few people looked at me wondering who the fuck I was, but Murray just glanced at me and nodded.

"Matt. Head into the back room, Erin's in there."

I appraised myself.

Kayla Bramwell, thirteen years. Lived on Marina View Drive, West Harbour. She'd left home at 7:30 a.m., heading for the bus stop on Hobsonville Road, normal school morning. Except she'd never arrived. The school had phoned home, her mother confirmed she'd left. Police were called soon after. Her phone was dead. Social media inactive. Nothing. And now they'd found her school jacket and her backpack near Soljans winery, by the State 16 and Old North Road roundabout, up near Kumeu.

There was a team with the family at their home. But I knew they wouldn't be getting any contact from the person who had taken her. This wasn't a ransom kidnapping. This was an abduction. And we didn't have much time.

I stood near the back for the briefing. I was here to observe and provide what help I could, but not being a sworn officer anymore, I had to keep out of it really. Murray kicked things off with the background, and then what the state of play was now – what had been done, who was where and what was currently happening, and what needed to be done – who was responsible for what.

I was well used to that feeling of ice flooding my spine, but it didn't make it any better now. There was a missing kid and the way I saw it, we had fuck all. Nothing. There was nowhere to go, nothing to follow. Not right now anyway. What could we do, scour the whole country north of where her stuff was found? Wait with the family? The bag and jacket had been rushed to ESR for immediate testing, but we wouldn't have a result for hours. Hours we didn't have.

I'd been churning this over ever since reading the news. Racking my brain, over and over. We'd missed nothing. Not a thing. Everyone was accounted for. No-one else had come out of the woodwork. But we couldn't ignore the timeline. Erin knew. It was why she had the Mist file out. We'd missed something, all right.

We'd nailed the whole group, except for Harding. But he was dead. So, job over. But obviously somebody had carried on with those kids up in Helensville, and now they'd been rescued, and the parents binned, there was nothing. No kids to prey on. So, whoever it was was still active. And whoever it was had gone hunting. *Just as they had back in '99*. Someone in Harding's crew.

Murray was still talking.

"Eighteen years ago, there was a similar abduction in this district. Operation Mist. Samantha Coates, fourteen. Went missing walking home from school in Hillcrest on the Shore. Some of her clothing was found out on Muriwai beach." He looked at me. "This is Matt Buchanan, former D. He worked that job. Matt, do you want to talk about that, and the developments that followed?"

All eyes turned on me.

"Yeah. Sam was presumed abducted and murdered, but it remained a missing persons case for years. Her death wasn't confirmed until last year. There was a burglary to a boat in Westhaven. Some of that property was found dumped in Ponsonby in the days after and got handed in. Amongst that was . . . a snuff video. Of Sam being raped and murdered. Her body has never been found."

Murmurs throughout the room. They knew the case. Had heard about it.

"The boat belonged to Gary Harding. Harding was tried and acquitted of a series of killings going back to 1995. A number of his associates were convicted of various offences linked to the same events. David Kitson, Damien Lendich. Thomas Calver. They're all in prison. They were all suspects in Sam's murder, except for Calver. He was inside when she went missing. There was no solid evidence linking the killing to anyone except Harding. But he died in a clan lab fire last year."

I looked at Murray and he took over. "What Matt is saying is that we have a clear suspect pool. Problem is, they're all either inside, or, in Harding's case, dead. So, we're looking for a link to these men."

Murray assigned people to supervisors who had already been tasked with areas of responsibility. Then we broke up. "Matt, in here." Murray beckoned me into the small HQ room with Derek and Erin.

"Matt, you know this ghost better than anyone. If it is linked."

I frowned. Just before he burned, Harding had mentioned someone else. And there was the second guy on the tape. Everyone had assumed it was Lendich or Kitson. But before I'd killed him, Harding had alluded to the fact that whoever it was, they were still out there. This was tearing me apart now, but I had to lie through my teeth.

"Well, I thought our ghost was Harding, to be honest. I've got nothing, Murray."

Erin nodded along with me. "No-one else even raised their head. You could trawl all the files from that trial. There isn't another suspect, or another associate, that even comes close."

"Fuck." Murray was stressed.

Time was disappearing. Something clicked in my head. "It's not all fucked. There's one guy who could point you in the right direction. I know he knows."

Murray looked at me, frowning. "Calver."

"Yup. If whoever took Kayla is linked with this old group, Calver knows them."

Murray made a call, but Corrections were having none of it. He was fucked off. "You've assaulted each other twice, the second time leading to a major investigation of your actions. They're clear. No more."

I fired up. "They're joking, right? Kayla's been abducted. She's going to die. What the fuck is wrong with them?"

"Derek and Erin will go." I looked doubtful. "In the meantime, stay in here. We need you in the HQ group. Sit with me, everything that comes in. We need your head in here, Matt. Find this guy."

I made a brew and started looking through the files and incoming paperwork. It was all just standard protocol shit.

As expected, Calver told Erin and Derek to get fucked. He was no snitch, didn't talk to cops. *Good one, Corrections.* When I heard that, I left the HQ. Gone for a piss, pinching the keys to an unmarked car on my way out. Everyone was so busy they didn't notice. I also borrowed Chris Patterson's swipe-card, on the excuse I needed to grab something from my car. Not because Chris had his Police ID in the same wallet . . .

I headed east, back across to the Shore, then north on Albany Highway until I hit the Avenue just after Albany village on the left. Then I floored it out to Paremoremo.

I was drawing the map in my head. Sam's clothing, Muriwai. Brianna, just north of Muriwai. That horror house, Helensville. Gabby, Kumeu. Kayla's bag, jacket . . . Kumeu. All the pieces were there, all connected. I had to get to Calver. I was in the middle of the web, but I didn't have anything. But I knew he did.

FIFTY-EIGHT

He was surprised, but I could see he was also relieved.

"Detective, a pleasure. You made it in. You really stepped things up."

He grinned. I hadn't seen him since I'd killed Harding. That had been ruled an accident, of course, despite an extensive scene examination and autopsy. But I knew that Calver knew. I could see it in his face. And I saw understanding there.

"Tom, you never fuckin' mentioned another person to me. But there is. A thirteen-year-old girl has been taken. We've worked together this far, but we've been talking dead people all the way. This girl, Kayla, she's alive. Probably. Let's get this done. But we're running out of fuckin' time."

"In more ways than one. Corrections will figure out it's you. They'll be in here any minute." He paused. His eyes leaked anger. But not at me. He carried on. "I thought he'd keep his head down, after what happened to Harding, and the rest. But he can't help himself." I frowned. And he came clean on why he'd held out on me. "I needed Harding, Detective. Needed him to go first. So did you." He took a breath. I interrupted.

"You owe, me, Tom. Now. Whatever you think happened with Harding, *you* needed that. Now help me. Kayla. The cops are running around out there, headless fuckin' chickens, with nothing. We're already four hours down—"

He held a hand up. "I've done twenty-one years in this shit hole, for something that I didn't do. And I've done the first six months of a sentence for something else I tried to stop. That's what I got. I don't expect you to believe me, but I've got nothing, nothing in this world, except my word—"

My turn to cut him off. "You want out? Tell the truth. I'll do what I can for you. Just fuckin' tell me."

He held his hand up again. "You don't need to bargain. But I can actually do better from in here, if you understand me." His face was deadly serious. "My turn to cross the line, Detective. Just get the cunt, and I'll take care of the rest—"

"Then talk to me."

But before he opened his mouth again the door behind him flew open. Two guards went in and grabbed his arms, pulling him backwards. The door behind me flew open too. Someone put a hand on my shoulder, then gripped my bicep and dragged me up.

"Matthew Buchanan, you're detained . . ." I didn't listen to them, just stared at Calver as he was pulled out. He stared back at me.

"Fletcher Road, childhood . . . grew up . . . you're always fuckin' hassling me, you cunt!"

He reverted to his cover story but I locked the words in. *Fletcher Road. Childhood. Grew up.* I can't say I listened to anything as the guards marched me down the corridor, into the same office I'd been to once before.

"Just phone Detective Inspector Tim Sutton," I said. "Here's his number . . ."

They phoned Tim who went berserk, but to his credit, smoothed things over. I didn't care if they charged me with anything, I just wanted out. Yes, I'd nicked an ID card. So what. Not my fault if people didn't check things too closely. I was allowed to return to my car but my phone buzzed before I started the engine. *Murray.* He wasn't even angry.

"What'd you get?"

"Fuck all. We got interrupted. But he gave me Fletcher Road, something about childhood, where someone grew up. That's all. I'm coming back."

"See you shortly."

I pulled into Henderson and found Murray in the back office. He swung around. He looked deflated.

"Erin's had a look into Fletcher Road. Harding grew up on it. It's out the back of Waimauku, off Muriwai Road."

"Harding?" *It's not him we give a fuck about. What the fuck are you on, Calver?* "What the fuck? Nah, he told me for a reason ..."

"Well, search me, Matt, cos we're no further ahead."

"I'm going up there. I'll ask around."

"We're running out of time ..." I was walking back out and Murray was calling after me. "Let's just find her, Matt ... so, if you're going to break the law again, you better make sure it's bloody worth it."

FIFTY-NINE

I got to Waimauku on State 16 and turned left onto Muriwai Road. Fletcher was about two K's down on the right. It was a narrow rural road which became metal just twenty-odd metres in. I drove past a gravel driveway on my right which led up a hill. Couldn't see the house. I was looking for something lived-in, something obvious. I carried on and passed a cream-coloured single level on my left. Just past it were some well-kept gardens. Perfect. I wanted a friendly neighbour. I did a U-turn, and pulled into the driveway. I got out and approached the front door under the cute A-frame awning, white pillars either side. I gave it a knock.

A young mother answered the door, kid in tow. She smiled. "Hi."

I pulled Chris' ID, holding the Police badge up but folding his photo over so she didn't see it, just like I'd done at the prison.

"Matt Buchanan, ma'am, Henderson Police. Sorry to disturb you, just after some help really."

She smiled again once she realised nothing was the matter. "Sure, what can I do for you?"

"I'm just after some local knowledge, so ideally someone who's lived on this road for a long time. You know, been here for the best part of thirty or forty years if that's possible? We're looking at something from a long time ago, it's nothing to be concerned about, but we're just after somebody who might know the area really well."

"Oh, easy. Jan Caldwell, she lives down the road." She indicated the way I had been going. "We've only been here for five years, but she's been here her whole life, it's the family home. She knows everyone. Lovely old lady. You can't miss her place, carry on down, you'll go past Taha Road on your right, then Mahana on your right, her place is just a bit further on, on your left. A-frame bit at the front, little pull-in for cars. Can't miss it."

I thanked her and jumped back in, reversing out and carrying on down Fletcher. It wound past rural properties and a combination of trees and fields. I past Taha, and kept going till Mahana appeared on my right. Further up it was exactly as she'd described. I could see the A-frame she'd mentioned, and pulled into the little layby. I switched the car off and walked up to the front door.

"Good afternoon, ma'am . . ." I began as she answered the door. She was short, curly grey hair, glasses on.

"We haven't had the Police around here for a long time." She didn't miss a beat.

I looked at the unmarked car, then back at her. "You're onto it."

She smiled. "Come in, young man. What can I do for you?"

I took my shoes off and followed her in. She closed the door behind me and led me into the lounge. It looked out over the fields, and a pond. Nice place.

"Tea?"

"No thank you, Mrs Caldwell." I took a breath. *Need to get straight to the point.* You could dawdle around something for ages, and cops were good at that. Cops also got caught up in what could or couldn't be said. But fuck that. Sometimes you just have to cut to the chase. "Have you lived here long? Long enough to remember a young Gary Harding?"

She put her hand to her mouth. "Oh . . . terrible, terrible. Yes, yes, Gary grew up further down from me. I knew his parents well. They moved away years ago now. I think the father passed a long while back, when Gary was little. But I saw the terrible things in the news, and heard he died last year?"

"Yeah, he was a drug cook, he made P. Died in a fire."

She nodded. Then shook her head. "He was always in trouble, even way back then. Knew he'd get up to no good. But I didn't have much to do with him after he was about fifteen, he moved away from here. When I watched that trial on TV, I . . . the terrible things they said he did. And he got off!"

I nodded.

"Well, it wouldn't surprise me at all if he'd done it, all of it." She was frowning. "There was something wrong with that boy. Once, the old man down on the left, Ivan O'Carroll, he had this tabby cat. Gary covered it in diesel one day, lit it on fire. I found it on the road. I think Gary's parents called Police about that. He would've only been about ten when that happened."

"Was he abused, do you think?"

"Well, their house was always a tip. Don't know, he was always an angry child. And you know, when that happens, you know something must be up. Was it abuse, was it genetic? A combination? I don't know."

Calver's words bounced around in my head. *Fletcher. Childhood.* I was fishing, for anything, for everything. Cos I didn't really know what I was looking for. "What do you remember about him? Hobbies, interests? Did he ever say anything to you, anything that stuck with you? Places he liked to hang out?"

She looked out the window. "No, nothing stands out. I mean I could sit here and try and remember conversations, but . . . something that stuck? Not really. He was just a rude boy, but, you know, not outrageously so. You could still talk to him. He never caused me any direct trouble. Oh, except one time, he ripped out all my hydrangeas. No, maybe it was because we shared the same street. But then, Ivan's cat . . ." she looked back from the window. "What exactly are you looking for?"

"I'm not exactly sure. A girl has gone missing. You would have seen the news. I think it's got something to do with his past. Someone he knew."

She nodded, concern moving across her features. "He used to go all over round here, he'd just wander and get up to stuff. I can't think of any specific place. Maybe the beach. He hung around with this one other boy, they were always together. Causing mischief. Gary, like I said, he never caused me any direct grief. That other boy, though, he was a strange one. Always looked at me funny. He lived with his mum. They moved away too, 'bout the time the Hardings did."

My mind turned over, once, paused. "A good friend of his?"

"Yeah, what was their name now? His mother was Sarah. Oh, of course . . ."

When she said the name, my heart stopped cold.

"Yeah, I'd have thought you might have known him, he was . . ."

But I was up and heading for the door, cutting her off. I didn't look back. Bit rude, but I was on autopilot again. I raced to the car, wrenched the door open. The anger I'd felt at Harding's place, it consumed me again, washed up me from my feet to my brain. I gripped the wheel and my mind started going in dangerous directions. I couldn't control the thoughts. I pulled harshly out of the layby, back the way I'd come, foot pressing down as I took the bends in the gravel road.

Against all good judgement, I juggled my phone in my left hand and dialled Erin. I gave her the name. "Should be about fifty. Lives Helensville somewhere, or South Head, Parakai last I'd heard. Can you find him in NIA? His address. Yup. It's him. It's him, Erin. Tell Murray."

I took the left onto Muriwai Road and accelerated, heading for the main highway. Speedo hitting one hundred and climbing. I heard Erin tapping into NIA over the phone. She was talking to herself as she did it. Forty-eight years, Huntly . . . nah." I could hear the mouse clicking as she checked records. "Here we go, fifty-one years, Helensville." Click, click. "Yep, this is probably him. Wishart Road." She gave me the number, and must have brought Google Maps up because she started passing me some directions. I locked them into my head. *Up State 16, right onto Kiwitahi, stay on that, left onto Old North, skirting the bush, becomes Wishart . . .*

Erin cut in again. "Matt, are you saying that he has Kayla?"

"Yes."

"But it says here that back in 1990 he joined—"

"I know."

"But in '95 he was—"

"I know."

I hung up. My speed was picking up and I needed both hands. And as much of my brain as I could muster. How had I missed this? Twenty-two years. Twenty-two long fuckin' years.

I'm coming for you, you cunt.

SIXTY

I slowed down about two hundred from the house. It was an older house set back off Wishart Road, and it backed onto a small block of pine forest. I switched off and looked at the lockbox in the passenger footwell. *Just wait. Wait for support.* But that video of Sam just kept swirling through my head. No fuckin' way was Kayla going to suffer that. We were already well behind the eight-ball, and even another thirty minutes could be all the difference. So, fuck it. If Kayla died now, that'd be me tapping out for good later today. I'd barely survived one failure. I couldn't do two.

I took the keys and unlocked the box, ripping the Glock from the compartment. I pulled it out of the holster which I ditched. I locked the slide back and checked the chamber. Picked up the mag from the compartment and pushed it in, hearing the click and then giving it a tug. Then I let the slide go forward. I stuffed the pistol into the waistband of my jeans and left the car, crossing the road onto the right side and taking to the pines bordering it. It was early afternoon but the trees were still shrouded in fog. The cold weather and cloud cover were preventing the sun beating through the pines to make it lift. I paralleled the road, keeping it on my left, knowing I'd have to eventually hit the house if I did that. I hit a knee-high wire fence and paused. Property boundary.

Standing under the pines, hidden in some secondary scrub, I checked ahead at the several metres of open ground I'd have to cover to make it to the house. To my left, the road provided a natural barrier. He wouldn't run that way. But to my right and behind me, the pine forest stretched away through the fog. I shivered. Looking back at the house, I spotted a camera covering the driveway. I moved to my right more, so I was looking at the side of the house. I considered my options. I didn't have many. Slow and steady, or full tilt.

I don't remember making the decision. I was out of the trees, heading for the right side, moving quick. I heard nothing as I ran. I noticed then the blue Holden wagon tucked up behind the house. There were piles of old wood, broken corrugated iron. I approached the back door. Still no sounds. I pulled the Glock from my jeans and raised it to my eye level with my right hand, reaching out with my left for the doorknob. I gave it a turn. Locked. I pushed on, moving further along the rear of the house, away from the direction I'd come. I moved below a window in a crouched position. My arse was pretty much dragging across the ground and my thighs were killing me. But a shot through a window and I'd be toast. There were no other ways in this side. *Fuck*.

I sat there and thought hard. But my head took its own course. The video of Sam started playing again. And then all of a sudden I was back on that rainy night in 1995, Gabby's blood staining my front, dripping down my arms. The anger rose. Then I heard it. Not loud, just a whimper. A half-cry. Not fighting, not angry. Sad. Broken. Then again. Crying. I retraced my steps to the back door, and this time I didn't give a fuck. I put my shoulder in beside the lock. The frame ruptured and splintered and I went in.

I screamed his name, followed by "Armed Police! Don't move!"

I had the Glock in both hands, up in the eye, scanning the kitchen I'd crashed into. I was taking in everything I saw but listening as well, anything to give me information to direct my next move. There was nothing in here. A hallway extended away in front of me. The cry must have come from the first room on my right. I ran to it, paused. I heard a door crash somewhere out of sight up ahead of me. Front door probably. Pause. *No. Fuck him for now. Kayla's here.* I reached for the bedroom door handle with my left hand, Glock up in my right. I turned it, gave it a push, stepped back. I heard the cry again then, louder, more urgent. I quartered the gap I'd opened in the doorway, then stepped in, pushing the door fully open with my left hand, moving in fast behind it, all the way into the blind spot behind the door. I'd picked up the bed in my vision as I'd cleared the room, but I needed to make sure there was nothing else here. Blind spot clear. *Bed.* Kayla was tied up, hands and feet tied to the top and bottom of the frame. She had a cloth tied around her face and was crying into it.

I spoke as I got to work on the cloth. "Kayla, it's okay. I'm with the Police. You're safe. My name's Matt, I'm here to get you out." As I struggled with the knot I could feel her sobbing change up a little, to relief. I pulled the cloth away and saw he'd stuffed another one into her mouth to really try and muffle any noise. I fished it out then got to work on her hands. I had to get her to safety, and I also had a probable armed offender on the loose. I needed quick answers from her so I could try and make decisions. "Broken bones, Kayla? I know what he's done, but anything that's gonna stop me moving you?"

"No, just . . . just . . ."

"It's okay, I know. You're safe now. We'll get you to the hospital." I got both her hands free and she clamped them round the back of my neck. She wasn't letting go. I untied her feet and lifted her, still trying to hold the Glock with my right hand. It wasn't working.

"Kayla, this is gonna hurt, but I need to change position. Can you stand?"

I gently put her on her feet, dropping the Glock onto the bed. I crouched, put my left shoulder in her stomach, and pulled her hands behind my head with my right. I pulled her over my left shoulder, standing up into a fireman's carry. I held her with my left arm, and with my right hand free I picked up the Glock from the bed. I moved with her out of the room back into the hall. Back to the kitchen, sweeping the hall behind me. I paused at the back door. *Fuck it.* Out, around the house, heading for the road. No sign of him. The Holden was still there. As I ran I caught my foot in the drainage ditch beside the drive. I went over, dropped the Glock, and dumped Kayla straight into the gravel ditch. She screamed out in pain. "Sorry, mate." Nothing else I could do. I felt around, found the pistol, stuffed it into my jeans again. *Fuck's sake. Just get her to the neighbours', you useless cunt.* I picked her up in both arms and hit the road, checking both ways. No sign of him. He must have gone into the pines. The nearest house was across the road, so I struck out for that. Kayla had her arms around my neck and held on for dear life. Just as well, cos I was starting to tire. She didn't make another sound though.

I got to the house and banged on the door. "Police! Help! I need help here!"

A young couple came racing to the door together. The girl went white when she saw Kayla. I put her down and the girl took her hand. The guy went back inside and grabbed a phone. My brain raced. *He's gone for the forest. He won't get far with that limp. And I need him now. Before anyone else turns up.* My heart was screaming at me though. *Don't leave Kayla, you cunt. Don't do it.* But these people had their shit together. As the guy came back with the phone up to his ear, I delivered some instructions.

"Tell them Buchanan has gone after the suspect, into the pine forest block. The suspect may be armed. We need an ambulance for Kayla, and more units here. There are already people on the way, but you may need to pass on some local knowledge."

The guy nodded. The girl looked up at me. "You're going? She's hurt . . ."

"I know. But the guy's gone, and we need to contain him. You'll be fine. He won't come back this way."

And just like that, I left them. I ran up their drive, crossing over the road and back into the pines.

SIXTY-ONE

The fog swirled around me. I couldn't see more than five to ten metres in any direction in this shit. Pine trunks loomed out of the white and grey. The air was damp, and it chilled my throat and lungs. I had the Glock up at eye level, in both hands, moving through the forest, quick as I could. The wet pine needles cushioned my steps, but they weren't helping me track him. I was just guessing, heading in the direction I would have gone if I was him. Diagonal, away from the house and the road. Into the middle of the pine block, then out the other side. I was searching, panning left and right of my track, looking for movement.

Hate coursed through me. My vision started to cloud, and I wiped my arm across my forehead. Gabby's dead eyes were staring up at me. *And he'd been right there.*

The fog blanketed everything as I moved between the pines, trunk to trunk. Hopefully they'd stop a round from whatever he was carrying. If he had a hunting rifle, I'd be a bit fucked. I couldn't hear much beyond the pounding in my ears, but if he had sprinted he'd be out the other side of the forest by now.

But he hadn't moved that quick. The limp, from when I'd shot him at Westgate in 2012, had slowed him down. Then he fucked up. I heard a snap up ahead as he stood on something still dry in the middle. I moved toward the sound, yelling out, trying to bluff him because I couldn't see shit. "Warren! I'm armed! Don't fucking move!" But *I* moved as quick as I could, trying to close some distance, while moving offline from where I'd called out. The smell of wet pine filled my nostrils. I stopped behind a trunk, sucked in air, trying to listen. Nothing. Nothing but the pounding in my ears, the drawing in of my own breath, the swirling fog.

The shot came from my left. I didn't see anything, just heard the explosion. My left arm took what felt like a punch, then more acute pain, bursting up near the shoulder. I groaned, gritted my teeth, dropped to my knees and fired blindly in that direction with just my right hand, letting off about six or seven rounds. *Had he seen me? Or had he been guessing too?* I heard him scream out. I moved about ten metres to my right, crawling now, on my knees, keeping low. I hugged a trunk, paused, sucking in air to try and breathe through the pain in my left arm. It started throbbing and I looked down at it. *Jesus.* The pain really hit me then. I slipped the pistol down my jeans, putting my right hand over my left bicep to try and stem the blood flow. I couldn't see the entry wound. Couldn't have been too big though cos my arm was still there. But it was still a fuckin' mess. *Fuck this.*

Seeing stars, I got myself to my feet, pulled the Glock out again and headed for the point I thought I'd heard the yell. I went slowly, pistol in my right hand, up to my eye, sight picture moving all over the place, up, down, left, right as I tried to hold my arm still and control my breathing. I wasn't doing a very good job of it. I was fucked. I was puffing, trying not to move my left arm, but it swung with each step, pain firing out from the wound and clouding my head. I kept the pistol as level as I could, following my eyesight. I was getting pretty close, and he would fire again any second. I dropped to my stomach, into the mud and pine needles. I kept low, crawling forward, keeping the Glock off the ground, up in my eye-line. The sight picture was more stable with my right arm supported on the ground. I couldn't put pressure on my left arm, I just let it drag, so I was sort of inching forward using my legs, lifting my right arm up and dropping it with each movement forward.

I came around a trunk and there he was, sprawled on the ground with his back to me, crawling slowly in the opposite direction. I got to my knees, then stood, pistol on him. I scanned his hands. *Nothing.* Scanned the area. A cut-down .22 lay on the forest floor between me and him. I scanned back to him. I saw the blood leaking out of his calf. I closed the gap slightly, but we were still about ten metres apart. He heard me, stopped crawling, turned. Looked into the Glock barrel. Stared into my face. And what he saw clearly frightened him. He got to his knees, shaking, eyes searching me for a way out.

"Matt . . . don't . . ."

Thoughts swirled in my head. *Second shooter at Westgate. Killed Pete and Steve. The videos. Anneke. Sam. Brianna.* How involved? *But Gabby. The panic to stem the flow of blood leaking from her chest. The coldness of her.*

My finger was on the trigger, gently taking up first pressure. I spoke slowly.

"I hope she fuckin' haunted you."

I lowered the barrel slightly, aiming at his chest. I kept first pressure. *God, I hope she haunted you.*

He had his hands up toward me, palms out in surrender. "Matt. You've no fuckin' idea . . . I can't help my . . . Harding, Calver. We were all gonna go down. They were getting rid of the evidence, after Anneke. Gabby just had to fucking 3T 'em, the enthusiastic bitch. I couldn't avoid it. We all panicked, we . . ."

"You knew exactly what you were doing."

"They'd chopped Anneke up! They had her body parts in that car, Matt. I wasn't gonna have Gabby fuck everything up! That was me inside for life. I'd been there. I raped her. So I made a call, and did it. Just don't fuckin' shoot me, please . . ."

"How did you do it? After you killed her? Did you shoot yourself? Or did one of them do it?" He raised his head, and as he looked at my face again his entire body began to shake. He didn't speak. I filled the silence. "Did she fuckin' haunt you? Your I-car partner? Your colleague?"

He was shaking good style now, trying to speak again but struggling. I didn't have long before someone would be here. I walked toward the cut-down .22 and kicked it a bit closer to him. I retreated several steps. The fog was lifting and I could almost see back out toward the road. I was about to bring the pistol back up when I heard it, like gentle thunder to the south. Then the throb of the rotors above the turbine engine. It was coming in quick.

Fuck it. End it. It doesn't matter. I thought through the options. Could I still make this look right? Probably. But I didn't know how good the cameras on Eagle were. I'd have thought the fog would still fuck them up, but I'd been wrong before more often than not. The observer may have had their FLIR on us already. But did I care? *I'm not going to end up back on that beach.* But what would stop that? Killing him? Or not killing him? *Fuck.*

I heard Eagle flare and settle somewhere out by the road, downwash blowing shit about. As the seconds ticked by, Warren got his balls back. He sneered at me once he knew I wasn't going to shoot him. "I'll take my chances with a jury, Matt. You're broken. Your oral evidence won't be worth shit."

I still had my Glock trained on him as the STG team came through the forest, weapons up, diamond formation, moving toward us. They would have been briefed on the move, and we were both pretty wet and dirty. They'd be unsure of ID, had to treat us the same. They were about twenty metres away and I could hear them yelling, one of them tapping his helmet with his fist as they closed in on us.

". . . on your heads! Hands on your heads! Drop the weapon!" We got the message. Warren complied. I moved slowly, putting the Glock down. Then I knelt, clasping my hands together on top of my head. They swarmed us, put him on his stomach into the pine needles, cuffed him. I stayed where I was. One of them had his M4 on my chest, another came in behind, cuffed me, patted me down. Then he picked me up under the arms, tried to get me to my feet. I groaned. It wasn't until I was turned around that whoever it was recognised me.

"Fuck. You all right, Matt?" I couldn't see the face under the balaclava, but I knew Craig's voice. We'd known each other for years, had been frontline together way back. He got on his radio. "Bravo one, alpha one, bring up the med bag . . ." he sat me back down, resting my back against his legs to keep my wound out of the mud and leaves. He let his M4 drop on its sling and pulled my shirt off to better assess the damage.

Things blurred together after that, I was in pain, just went with the flow. Eagle's rotors were still turning. I heard the sirens then, lots of them.

I prayed Kayla was doing all right.

I saw Warren get carried back toward the road by the STG guys. We locked eyes and his face creased into another sneering grin.

And I smiled back at him. Because I knew where he'd end up. And I remembered there was a Plan B.

SIXTY-TWO

The cold wind blew across the hills, rustling the larger trees. I looked across the gully at the headstones on the opposite hill, the tall trees behind. It was about to get started.

After being choppered to Auckland Hospital by the Westpac crew, I'd spent the next week recovering in there after some minor surgery. I'd had a few visitors, and Erin had kept me updated. They'd found Sam's body. Or what was left of her anyway, in the retreated dunes in the Woodhill Forest. Warren had showed them the resting place in return for an amended charge of accessory after the fact. Blame was placed squarely on Gary Harding. Karen, Rob, Holly . . . they had been okay with that. They finally had Sam, which was what they'd wanted all along. They knew Harding was dead, they knew Warren was going away. I was okay with it too, because Warren wasn't just going for that and Kayla's abduction. They'd also charged him with Gabby's murder. And the thousands of photos and videos they'd found on his devices added to the fire. Some of them were as dark as the shit from Harding's boat. Some were copies of others we'd found on Harding and Kitson already. He wasn't getting charged in relation to Pete or Steve. Too hard to prove. But whatever. I didn't care so much for the charges themselves. Kayla was safe. The Coates were going to be all right. And so would I.

Because I knew Warren was heading for Paremoremo.

I was standing with Erin and Hailey, just behind Karen, Rob and Holly, looking at the hole in the ground. It was an all-too-familiar scene. I'd done this too many times. But this one, this one was different. It was closure. It was the conclusion to something that had held me hostage for eighteen years. The service had been incredible. People had packed out the hall here at Schnapper Rock. They'd focused on Sam's life during the service, not on how it had ended, or the years since. Holly had delivered a speech that brought me to tears. I was past trying to hide the way I felt about shit. I was starting to improve. Hailey didn't fare much better on the tears front. She hadn't been too involved over the years with the Coates, but obviously my involvement had rubbed off on her, and seeing her dad crying just set her off.

With an arm around Hailey, we watched as they lowered the coffin down. Karen turned around to me. Her eyes were wet, but the look on her face wasn't sadness. She smiled. Holly glanced back at me too, wiping her tears.

The priest said the usual, and then it was time to chuck the dirt on. It was always the same. No one moved initially. Then somebody, usually a younger guy, steps up and grabs a handful, chucking it on. It was the same today. I don't know who the guy was, maybe a cousin or old school friend. He grabbed a handful of dirt, held it. "Fly free, Sammy" he breathed as he dropped the dirt into the hole on top of the coffin. That opened the floodgates. People moved forward, grabbing handfuls and dropping them in. Some spoke as they did it. Some didn't, keeping their thoughts to themselves. I waited. While I waited, my thoughts wandered.

Karen and Holly hadn't seen the video. They'd been warned, Rob too, but he insisted. After watching it, he'd explained it to his family. And he wouldn't let them see it. He'd been seeing a psych ever since, to try and work through it. After I'd dumped the video and the other shit in Ponsonby's Western Park, near the sculpture, it had of course been handed in. The first cop from Auckland Central who watched it had taken six months off work. Erin had acquired it eventually as they worked things out. She'd seen it. And she'd refused to let me watch it. I'd had to put on a show, because that's what I would have done, had I known nothing about its origins. I ordered, demanded, pleaded and begged. But Erin managed to convince Tim and the other bosses that it would be too traumatic for me. *If only they fuckin' knew.*

But if I hadn't found it, watched it, who knows? Would I have still ended up on that beach, in the dunes, north of Muriwai? *Maybe. Maybe not.*

Holly bent down and flicked the latch on a wooden box at her feet. She picked it up, and Karen opened the lid. A white dove took flight, rising and then hanging around, catching the air currents, testing them, before picking a direction and disappearing.

Rest easy, Sam. Time to enjoy yourself. I'm sorry it took me so long.

I put my arm back round Hailey and we walked up the hill with Erin. She continued on to the car, leaving Hailey and me to ourselves as we stopped at Kate's memorial in the rose garden. It wasn't far from Brianna's. As we stood there together, I looked at my daughter. Fuck, was I proud. She'd brought herself through, and that was all her, not me. I was only standing there because of her. She'd saved my life twice. Once without knowing it. I couldn't keep putting her through this sort of shit. She had her whole life, her whole career ahead of her.

Katie, I think I'm coming right. But for Hailey's sake, if I end up on that fuckin' beach again, you better bloody well do something.

EPILOGUE

Nine months later

I picked up the cup and sipped the coffee. *Fuckin' cold morning.* I reached for the iPad with my left arm. It still hurt when I stretched it out fully. I unlocked the tablet, pulled up the news. The headline made me put my cup down. I sat up straight and opened the article.

Serial killer ex-cop dies in prison.
   I started reading.

Warren Malcolm, who served with the Police from 1990 until 2001, died in his cell at Paremoremo yesterday afternoon of suspected self-inflicted injuries . . .

   There was some shit about his time in the Police.

. . . Malcolm was serving a life sentence with seventeen years non-parole after being convicted of a series of offences . . . murder of Constable Gabrielle Stewart in 1995 . . . an accessory to the murder of Samantha Coates in 1999 . . . abduction of a thirteen-

year-old girl last year . . . prison guards found him and immediate medical aid was provided. Paramedics attended but he could not be resuscitated . . .

They had all the depression and suicide hotline numbers at the end of the article, suggesting he'd killed himself. But I knew differently. I imagined Tom, grey-haired, sitting calmly in his cell. His pardon was progressing, but he'd deliberately slowed the process so he could remain inside the prison. I wondered how he'd actually managed to do it. And maybe he'd finally redeemed himself in his own mind. I thought about his comparison – about us being two sides of the same coin. And decided he'd been right after all.